THE DEVIL

TO PAY

THE DEVIL

TO PAY

Ellery Queen

Thorndike Press　　　　**Chivers Press**
Waterville, Maine USA　　**Bath, England**

This Large Print edition is published by Thorndike Press®, USA and by Chivers Press, England.

Published in 2003 in the U.S. by arrangement with The Frederic Dannay Literary Property Trust, The Manfred B. Lee Family Literary Property Trust and their agent, JackTime of 3 Erold Court, Allendale, NJ 07401.

Published in 2003 in the U.K. by arrangement with The Frederic Dannay Literary Property Trust & The Manfred B. Lee Family Literary Property Trust.

U.S. Softcover 0-7862-5680-X (Paperback Series)
U.K. Hardcover 0-7540-7363-7   (Chivers Large Print)
U.K. Softcover 0-7540-7364-5   (Camden Large Print)

The text of this Large Print edition is unabridged.
Other aspects of the book may vary from the original edition.

Set in 16 pt. Plantin by Minnie B. Raven.

Printed in the United States on permanent paper.

British Library Cataloguing-in-Publication Data available

Library of Congress Cataloging-in-Publication Data

Queen, Ellery.
    The devil to pay / Ellery Queen.
      p. cm.
    ISBN 0-7862-5680-X (lg. print : sc : alk. paper)
    1. Stockbrokers — Crimes against — Fiction.   2. New York (N.Y.) — Fiction.   3. Novelists — Fiction.   I. Title.
PS3533.U4D485 2003
813'.52—dc21   2003054024

THE DEVIL

TO PAY

CONTENTS

I am informed that certain persons of high ego or low conscience spend all their waking hours in the soul-searching effort to find resemblances between themselves and the multifarious off-spring of the literary imagination.

Consequently I feel constrained to assert the self-evident fact that what follows in these pages is a work of fiction; and that, if any character in it resembles any real person whatsoever in name, physique, idiosyncrasy, mental equipment, cultural or professional background, or general morality, such deplorable resemblance should be construed as an act of God with which the author had nothing consciously to do.

E.Q.

PART
ONE

1

MUCH ADO ABOUT SOMETHING

Hollywood, like the Land of Oz, possesses a quaint and fluty flavor: it is the place where tin Christmas trees suddenly sprout around lamp-posts in December under a ninety-degree sun, where restaurants take the shape of lighthouses and hats, ladies on Saturday nights stroll the boulevards in trousers and mink coats leading baby leopards on a leash, where morning newspapers cost five cents and evening newspapers two, and people wait in queues for unexhausting hours to witness other people pressing their hands into juicy cement.

A trivial happening in Hollywood, therefore, is hugely less trivial than if the identical event occurs in Cincinnati or Jersey City, and an important one incalculably more important.

So when the Ohippi Bubble burst, even people who were not stockholders devoured the Los Angeles dispatches, and overnight "Ohippi" became as familiar a catchword as "quintuplets" and "the nine old men."

This is not to belittle the event itself. In collapsing Ohippi paradoxically stood on its own feet as a major calamity. And while the issue was not fought in the courts, owing to little Attorney Anatole Ruhig's foresight, a veritable battle-royal raged in print and on the streets. A wonderfully martial time it was, with Solly Spaeth's lanky son firing long-range bursts from the editorial offices of the *Los Angeles Independent* and unhappy stockholders alternately howling and scowling at the iron gate of *Sans Souci,* behind which Solly sat imperturbably counting up his millions.

It was really the Eastern diagnostician's fault, for Solly would never have settled in California had the doctor not recommended its climate, its golf, and its sunbaths. Imagine Solomon Spaeth being content to do nothing but squint along the mountain-range of his belly as he lolled in the sun! It was fated that Solly should begin restlessly ruminating his capital, which was lying as idly as he in various impregnable but unexciting banks.

So Solly rose, covered his nakedness, looked hopefully about, and found Rhys Jardin and little Anatole Ruhig. And it was from their happy fusion that the celebrated and subsequently notorious Ohippi Hydro-

Electric Development emerged.

(Solly met Winni Moon at the same time, but his interest in Winni was esthetic rather than commercial, so that is a different part of the story. Solly was never a man to neglect the arts. Winni became his protégée, and it is fascinating to recall that her career dated from that sensitive juxtaposition of souls.)

The organization and development of Ohippi Hydro-Electric took genius in those days, when heavy industry was prostrate and premonitory rumblings of holding-company legislation were audible in Washington; but Solly had genius. Nevertheless, he could not have succeeded without Rhys Jardin, who played the rôle of industrial angel with superb technique. Rhys, that sterling yachtsman, golfer, gymnast, and collector of *objets de sport,* was indispensable to Solly for entirely different reasons: he possessed the necessary supplemental capital, he carried the magic Jardin name, and he knew nothing whatever about big business.

When Ohippi moved from the financial pages into the offices of the Homicide Detail of the Los Angeles Central Detective Bureau the case, already precious, became

15

a managing editor's dream; and Fitzgerald went slightly mad.

Fitz had been a classmate of Rhys Jardin's (Harvard '08) and he was also technically Walter Spaeth's employer. But the set-up was so alluring — the floods, Winni Moon and her scented chimpanzee, that provocative little detail of the molasses, the old Italian rapier, the scores of thousands of potential murderers — that Fitz shut his eyes to the ethical questions involved and let fly with both presses.

Of course, every newspaperman in Los Angeles became wall-eyed with civic pride and professional joy, and the items that flooded the papers dealt with everything from Winni's dainty bathing habits to an old still-picture of Pink, bow in hand, as Chief Yellow Pony, from that forgotten epic of the plains, *Red Indian*. They even dug out of the morgue a photograph of Rhys Jardin winning the 1928 Southern California amateur golf championship.

One feature writer, running out of material, fell back upon statistics. He pointed out that, as usual, nearly every one in the case came from anywhere but Hollywood.

Rhys Jardin was originally a Virginian, the Jardins having been one of the few first families of that great commonwealth with traditional riches as well as rich traditions.

Solly Spaeth had been spawned in New York.

Walter Spaeth — who as a result of his father's migratory instincts might have been born on mountain, plain, or sea — happened to see his first sunbeam in a Chicago hospital, where his mother saw her last.

Winni Moon had been christened Freda Möndegarde in a cold little Swedish church in the South Dakota wheatfields. (Her unavoidable destination had been Hollywood, since she was blonde and swivel-hipped, had been the star of her high-school dramatic society, had once waited on table in an Eatery run by a Greek named Nick, and had then won a State-fair beauty contest, sharing honors with the prize milch-cow.)

Anatole Ruhig had been born in Vienna, an error he quickly rectified; he passed the bar in Kansas City and was drawn to Hollywood by magnetic attraction, like an iron filing.

Pink came from Flatbush, Brooklyn.

The reporter even included Fitzgerald, to that gentleman's wrath. Fitz, it seemed, was a Boston Irishman with a weakness for truth and whisky who had been called to

California by chronic sinusitis and the plight of Tom Mooney.

And so it went. Mr. Ellery Queen, himself a native of West Eighty-seventh Street, Manhattan, amused himself once, during the darker hours of the puzzle, by studying these interesting but futile data.

The only indigenous Californian involved in the case was Rhys Jardin's unpredictable daughter, Valerie.

"I didn't think," said Walter Spaeth the first time he met her, which was at a private polo game in Beverly Hills, "that any one's actually born here, Miss Jardin."

"Is that the smallest talk you have?" sighed Val, peeling an orange.

"But why Hollywood?" insisted Walter, eying her up and down. He wondered how the felt bowler stuck on the side of her head managed to defy the law of gravity, but that great problem was soon forgotten in a consideration of her mouth.

"I wasn't consulted," said Miss Jardin with annoyance. "Go away, you're spoiling the —" She began to dance. "Good boy, pop! 'At' it, Pink!" she screamed, waving the orange. "Watch that roan!"

Presumably Pink did so, for out of the mêlée shot two horsemen, the ball pre-

18

ceding them in a beautiful arc.

"That's the end of that," said Miss Jardin with satisfaction. "Oh, are you still here, Mr. Spaeth?"

The first horseman, a youngish fellow with longish legs clamped about a brownish pony, thundered up the field smacking the ball toward the goal with dismaying accuracy. Between him and his pursuers raced another youngish fellow with freckles, red hair, and preposterously broad shoulders. The ball bounced between the goal-posts, the first rider brought up his mallet in salute, and his red-haired guard completed the amenities by grinning and putting his thumb to his nose. Then they cantered back to mid-field.

"Oh, I see," said Walter. "The first one is pop, and the second is Pink."

"A detective," said Val, looking interested. "However did you know?"

"Red hair — Pink — they seem to go together. Besides, I don't get the feeling that your father would thumb his nose. Who's Pink?"

"Why?"

"Your boy-friend?"

"So that's the way the wind's blowing," remarked Miss Jardin shrewdly, sinking

19

small teeth into the orange. "Three minutes, and the man's poking his nose into my private affairs! You'll be proposing next."

"I beg your pardon," said Walter stuffily. "If I'm boring you —"

"Aren't you the one!" smiled Val. "Come here, little boy."

Walter wavered. Women of the modern school worried him. The only female he had ever known closely was Miss Titus, an aged English lady who had tutored him and tucked him into bed until he was old enough to go to Andover; and Miss Titus until her departure for a better world had deplored every feminist fad which passed her by, from smoking and knee-length skirts to suffrage and birth control.

Walter looked Miss Jardin up and down again and decided he would like to learn about women from her. He settled himself on the rail. "Your father is terribly young-looking, isn't he?"

"Isn't it disgusting? It's the vitamins and the exercise. Pop's a sports fiend. That's where Pink comes in — just," said Valerie dryly, "to relieve your mind, Mr. Spaeth. Pink's a phenomenon — can play and teach any game ever invented, and besides he's a dietitian. Vegetarian, of course."

"Very sensible," said Walter earnestly. "Are you one?"

"Heavens, no. I'm carnivorous. Are you?"

"It's a debased taste, but I'll admit I do like to sink a fang into a *filet mignon*."

"Swell! Then you may take me to dinner tonight."

"Well — say — that would be fine," mumbled Walter, quite unconscious of how the magic had been done. He wondered with desperation how this delectable conversation might be prolonged. "Uh — he *does* look like your brother. I mean, as your brother might look if you had —"

"I'm taken for pop's older sister already," said Val tragically.

"Go on," said Walter, examining Val all over. "You're the young connubial type."

"Mr. Spaeth, you're positively clairvoyant! I sew the meanest seam, and I've always been marked A in bedmaking."

"I didn't mean exactly that." She did have the most remarkable figure, Walter thought.

Valerie eyed him sharply. "What's the matter? Am I coming out anywhere?"

"There's something wrong with the movie scouts!"

"Isn't it the truth? Just like the Yankees

letting Hank Greenberg go to the Tigers —
a Bronx boy, too."

"You'd photograph well," said Walter,
edging closer. "I mean — you've a nose
like Myrna Loy's, and your eyes and
mouth remind me of —"

"*Mr.* Spaeth," murmured Val.

"My mother's," finished Walter. "I have
her picture. I mean — how did they ever
miss you?"

"Well, it's like this," said Valerie.
"They've camped on my tail for years, but
I've always turned 'em down."

"Why?"

"I'd never succeed in the movies," said
Val in a hollow voice.

"That's nonsense!" said Walter warmly.
"I'll bet you can even act."

"Shucks. But you see — I was born right
here in Hollywood; that's one strike on me.
Then I hate sables and flat heels. And I'm
not a homesy girl sick of it all. So don't
you see how hopeless it is?"

"You must think I'm a fool," growled
Walter, whose large ears had been growing
redder and redder.

"Oh, darling, forgive me," said Val con-
tritely. "But you *are* wide open for a left
hook. Finally there's kissing. Look!" She
seized him, squeezed him with passion,

22

and kissed him fiercely on the lips. "There, you see?" she sighed, biting into the orange again. "That's how it is with me."

Walter smiled a flabby smile at the polo fiends around them and wiped the lipstick off his mouth.

"What I meant to say," continued Val, "was that in the movies you've got to go through all the *motions* of passion, but when it comes right down to it they just peck at each other. When I kiss, I *kiss*."

Walter slid off the rail. "How do you spend your time?" he asked abruptly.

"Having fun," mumbled Val.

"I knew there'd be something wrong with you. You never got those hands over a wash-tub!"

"Oh, God," groaned Valerie, "a reformer." She popped the last segment into her mouth. "Listen, my lean and hungry friend. Pop and I, we live and let live. We happen to have some money, and we're trying to spend it as fast as we can before it's taken away from us."

"You're the kind of people," said Walter bitterly, "who cause revolutions."

Val stared, then burst into laughter. "*Mr.* Spaeth, I do believe I've misjudged you. That's the cleverest line! Isn't the next step a suggestion that we stage a private sit-down strike in the nearest park."

"So that's what you meant by having fun!"

Valerie gasped. "Why, I'll slap your sassy face!"

"The trouble with you people," snapped Walter, "is that you're economic royalists, the pack of you."

"You just heard somebody say that!" flared Valerie. "Where do you come off lecturing me? I've heard about you and your father. You're just as fat leeches as we are, feeding on the body politic!"

"Oh, no," grinned Walter. "I don't care what you call yourself or my old man, but *I* work for a living."

"Yes, you do," sneered Val. "What's your racket?"

"Drawing. I'm a newspaper cartoonist."

"There's work for a man. Yes, sir! See to-morrow's funny section for the latest adventures of Little Billy."

"Is that so?" yelled Walter.

"Mr. Spaeth, your repartee simply floors me!"

"I draw political cartoons," yelled Walter, "for the *Los Angeles Independent!*"

"Communist!"

"Oh, my God," said Walter, waving his long arms, and he stamped furiously away.

★ ★ ★

Valerie smiled with satisfaction. He was a very young man, and he did look like Gary Cooper.

She examined her mouth in her hand-mirror and decided she must see Mr. Walter Spaeth again very soon.

"And tonight's date," she shouted after him, "is definitely off. But DEFINITELY!"

2

LA BELLE DAME SANS SOUCI

There were other nights, however, and other meetings; and it was not long before Mr. Walter Spaeth despairingly concluded that Miss Valerie Jardin had been set upon earth for the express purpose of making his life unbearable.

Considering Miss Jardin *in toto,* it was a pleasant curse; that was what made it so vexatious. So Walter wrestled with his conscience daily and nightly — Walter was an extremely spiritual young man — and he even plunged into Hollywood night life for a time with a variety of those beautiful females with whom Hollywood crawls.

But it all came out the same in the end — there was something about the idle, flippant, annoying Miss Jardin to which he was hopelessly allergic.

So he crept back and accepted every electric moment Miss Jardin deigned to bestow, thrashing feebly in his exquisite misery like a flea-ridden hound being scratched by his mistress.

Being totally blind to the subtleties of

feminine conduct, Walter did not perceive that Miss Jardin was also going through a trying experience. But Rhys Jardin, physically a father, had had to develop the sixth sense of a mother in such matters.

"Your golf is off six strokes," he said sternly one morning as Pink mauled and pounded him on the rubbing table in the gymnasium, "and I found a wet handkerchief on the terrace last night. What's the matter, young lady?"

Val viciously punched the bag. "Nothing's the matter!"

"Filberts," jeered Pink, slapping his employer. "You had another fight with that wacky twerp last night."

"Silence, Pink," said her father. "Can't a man have a private conversation with his own daughter?"

"If that punk calls you a 'parasite' again, Val," growled Pink, digging his knuckles into Jardin's abdomen, "I'll knock his teeth out. What's a parasite?"

"Pink, you were listening!" cried Val indignantly. "This is one heck of a household, that's all *I* can say!"

"Can I help it if you talk loud?"

Val glared at him and plucked a pair of Indian clubs from the rack in the wall-closet.

"Now, Pink," said Rhys, "I won't have eavesdropping. . . . What else did Walter call her?"

"A lot more fancy names, and then she starts to bawl, so he hauls off and kisses her one."

"Pink," snarled Val, swishing the clubs, "you're an absolute *louse*."

"And what did my puss do?" asked Rhys comfortably. "A little more on the pectorals, Pink."

"She give him the chorus girl's salute — like she meant it, too. I mean, that was a *kiss*."

"Very interesting," said Val's father, closing an eye.

Val flung one of the Indian clubs in the general direction of the rubbing table, and Pink calmly ducked and went on kneading his employer's brown flesh. The club cracked against the far brick wall.

Val sat down on the floor and wailed: "I might as well entertain my friends in the Hollywood Bowl!"

"Nice boy," said her father. "Nice lad, Walter."

"He's an oomph!" snapped Val, jumping up. "He and his 'social consciousness'! He makes me *sick*."

"Well, I don't know," said Pink, massaging. "There's something in it. The little guy don't get much of the breaks."

"Pink, you keep out of this!"

"See what I mean?" complained Pink. "This master and man stuff. I should keep out of it. Why? Because I'm a wage slave. Turn over, Rhys."

His employer docilely turned over and Pink set about trying to crack his spine. "You don't have to see the boy, Val — ouch!"

"I should think," said Val in a frigid voice, "that I'm old enough to solve my own problems — without interference." And she flounced off.

And Walter *was* a problem. Sometimes he romped like a child, and at other times he positively snorted gloom. One moment he was trying to break her back in a movie kiss, and the next he was calling her names. And all because she wasn't interested in labor movements and didn't know a Left Wing from a Right, except in fried chicken!

It was all very confusing, because of late Val had had practically to sit on her hands; they had developed a sort of incorporeal itch. Either they wanted to muss his unruly black hair and stroke his lips and run over his sandpaper cheeks — he *always* seemed to need a shave — or they yearned to hit him on the point of his dear longish nose.

The situation was complicated by the fact that Solomon Spaeth and her father had gone into business together. Rhys Jardin in business, after all these splendid idle years! Val could not decide whether she disliked rubicund Solly more for his oozy self than for what he was doing to her father. There were tedious conferences with lawyers — especially a wet-faced little one by the name of Ruhig — arguments and contracts and negotiations and things. . . . Why, Rhys neglected his yachting, golf, and polo for three whole weeks — he barely had time for his Swedish exercises under Pink's drill-sergeant direction!

But that wasn't the worst of it. It was what happened at *Sans Souci* after the contracts were signed.

Sans Souci dated from the careless, golden days. It occupied half a dozen acres high in the Hollywood hills and was designed for exclusiveness, with a ten-foot fence of stout peeled-willow stakes all round to keep out hucksters and trailer tourists, and a secondary paling of giant royal palms to make their envious mouths water.

Inside there were four dwellings of tile, stucco, plaster, and tinted glass which were supposed to be authentic Spanish and were not.

The development was shaped like a saucer, with the four houses spacing the rim and all the rear terraces looking down upon the communal depression in the center, where the democratic architect had laid out a single immense swimming pool surrounded by rock gardens.

Rhys Jardin had bought one of the houses because the realtor was an old acquaintance in need — an empty gesture, for the bank foreclosed promptly after the depression began and the realtor shot his brains out by way of his mouth. Valerie thought the place ghastly, but their dingy expensive shack at Malibu and their bungalow-villa on the Santa Monica Palisades always seethed with people, so *Sans Souci*'s promise of privacy attracted her.

The second house was occupied by a male star with a passion for Dandie Dinmonts, whose barking made life a continuous agony until their owner suddenly married an English peeress who carried him and his beasts off to dazzle the British cinema public, leaving the house happily unoccupied except for brief annual visits.

The third house was tenanted for a time

31

by a foreign motion picture director who promptly had an attack of *delirium tremens* at the edge of the pool; so that worked out beautifully, because he was whisked off to a sanitarium and never returned.

The fourth house had never been occupied at all.

That is, until Solly Spaeth bought it from the bank "to be nearer my associate," as he beamingly told Valerie, "your worthy and charming father."

And when the insufferable Solly moved in, Walter moved in, too.

There was the rub. Walter moved in. The creature was so *inconsistent*. He didn't *have* to live there. In fact, he had been living alone in a furnished room in Los Angeles until his father took the *Sans Souci* estate. The Spaeth's didn't get along — small wonder, considering Walter's ideas! But suddenly it was peaches and cream between them — for a whole week, anyway — with Solly bestowing his oleaginous benediction and Walter accepting it glumly and moving right in, drawing board, economic theories, and all.

And there he was, only yards away at any given hour of the day or night, making life miserable . . . preaching, criticizing her charge accounts and décolletage and the cut of her bathing suits, fighting with his father like an alley cat, drawing inflammatory cartoons for the *Independent* under the unpleasant *nom de guerre* of WASP, heatedly lecturing Rhys Jardin for his newly assumed "utilities overlordship," whatever that meant, scowling at poor Pink and insulting Tommy and Dwight and Joey and all the other nice boys who kept hopefully bouncing back to *Sans Souci* . . . until she was so angry she almost didn't want to return his kisses — *when* he kissed her, which wasn't often; and then only, as he hatefully expressed it, "in a moment of animal weakness."

And when Winni Moon came to live at the Spaeth house as Solly's "protégée," with her beastly beribboned chimp and a rawboned Swedish chaperon who was *supposed* to be her aunt — you would have thought a self-respecting moralist would move out *then*. But no, Walter hung on; and Valerie even suspected the impossible Winni of having designs on her benefactor's son, from certain signs invisible to the Spaeths but quite clear to the unprejudiced female eye.

Sometimes, in the sacred privacy of her own rooms, Valerie would confide in little Roxie, her Chinese maid.

"Do you know what?" she would say furiously.

"Yisss," Roxie would say, combing out Val's hair.

"It's *fantastic*. I'm in love with the beast, damn him!"

Walter leaned on his horn until Frank, the day man, unlocked the gate. The crowd in the road was silent with a rather unpleasant silence. Five State troopers stood beside their motorcycles before *Sans Souci*, looking unhappy. One little man with the aura of a tradesman leaned glassy-eyed on the shaft of a homemade sign which said: Pity The small Invester.

The crowd was composed of tradespeople, white-collar workers, laborers, small-business men. That, thought Walter grimly, accounted for the inactivity of the troopers; these solid citizens weren't the usual agitating mob. Walter wondered how many of the five troopers had also lost money in Ohippi.

Driving through the gate and hearing Frank quickly clang it shut, Walter felt a little sick. These people knew him by now, and the name he bore. He did not blame them for glaring at him. He would not have blamed them if they had tossed the troopers aside and broken down the fence.

He ran his six-cylinder coupé around to the Jardin house. More than a dozen cars were parked in the Jardin drive — sporty cars of the same breed as their owners, Walter thought bitterly. Valerie must be fiddling again — while Rome burned.

He found her in the front gardens radiantly holding off all the sad young men and their ladies with one hand and offering them *delicatessen* with the other. At first Walter blinked, for it seemed as though Val was plucking salami and sausages from the rose bushes; and he had never heard of bologna sandwiches and one-drink cocktail bottles growing on palm boles before. But then he saw that the refreshments had been artfully tied to the arboreal landscape.

"Oh, it's Walter," said Val, the radiance dimming. Then she stuck out her chin. "Walter Spaeth, if you mention one word about the starving coal-miners I'll scream!"

"Look out," giggled a young lady, "here's Amos again."

"Wasn't he the prophet who flapped his arms so much?'

"Goodbye, Val," said Tommy. "I'll see you in the first tumbril."

"Val," said Walter, "I want to talk to you."

"Why not?" said Val sweetly, and excused herself.

She maintained the sweet smile only until they were behind a cluster of palms. "Walter, don't you *dare* spoil my party. It's a brand-new idea, and I've got Tess and Nora and Wanda simply tearing their permanents —" She looked a little more closely at his face. "Walter, what's the matter?"

Walter flung himself on the grass and kicked the nearest palm. "Plenty, my feminine Nero."

"Tell me!"

"Bottom's dropped out. Hell's loose. River topped the levees last night — out of control. The whole Ohio Valley and part of the Mississippi Valley are under water. So there, may they rest in peace, go the Ohippi plants."

Valerie felt a sudden chill. It didn't seem fair that the floods in a place half a continent away should creep into her garden and spoil everything.

She leaned against the palm. "How bad is it?" she asked in a croupy little voice.

"The plants are a total loss."

"First the stock-market drop, and now

36

— Poor pop." Val took off her floppy sunhat and began to punch it. Walter squinted up at her. It was going to be tough on the kid, at that. Well, maybe it would do her good. All this criminal nonsense —

"It's your father's fault!" cried Val, hurling the hat at him.

"Ain't it the truth?" said Walter.

Val bit her lip. "I'm sorry, darling. I know how much you hate what he stands for." She sank down and laid her head on his chest. "Oh, Walter, what are we going to do?"

"Hey, you're wetting my tie," said Walter. He kissed her curls gently.

Val jumped up, dried her eyes, and ran away. Walter heard her call out in a marvelously bright voice: "Court's adjourned, people!" and a chorus of groans.

Just then it began to drizzle, with that dreary persistence only the California clouds can achieve during the rainy season.

It's like a movie, thought Walter gloomily, or a novel by Thomas Hardy. He got to his feet and followed her.

They found Rhys Jardin patrolling the flags of his terrace at the rear of the house. Pink, in sweat-shirt and sneakers, was staring at his employer with troubled eyes.

"Oh, there you are," said her father. He immediately sat down in the porch swing. "Come here, puss. The rain's spoiled your party, hasn't it?"

"Oh, pop!" said Val, and she ran to him and put her arms about his neck.

The rain pattered on the awning.

"Well, Walter," smiled Rhys, "as a prophet you're pretty good. But not even you foresaw the floods."

Walter sat down. Pink heaved out of his deck-chair and went to the iron table and poured himself a drink of water. Then he said: "Nuts!" and sat down again.

"Is anything left?" asked Val quietly.

"Don't look so tragic, Val!"

"Is there?"

"Well, now that you ask," smiled Rhys, "not a thing. Our negotiable assets are cleaned out."

"Then why did you let me run this party today?" she cried. "All that money going to waste!"

"I never thought I'd live to see the day," said Pink lightly, "when Val Jardin would start squeezing the buffalo."

"Do we have to give up the Malibu place, the house in Santa Monica?" asked Val with difficulty.

"Now don't worry, puss —"

"This — this house, too?"

"You never liked it, anyway."

Val cradled her father's head in her arms. "Darling, you'll have to give up your yachting and golf clubs and things and go to work. How will you like that?"

The big man made a face. "We can realize a lot of money from the real estate and the furnishings —"

"And we'll get rid of Mrs. Thomson and the housemaids and Roxie —"

"No, Val!"

"Yes. And of course Pink will have to go —"

"Nuts," said Pink again.

Val became quiet and sat back in the swing, sucking her lower lip. After a while Walter said uncomfortably: "I know my anti-holding-company cartoons didn't help Ohippi, Mr. Jardin. But you understand — Newspapermen can't —"

Jardin laughed. "If I'd listened to your advice rather than your father's we'd all be a lot better off."

"The lousy part of it is," grunted Pink, "that your old man could still save Ohippi. Only he won't. There ought to be a law!"

"What do you mean?" asked Walter slowly.

Pink waved his arms. "Well, *he* cleaned up, didn't he? Why shouldn't he —"

"My father cleaned up?"

"Keep quiet, Pink," said Rhys.

"Just a moment. I've a right to know!"

"It's not important any more, Walter," said Rhys mildly. "Forget it."

"Forget your grandfather!" yelled Pink. "Go on, tell him about that cat-fight you had with Spaeth this morning!"

Jardin shrugged. "You know, your father and I were equal partners. Whenever he arranged to form a new holding company — he created seven before the government stepped in — the corporation would retain control of the common stock and put the remaining forty-nine percent on the market. The preferred stock we held back, splitting share and share alike."

"Yes?" said Walter.

"Pop. Don't," said Val, looking at Walter's face.

"Go on, Mr. Jardin."

"Knowing nothing about these things, I trusted your father and Ruhig completely. Ruhig advised me to hold on to my preferred — it did seem wise, because the basic Ohippi plants were perfectly sound. Secretly, however, through agents, your father sold his preferred as the companies

40

were created. And now, with all the stock-holders caught, he's sitting back there with a fortune."

"I see," said Walter; he was pale. "And he led me to believe —"

"With the dough he's made," raved Pink, "he could rebuild those power plants and put 'em on their feet again. We got some rights, ain't we? We —"

"You lost money, too?"

Rhys Jardin winced. "I'm afraid I sucked in a lot of my friends — in my early inno-cence."

"Excuse me," said Walter, and he rose and went down the terrace steps into the rain.

"Walter!" cried Val, flying after him. "Please!"

"You go on back," said Walter, without stopping.

"No!"

"This is my business. Go back."

"Just the same," said Val breathlessly, "I'm coming."

She clung to his arm all the way around the pool and up the rocky slope to the Spaeth house.

Val remained nervously on the Spaeth terrace. "Walter, please don't do anything

41

that —" But it was half a whisper, and Walter was already stalking through the glass doors into his father's study.

Mr. Solomon Spaeth sat at his oval desk the picture of baronial gravity, shaking his head a little at the rapid-fire questions of a crowd of newspapermen. His reading glasses rested on the middle of his fat nose, and with his paunch and thin gray hair and sober air he did not remotely resemble the devil and worse that the stockholders at the gate were calling him.

"Gentlemen, please," he protested.

"But how about the flood story, Mr. Spaeth?"

"Are you going on?"

"Where's that statement you promised?"

"I'll give you just this." Solly picked up a paper and fussed with it. The reporters grew quiet. Solly put the paper down. "Owing to the catastrophe in the Ohio and Mississippi Valleys," he said gravely, "our field men report the complete ruin of our equipment. That hydro-electric machinery would cost millions to replace, gentlemen. I'm afraid we shall have to abandon the plants."

There was a shocked silence. Then a man exclaimed: "But that means a loss of a hundred cents on the dollar to every investor in Ohippi securities!"

Solly spread his hands. "It's a great misfortune, gentlemen. But surely we can't be held responsible for the floods? Floods are an act of God."

The reporters did not even notice Walter in their scramble for the door.

Walter stood still near the terrace doors. His lips were twisted a little. . . . His father rubbed his right jowl thoughtfully for a moment, and then began to read the afternoon papers.

Winni Moon was drifting about the study with a vague, pleased smile, touching things here and there; a small fire cracked in the gate; and Jo-Jo, Winni's chimpanzee, was whirling on her pink haunches near the hearth like a dervish, chattering crossly. Jo-Jo whirled incessantly, for she despised the smell of herself, although she was sprinkled with a scent that set Solly back fifty dollars an ounce.

On the terrace, watching, Val tingled with hostility. The Moon worm was wearing the boldest creation in burgundy crêpe, with shirrings at the wrists that "dramatize your every gesture, madame" — Val knew the line *so* well — and her thick wheat-colored hair was done up in a convoluted braid, like a figure eight lying on its side on top of her head.

Hostess gown. Hostess! Protégée! Val's fingers curled for something to pluck and rend.

"Oh," cried Winni, "here's Walter!" And she pounced.

Her clinging act, thought Val bitterly. True, Walter was fending her off with one arm, but that was probably because he knew Val was watching.

"Wally dear, isn't it awful? The floods, and all those people in the woad. You'd think it was the storming of the Castille, at the very weast! I've simply begged Solly — your father to make the police dwive them away —"

Walter shouted: "Lay off me!"

"Why, Walter!"

Solly took off his glasses. After a moment he said: "Get out, Winni."

Winni smiled at once. "Of course, daddy. You two men must have —" She clapped her hands prettily. "Jo-Jo!"

Oh, you — *thing!* thought Val, seeing it all from the terrace through the glass doors.

The unhappy beast leaped to Winni's shoulder and she went out with it, her hips swaying from side to side under the clinging stuff as if they were set in gimbals. She turned, smiled again, and carefully closed the study door.

Thing! THING!

Walter strode forward and faced his father across the marbled leather top of the desk.

"Let's get down to cases," said Walter. "You're a crook."

Solomon Spaeth half-rose from his chair; then, blinking, he sat back. "You can't talk to me that way!"

"You're still a crook."

Solly's complexion deepened. "Ask the United States Attorney! There's nothing illegal about my operations."

"Oh, I'm sure of that," said Walter, "with Ruhig to handle it. But that doesn't make you any the less a crook."

"If you call me that once more —" began his father balefully. Then he smiled. "Pshaw, you're excited, Walter. I forgive you. Have a drink?"

"I don't want your forgiveness!" roared Walter.

Walter, Walter, thought Val desperately.

"Before the floods our cash position was sound. It was just the government — Congress undermined the confidence of the public —"

"Look," said Walter. "How much money

45

have you made out of the sales of your preferred stock since you began creating holding companies around Ohippi?"

"A few dollars, Walter," said Solly soothingly. "But so could Jardin, only he says he hung on to his stock."

"You got that rat Ruhig to advise him to hold on!"

"Who says so? Who says so?" spluttered Solly. "Prove that. Let him prove —"

"You weren't satisfied with swindling the investing public, you had to doublecross your partner, too!"

"If Jardin says I doublecrossed him, he's a liar!"

Val gritted her teeth. You oily rascal! she thought. If only you weren't Walter's father . . .

"Jardin's broke, and you know it!" shouted Walter.

A strange smile fattened Solly's features. "Is that so? Really? Did Jardin tell you that?"

Valerie felt her heart skip a beat. And there was almost a dazed look on Walter's face. What did the man mean? Was it possible that —

"The fact remains," muttered Walter, "you've made millions while your stockholders have been wiped out."

Spaeth shrugged. "They could have sold at peak, too."

"And now you're abandoning the plants!"

"They're useless."

"You could put them back on their feet!"

"Rubbish," said Solly shortly. "You don't know what you're talking about."

"You could put those millions back where they belong — in the plants. You could get Ohippi operating again at a profit when the floods recede!"

Spaeth pounded the desk, swallowing. "Since the Securities Act of 1934 the government is liquidating holding-company structures —"

"And a damned good thing, too!"

"The turn would have come soon, anyway, even without the floods. There's just no point in reinvesting; there's not enough money to be made. You don't know what's happening in this country!"

"You made those filthy millions out of Jardin and the public," growled Walter, "and it's your moral responsibility to save their investments."

"You're a fool," said Solly curtly. "Come back and talk when you've got some sense in your head." And he put on his glasses again and picked up a paper.

Valerie, watching Walter's face, peering around the terrace wall, felt panic. If only she dared go inside — take Walter away before he —

Walter leaned across his father's desk and gently took the paper away and tossed it into the fireplace. Sully sat very still.

"You listen to me," said Walter. "I'll overlook your crookedness, the way you took Jardin, your lie to me about how hard you were hit. But you're going to do one thing."

Solly whispered: "Walter, don't get me excited."

"You're going to save those plants."

"No!"

"It's my hard luck to own your name," said Walter thickly, "so I've got to take the stink out of it. You've ruined the father of the woman I'm going to marry, and you're going to make it up to both of them, do you hear?"

"What's that?" screamed Solly, bouncing out of his chair. "Marry? The Jardin girl?"

"You heard me!"

Val went over to the top step of the terrace and sat down limply in the rain. She felt like crying and laughing at the same time. The darling, darling idiot — proposing like that . . .

"Oh, no, you're not," panted Solly, shaking his finger in Walter's face. "Oh, no, you're not!"

Tell him, Walter, thought Val, hugging her knees ecstatically. Tell the old boa-constrictor!

"You're damned right I'm not!" shouted Walter. "Not after what you've done to her! What do you think I am?"

Val sat open-mouthed. Surprise! Oh, God, you secondhand Don Quixote. She might have known. He'd never do anything the sane and normal way. Val felt like crawling off the terrace into the rock garden and taking refuge under a stone.

In the study there was a curious silence as Solomon Spaeth scurried around his desk again and opened a drawer. He flung a handful of newspaper clippings on the desk.

"Ever since the stocks began to fall," yelled Solly, "you've been drawing these filthy cartoons in that Red rag you work for. Oh, I've been saving 'em! You've drawn me as —"

"Not you — the stinking system you stand for!"

"A rat, a vulture, a wolf, a shark, an octopus!"

"If the shoe pinches —"

Solly hurled the clippings into the fire.

49

"I've given you your way too much! I let you pick your own vocation, childish as it is, let you brand me publicly as a damned menagerie. . . . I warn you, Walter! If you don't stop this nonsense right now —"

Walter said in a strained voice: "Put your money back into the plants."

"If you don't forget this ridiculous idea of marrying a pauper —"

"Next week *East Lynne*."

"You'll marry money!"

"Now you're thinking in terms of dynasties. Have you got the royal sow picked out yet, your Majesty?"

"By God, Walter," shrieked Solly, "if — you — don't — !"

He stopped. Their eyes locked. Val held her breath.

Solly snatched the telephone and shouted a number.

Walter waited grimly.

"Ruhig! Give me Ruhig, you fool!" Spaeth glared at his son. "I'll show *you*. I've had a bellyful of — Ruhig? . . . No, no, stop babbling! Ruhig, you come right over here with a couple of witnesses. . . . For what? To draw up a new will, that's for what!"

He hung up, panting, and adjusted his glasses with shaking fingers.

"I suppose," laughed Walter, "you think

you've dealt me the mortal blow."

"You'll never get your hands on my money, damn you!"

Walter walked over to the glass doors in silence. Val got up, holding her throat. But then he went back, passed his father's desk, and opened the study door.

Winni Moon almost fell into his arms; there was a silly smile on her face. Walter brushed by her without a glance, and she disappeared.

Spaeth sat down, breathing heavily through his mouth. Val, on the terrace, felt completely numb.

A few moments later she heard Walter returning. She looked, and saw a valise in one hand and a drawing board in the other.

"I'll call for the rest of my stuff to-morrow," said Walter coldly.

His father did not reply.

"And this isn't the end of it, either," continued Walter in the same bleak way. "That money goes back to the people you took it from, do you understand? I don't know how I'll do it" — he opened the glass doors — "but by God, I'll *do* it."

Solly Spaeth sat still, only his head bobbing a little.

Walter went out onto the terrace. He

nudged Val's soaked shoulders with the edge of the drawing board.

"Could you put me up tonight, Val? I can't start looking for a place until to-morrow."

Val looped her arms around his neck and clung. "Walter. Darling. Marry me."

She felt him stiffen. Then he said lightly: "I'd rather live with you in sin."

"Walter — dearest. I'm mad about you. I don't care what your father's done. We'll manage somehow. Don't keep hauling the burdens of the world around on your shoulders. Forget what's happened —"

Walter said in a gay voice: "Come on, let's run for it. You've just about ruined that precious croquignole bob of yours as it is."

Val's arms fell. "But, Walter. I asked you to *marry* me."

"No, Val," he said gently.

"But, Walter!"

"Not yet," said Walter; and there was something in the way he said it that turned the rain down her back to ice-water.

3

DESIGN FOR LEAVING

A great flood rushed down upon *Sans Souci* in the middle of the night, and Walter and Val and Winni Moon and Jo-Jo and Pink and Rhys Jardin clung shivering to the highest gable of the roof in the darkness, hearing the water gurgle hungrily as it rose.

Suddenly there was a moon, and the man in it bore the ruddy features of Solomon Spaeth. Then the moon went down into the black waters and was drowned, still leering, and the gray day began to dawn; and Val saw nothing but water, water everywhere, and she felt terribly thirsty, and she awoke with her tongue sticking to the roof of her mouth.

A pseudopod of sunlight tried to climb into her bed, but it was too weak; and soon it vanished altogether under the cold swollen clouds of the real day.

Val shivered again and crept out of bed, by habit looking around for Roxie. But Roxie was gone — Roxie and Mrs. Thomson the housekeeper and all the rest; and, as in the dream, Val felt that the end of the world had come.

She was sitting helplessly before her dressing table in the bathroom, looking at the eight-ounce crystal bottle of *Indiscret*, when Rhys knocked, and came in, and said: "What's the exact moment, puss, that bacon becomes cinders?"

Val jumped up. "Pop! You haven't been trying to make breakfast? Don't do another thing. I'll be down in a jiffy."

Rhys held her at arm's length. "I'm glad you're taking it this way, puss."

"*Will* you go downstairs?"

"If Pink goes, we'll have to get a cook."

"Don't need one. I can cook like a fiend."

"You're not going to be slave to a stove, Val. We'll be able to afford it."

Val sniffed. "Yes, until the money's eaten up. How did you make out with the real estate?"

He shrugged. "I got a fair price for the Santa Monica and Malibu places, but this one represents a considerable loss."

"Did that movie man take the yacht?"

"Literally — the pirate!"

Val kissed his brown chin. "Please don't worry, darling; *I'll* show you how to economize! Now get out."

But when she was alone again Val looked a little ill. To give up all these lovely, precious things was like facing the amputation of an arm. Val thought of the auction sale to come, mobs of curious people trampling over everything, handling their most intimate possessions . . . and stopped thinking.

She burned the toast and charred the bacon and over-fried the eggs and under-boiled the coffee, and Rhys gobbled it all and maintained with a plausibility that almost fooled her that he had never eaten such a delicious breakfast in his life. The only thing that really tasted good was the orange juice, and Pink had prepared that before he left. Walter was right — she *was* useless! And that made her think of Walter, and thinking of Walter made her lips quiver, and after she pushed Rhys out of the departed Mrs. Thomson's no longer spotless kitchen Val sat down and wept into the dish-washing machine. It was a sort of requiem, for Val was positive it was the last time they would ever be able to afford such a wonderful thing.

It was even worse later.

The auction people turned up and completed the details of the task begun a week before — cataloguing the furniture and art-objects. They ran all over the house like oblivious ants.

The telephones rang incessantly — the purchaser of the yacht with a complaint, a multitude of lawyers with questions about this piece of property and that, insistent reporters; Rhys kept dashing from one telephone to another, almost cheerful, followed everywhere by Pink, who looked like a house-dog which has just been kicked.

Valerie was left to her own devices in the midst of this hurly-burly; she had nothing to do but get out of the way of hurrying strangers. A man practically dumped her on the floor retrieving the antique Cape Cod rocker in which her mother had sung her to sleep; Val felt like giving him the one-two Pink had taught her, but the man was away with his loot before she could get her hands on him.

She drifted about, fingering the things she had grown up with — the heavy old silver, those precious little vessels made of old porcelain backed with pewter which Rhys had picked up on his honeymoon in Shanghai, the laces and velvets and lamps, the lovely old hunting prints. She fingered the books and stared at the pictures and spent a difficult moment before the grand old piano on which she had learned to play

— never very well! — Chopin and Beethoven and Bach.

And Walter, darn him, didn't even call up *once!*

Val used up two handkerchiefs, artfully, by crying in corners.

But whenever her father bustled into view she said something gay about their new furnished apartment at the *La Salle* which Walter, who had taken rooms there, had recommended. How thrilling it was going to be living there! Yes, agreed Rhys, and different, too. Yes, said Val — that ducky little five-room place — hotel service — built-in radio — even a really fair print or two on the walls. . . . And all the while little frozen fingers crawled down her back.

She found Pink in the dismantled gymnasium, sweating powerfully over a litter of golf-bags, skis, Indian clubs, and other sporting paraphernalia.

"Oh, Pink," she wailed, "is the *La Salle* really so awful?"

"It's all right," said Pink. "Anything you want, you ask Mibs."

"Who's Mibs?"

"Mibs Austin. Girl-friend of mine."

"Why, Pincus!"

Pink blushed. "She's the telephone oper-

57

ator there. She'll take care of you. . . . Just *one* of 'em," he said.

"I'm sure she's sweet. . . . After all," said Val absently, "Walter does live there."

"And me," said Pink, wrapping a pair of skis. "I sort of rented me a 'phone booth there, too."

"Pink, you didn't!"

"I got to live somewhere, don't I!"

"You *darling!*"

"Anyway, who's going to cook? *You* can't. And all Rhys can make is Spanish omelet."

"But, Pink —"

"Besides, he needs his exercises. You can't give him his rubdown, either."

"But, Pink," said Val, troubled, "you know that now — we weren't figuring on extra expenses —"

"Who said anything about pay?" growled Pink. "Get out of here, squirt, and let me work."

"But how are you going to — I mean, have you any plans?"

Pink sighed. "Once I was going to start a health farm and make me some real dough out of these smart guys that run to rubber tires around the middle, but now —"

"Oh, Pink, I'm so sorry about your losing all your money!"

"I got my connections, don't worry. I can always go back to being an expert in the movies — double for some punk with a pretty pan who don't know how to hold a club but's supposed to be champ golfer of the world — that kind of hooey."

"Pink," said Val, "do you mind if I kiss you?"

Pink said gruffly: "Keep 'em for Little Boy Blue; he has 'em with cream. Val, scram!" But his nutbrown face reddened.

Val smiled a little mistily. "You're such a fraud, Pincus darling." And she kissed him without further opposition.

The auctioneer cleared his throat. "And now, ladies and gentlemen, a few announcements before the sale commences. As you know, this is not a forced sale. So the owner, Mr. Rhys Jardin, has exercised his privilege of making last-minute withdrawals. If you will kindly note these changes in your catalogue . . ."

Val, sitting beside her father in the front row of chairs, felt him tremble; she did not dare look at his face. She tried to preserve an air of "Who cares?", but she knew the attempt was a miserable failure.

". . . the sixty-foot yacht *Valerie* has been withdrawn from the auction, having been

59

disposed of in a private sale yesterday. . . ."

Walter was here — sitting in the rear, the coward! The least he might have done was say hello — or isn't it a lovely day for an execution — or something like that. But Walter was acting very strangely. He hadn't even glanced at her before the people took seats, and he was so pale —

". . . your number one-two-six, a collection of four hundred and twenty-two assorted sporting prints. Also your number one-five-two, a collection of small arms. Also your number one-five-three, a collection of medieval arrowheads. Due to the great interest in the sporting-print collection, Mr. Jardin wishes me to announce that it has been donated to the Los Angeles public library association."

There was a little splatter of applause, which quickly died when some one hissed. Val felt like hiding her head. A man's voice behind them whispered: "I understand he's given the arrowheads to the Museum."

"He must be stony broke," whispered a female voice.

"Yeah? Maybe."

"What do you mean?"

"Shh! Isn't that him in front of us?"

Val's hands were tight in her lap. She heard her father expel a long, labored breath. People were such pigs. Vultures! Wheeling over the carrion! Even that Ruhig person had had the unadulteratcd gall to attend the auction. He was sitting well down front, beaming at all the hostile glances converging on his pudgy cheeks.

"Also withdrawn is number seven-three, a miscellaneous lot of sporting equipment — golf clubs, bags, fencing foils, tennis rackets, *et cetera*."

She felt Rhys stir with surprise. "No, pop," she whispered. "It's not a mistake."

"But I included them —"

"I withdrew them. You're *not* going to be stripped bare!"

He groped for her hand and found it.

"Everything else will be sold on this floor regardless of bid. Everything is in superb condition. The art-objects and antiques have all been expertized and found genuine. Each lot is fully described in your catalogue. . . ."

Come *on*. Get *started*. . . . It was worse, far worse, than Val had imagined it would be. Oh, Walter, why don't you move down here and sit by me and hold my hand, too!

"Lot number one," said the auctioneer in a brisk chant. "Lowestoft china, 1787, with the New York insignia, design female and eagle, two hundred pieces, rare antiquity and historic value, who'll start it with five thousand dollars? Do I hear five thousand on lot number one? Five thousand?"

"Two thousand," called out a cadaverous man with the predatory look of a rabid collector.

The auctioneer groaned. "Gentlemen, gentlemen. A crude imitation of these superb antiques brought seven thousand in a private sale only a few years ago —"

"Twenty-five hundred," said a calm, rather husky voice from the rear.

"Three thousand," droned the cadaverous man.

"Thirty-five," said the husky voice.

"Thirty-five! Who says four thousand?"

"Four thousand," said Mr. Anatole Ruhig.

"Five? Do I hear five?"

"Forty-five hundred," said the husky voice.

"Forty-five bid! Five, anyone? You, sir? Mr. Ruhig? Forty-five once, forty-five twice, forty-five . . . Sold to the gentleman for forty-five hundred dollars."

Robbery! screamed Val silently. The Lowestoft had come down in the family. It was worth many, many thousands. Robber!

She craned with the others to see the husky-voiced thief. He was a spare young man with a close black beard covering his cheeks and chin, and he wore *pince-nez* glasses. Val after one malevolent look turned her eyes front. Robber!

Lot number two went up; Val heard the rattle of auctioneer's patter and bids only dimly. Poor Rhys was so rigid. It was horrible having to be here. . . . When the voices stopped it appeared that the husky one belonging to the bearded young man had again prevailed. The beast — buying poor mother's b-bedroom suite!

Lot number three — history repeated itself. There were murmurs from the floor, and the auctioneer looked enchanted. Mr. Anatole Ruhig, who seemed to have a passion for antiques, looked definitely unenchanted. Black looks were hurled at the unconquerable bidder. . . . Far in the rear, Mr. Walter Spaeth sat slumped in a chair, his right hand absently sketching on the back of an envelope the head of the bearded young man, who was sitting in the row before.

Lot number four. Number five. Six. Seven. . . .

"It's a frame-up," said some one loudly. "He doesn't give any one else a chance!"

"Quiet! Please! Ladies and gentlemen —"

"This isn't an auction, it's a monologue!"

Three people rose and went out in a dudgeon. Mr. Anatole Ruhig was by this time regarding the villain of the piece thoughtfully. The cadaverous one rose and left, too. Val looked around in a panic; Rhys frowned at the greedy one.

Lot number eight, nine, number ten. . . .

"I'm going!"

"So am I!"

The bearded young man coughed. "Common courtesy compels me to warn those who still remain that you may as well leave, too, unless you choose to remain as mere spectators."

"I beg your pardon sir —" began the auctioneer, who did not like the way things were going.

"I was about to add," the bearded young man called out to the auctioneer, "that we can all save a lot of wear-and-tear on our vocal cords if we face the fact."

"The fact?" said the auctioneer in bewilderment, rapping for order.

"The fact that I humbly intend," continued the young man, getting to his feet and revealing considerable flannel-clad length, "to buy every lot in this auction, regardless of opposition bidding."

And he sat down, smiling pleasantly at his neighbors.

"Who is he?" muttered Rhys Jardin.

"Don't you know?" whispered Val. "I can't understand —"

"This is highly irregular," said the auctioneer, wiping his face.

"In fact," said the young man hoarsely from his seat, "to save time I'm prepared to offer Mr. Jardin a lump sum for the entire catalogue!"

The man behind Val jumped up and shouted: "It's a conspiracy, that's what it is!"

"I see the whole thing," cried some one else.

"Sure! It's a trick of Jardin's!"

"He's pulling a bluff!"

"Run a fake auction to make the public think he's broke, and then plant this man to buy the whole thing back for him!"

"With his own money! *My* money!"

"Ladies and gentlemen! Please —" began Rhys, rising with a pale face.

"Sit down, you crook!" screeched a fat sweaty lady.

"No, no, he's nothing of the sort," protested the young man who had caused all the trouble. But by this time every one was shouting with indignation, and the young man's voice was lost in the noise.

"You take that back!" screamed Val,

diving for the fat lady.

"Officer! Clear the room!" roared the auctioneer.

When order was restored Val scrambled over two chairs getting to the bearded young man. "You worm! Now see what you've done!"

"I'll admit," he said ruefully, "I didn't foresee a rising of the masses. . . . Mr. Jardin, I think? Of course my proposal was seriously intended."

"Breaking up auctions," grumbled the auctioneer, scowling; for obviously with such a spirited bidder on the floor he would have realized a greater gross sum and consequently a handsomer commission.

"I decided on impulse, Mr. Jardin, and didn't have time to make an offer in advance of the sale."

"Suppose we talk it over," said Jardin abruptly; and the three men put their heads together. Mr. Anatole Ruhig rose, took his hat and stick, and quietly went away.

The young man was a persuasive bargainer. In five minutes Jardin, completely mystified, had agreed to his offer, the auctioneer sat grumpily down to write out a bill of sale, and the young man dragged a large wallet out of his pocket and laid on the desk such a pile of new thousand-dollar bills that Val felt like yelling "Economic royalist!"

"Just to avoid any embarrassment about checks," he said in his hoarse voice. "And now, if there's nothing else, I have a group of vans waiting outside."

And he went out and returned a moment later with a crew of muscular gentlemen in aprons who looked around, spat on their hands, listened to their employer's whispered instructions, nodded, and went to work without conversation.

"Who is he, anyway?" demanded Pink, glaring at the beard.

"Profiteer," snapped Valerie. That made her think of Walter, so she drifted over casually to where he still sat.

"Hello."

"Hello."

Silence. Then Val said: "Aren't you ashamed of yourself?"

"Yes," said Walter.

What could you do with a creature like that? Val snatched the envelope on which he was sketching out of his hands, crumpled it, threw it at him, and flounced away.

Walter picked up the envelope and absently pocketed it.

"There you are," said a bass voice, and Walter looked up.

"Hullo, Fitz. How are you?"

Fitzgerald sat down, wheezing. "Lousy. I thought California would stop these sinus headaches of mine, but I'll be a monkey's uncle if they aren't worse." Fitz had been in California over ten years and he complained about his sinusitis on the average of a dozen times each day. "Where's the drawing?"

"Which one?"

"Today's — yesterday's — any day's," growled Fitz. "What do you think I'm paying you for — your good looks? With all this Ohippi dirt in the air, you go on a bat!"

"I was busy."

"I haven't had a cartoon for a week — I've had to fill in with old ones. Listen, Walter . . . Say, what's going on here?"

"As if you didn't know, you long-eared jackass."

"I heard outside somebody stampeded the works."

"There's nothing wrong with your nose, either."

Fitz was a bulky Irishman with eyebrows like birds' nests, imbedded in which were two very glossy and restless eggs. He was also unpredictable. He left Walter like a genie.

68

"Hullo, Rhys. Say, Rhys, I'm damned sorry about everything. Would have come over sooner, but I thought you'd rather not jaw about it."

"Good of you." Jardin looked around; the room was getting bare. "You're in at the death, anyway," he said grimly.

"Tough break." Fitz shot sidewise glances at the bearded young man, who was watching his men calmly. "Who's the buyer? Hullo, Valerie."

Just then the young man turned his bearded face toward them, and Fitz's eyebrows almost met his puffy cheeks.

"Hello, Mr. F-Fitzgerald," said Val, watching a commode sail by. There was still a deep scratch in one leg where she had kicked it the time Mrs. Thomson had whacked her for printing "Thomson is a turkey" in yellow crayon on the drawer.

But Fitz ignored her. He lumbered over to the bearded young man and said: "Hey, you're somebody I know."

"Yes?" said the young man politely, and he moved off.

Fitz followed him. "Name's Queen, isn't it? Ellery Queen?"

"Sharp eyes," said the young man. He moved off again.

Fitz seized his arm. "Know who bought

your stuff, Rhys?" he bellowed. "Ellery Queen, the master-mind!" But the master-mind was gone with a single twist. Fitz thundered after him, leaving a bewildered group behind. As he passed Walter he snapped: "Report to the office, damn you. Queen! Hey!"

He caught up with Ellery outside the house. Several of the vans had filled up and were gone; the men were packing the last two.

"Now don't be unpleasant," sighed Mr. Queen.

"I'm Fitzgerald of the *Independent*," said Fitz briskly, grasping Ellery's arm like a grappling-iron.

"You're an ass."

"What's that?"

"If I'd wanted my identity known, Mr. Fitzgerald, don't you think I'd have advertised it myself?"

"So that accounts for the phony brush!"

"Not at all. I broke out in a nasty facial rash a few months ago — probably an allergy — and I couldn't shave. Now that the rash is gone I'm so pleased with my appearance I've kept the beard."

"With me it's sinus," said Fitz. "However, it still smells. How about the voice? Got a rash on your vocal cords?"

"Very simple, my dear Watson. The moment I stepped off the train into your balmy California rains I caught laryngitis, and I've still got it. I should be in bed," said Ellery bitterly.

"Why aren't you? What's the gag? What are you doing in Hollywood? Where'd you get the dough? Are you getting married and furnishing your love-nest?"

"If this is an interview," said Ellery, "I'm a deaf-mute overcome by complete paralysis."

"Say, who do you think you are? Managing editors don't leg it." Fitz eyed him keenly. "It isn't if you say so."

"I say so."

"Now how about satisfying my layman's curiosity?"

"It's no gag. I'm in Hollywood on a writing contract to Magna — God knows I don't know anything about writing for the screen, but they don't seem to care, so I don't either. And no, I'm not being married."

"Wait a minute! Why are you buying the Jardin stuff?"

Ellery watched the last two vans drive off. He moved out from under the porte-cochère into the drizzle and stepped hastily into his rented car.

"Goodbye, Mr. Fitzgerald," he said amiably, waving. "It's been nice seeing you." And he drove off.

The Jardins and Walter and Pink stood in silence in the denuded living-room.

"Are the — are the trunks gone?" asked Val at last in a small voice. "And . . . everything else?"

"Yes, Val."

"Then I don't suppose there's anything —"

"Come on, let's get going," growled Pink, "before I bust out crying."

They marched out of the empty house in a body, close together, like condemned criminals on their way to the wall.

Outside Val picked a rose off a bush and absently pulled it to pieces.

"Well! Here we go," said Rhys in a cheery voice. "It's goodbye to all this. I think we're going to have a lot of fun, puss." He put his arm around her.

"All the common people have fun," said Pink. "Perk up, squirt."

"I'm all right," protested Valerie. "Of course, it's a little strange. . . ."

"Let's go," said Walter in a low voice.

He preceded them down the private drive toward the pillbox at the gate, hands jammed into the pockets of his topcoat. He did not look back at either the Jardin house — or that other.

A crowd was waiting in the road beyond the gate, making mob noises; but the noises stopped as the little procession came toward them. Frank, the day man, his empty left sleeve flapping, hurried from the pillbox toward their two cars, which were parked near the gate.

It became more and more difficult to keep that steady pace. Val felt a little faint. It was like the French Revolution, with the mob of *citoyens* waiting greedily for the victims, and the guillotine looming ahead. . . .

Frank held the door of Jardin's small sedan open — the only car they had kept.

"I'm sorry, Mr. Jardin. I'm awfully sorry," said Frank. In getting into the sedan Rhys had caught his coat on the door-handle, and the camel's-hair fabric just below the right pocket ripped away in a triangular flap.

Pink said: "You tore your coat, Rhys," but Jardin paid no attention, groping blindly for the ignition-key. Valerie crept into the rear seat and slipped far down on her spine; she avoided Walter's eyes as he closed the door behind her. Pink jumped in beside Jardin.

"I'm sorry, sir," said Frank again, in a weepy voice.

"Here." Jardin leaned out and pressed a large bill into the gateman's hand. "Split it with Walewski, Frank. Goodbye."

"Thanks, thanks!" Frank scuttled off to the gate.

"Well," smiled Rhys, starting the car, "what shall it be? A snack at the Troc?"

"It's too expensive there, pop," murmured Val.

"How about Al Levy's? Or the Derby?"

"Better get going," remarked Pink dryly, "before that mob out there starts yipping for blood."

Rhys fell silent and shifted. Val looked back. Walter was getting into his coupé, slowly. Then he stopped and stepped back and looked across the lawns toward the Spaeth house. Far away. Solomon Spaeth stood alone, in motion. He was waving and his mouth was open. Apparently he was shouting something, but his voice did not carry.

Walter's lean jaw hardened. Val saw the taut whitening line. He got into his car without a sign that he had seen.

"It's like the end of a bad dream," thought Val, shivering. "For all of us."

Then they were pushing slowly through

74

the silent crowd and she sat up straight
and tried to look as she fancied Marie An-
toinette had once looked in a somewhat
similar situation.

4

— AND SUDDEN DEATH

After lunch Pink said he had to see a dog about a man and Jardin dropped him at the Magna studio on Melrose.

"We may as well face it, Val," said Rhys when Pink had gone. "We'll have to go there some time."

"Why not now?" smiled Val. She felt better, because the sherry had been good and so had the chicken patties. And it was true — they might as well get used to the notion that they were proletarians just as quickly as they could. The only fly in the afternoon's ointment was Walter; he had left them abruptly, with a gloom that was odd even for him.

Val brooded about Walter as Rhys drove up to Santa Monica Boulevard and turned west on the car-tracks. She would definitely have to do something about Walter. Things couldn't go on this way. It was absurd of him to reject her proposal of marriage — absurd and a little dangerous, considering that last quarrel with his father and the look in his eye.

"Here we are," said Rhys bravely.

Val sat up. There they were, one square from Hollywood Boulevard's bedlam — in front of the *La Salle.*

"Parking," said Rhys, "is going to be a problem."

"Yes," said Val. "Won't it?"

Rhys finally found a tiny space near a curb, and he parked and they got out and looked at each other and squared their shoulders and entered the hotel.

"You must be the Jardins," said a small blond girl with a blond dip over one eye. "Pink 'phoned me about you. I'm Mibs Austin."

"Hello, Mibs," said Val, looking around at the lobby.

Miss Austin took the earphones off her head and leaned earnestly across the register. "Now don't let *anything* worry you, honey. I just about run this dive. Watch out for Fanny, the woman who'll clean your apartment; she skips corners. The radio needs a new thingumbob — I've told the manager about it. And, Mr. Jardin, the valay here is very high-class."

"I'm sure we'll love it," said Val.

"Oh, and your stuff came, too," said Miss Austin. "I watched myself. They didn't break a single thing."

"Stuff?" echoed Val. "What stuff? Oh, you mean the trunks. Thanks, Mibs; we're terribly grateful for everything."

They took the wheezy elevator to the third floor, rear — it was thirty dollars a month cheaper in the rear — leaving Miss Austin behind to stare. Trunks? Who said anything about trunks?

Rhys pushed the key slowly into the lock of 3-C, and slowly opened the door, and Val slowly went in and said: "Oh!"

The pseudo-modern furniture, the noisy drugget, the questionable prints — all, all had vanished. In their places were the things the moving men had carried out of *Sans Souci* under the mysterious Mr. Queen's vigilant eye only a few hours earlier.

Rhys said: "I'll be double-damned." He dropped his coat onto his own sofa and sank into his own leather chair.

Val flew to the telephone. "Mibs! Who brought our furniture here? I mean, how did —"

"Wasn't it supposed to be? The man said —"

"Mibs! Who?"

"The movers. They just brought the van loads and dumped 'em. We had orders to take out the hotel furniture this morning."

"Oh," said Val. "And who was it ordering *that?*"

"Why, the gentleman in 4-F. What's his name? That Mr. Spaeth. Oh! Miss Jardin, is that the Spaeth — ?"

"Hello," said Walter from the doorway, and Val dropped the 'phone to find him grinning at her like some friendly mugwump.

"Walter, you *fiend*," sobbed Valerie, and she ran into her bedroom and slammed the door.

"Was it you?" asked Rhys.

"It's all here," said Walter gruffly. "I mean everything we could cram into five rooms. Here's the warehouse receipt for the rest, Mr. Jardin."

"Warehouse receipt?" said Rhys in an odd voice.

"I've put the leftovers in storage for you."

Rhys laughed a little blankly and rubbed the back of his neck. "I'm afraid what's happened today is getting to be a little too much for my primitive brain. And that Queen fellow — who was he?"

Walter dropped his hat and coat on the sofa and sat down to light a cigaret. "Funny thing. He's just come to the Coast on a movie-writing contract — he's a

writer as well as a detective, you know —
and an old school chum of mine in New
York told him to look me up. So I asked
him to act as my proxy. He did it well,
don't you think?"

"But, Walter, why?" asked Rhys gently.

Walter scowled at his smoke. "Well . . . I
know how stiff your neck is. You wouldn't
have accepted money. So to avoid arguments . . ."

Jardin rose and went to the window and
pulled up the Venetian blinds and threw
the windows open; the drizzle had stopped
and the sun was trying to shine again.
Traffic noises roared into the room from
the rear street below. He closed the windows at once and turned around, a little
shrunken.

"It's wonderfully decent of you, Walter.
But I simply can't accept it. Besides, Val
has told me about your father cutting you
out of his will."

"I've some money of my own from my
mother's father — plenty more left."

Rhys smiled sadly. "I've deposited the
cash, and it's too late today to draw it out
again. But, Walter, the first thing —"

"Forget it."

"Walter, you make it awfully difficult."

They eyed each other in silence, at an

impasse. Then Val sobbed from the bedroom: "The least you could do, you swine, is come in here and console me!"

Walter rose with a foolish grin.

"I think," murmured Rhys, "I'll go out for some air." He picked up his hat and left as Walter went into the bedroom.

A little later the telephone rang and Val ran into the living-room, fussing with her hair, to answer it. All trace of tears had vanished. Walter followed, looking even more foolish, if that was possible, than before.

"Yes," said Val. "Just a moment. It's for you, Walter. The telephone operator wants to know if you're up here."

Walter said: "Hullo," still looking foolish, then he said nothing at all as he listened to a voice, the foolish look slowly turning grim. Finally he muttered: "I'll be right over," and hung up.

"What's wrong?"

Walter reached for his hat and coat. "My father."

Valerie went cold. "Don't go, Walter."

"I've got to settle this thing once and for all."

She flew to him, clinging. "Please, Walter!"

Walter said gently: "Wait for me. I'll be

81

back in half an hour and we'll drive out Wilshire to the beach for dinner." And he pushed her away and went out.

Val stood still for a long time. The old half-quenched fears began to burn brightly again. She picked up the coat left on the sofa and took it into the foyer, hardly aware of what she was doing.

But as she was hanging the coat up in the foyer closet awareness returned. She held the coat up and looked at it more closely. It was Walter's! He had taken Rhys's by mistake — they were both tan camel's-hair of the same belted style, of a size.

And as she turned the coat over in her hands, something fell out of one of the pockets and struck her foot.

It was an automatic, very black and shiny.

Val recoiled in instant reflex. But after the first horrible moment she pounced on it and thrust it hastily back into Walter's coat, unreasoningly glad her father was not there to see it. Then she took it out of the pocket and, handling it as if it were a scorpion, carried it into her bedroom and buried it in the deepest bureau drawer, her heart pounding.

A gun. Walter. . . . She was so frightened

82

she sat down on her bed to keep from rec-
ognizing the weakness in her knees. Walter
had never had a gun. Walter hated guns, as
he hated war, and poverty, and injus-
tice. . . .

She rose a little later and began to unpack her trunks, trying not to think.

Rhys returned in ten minutes, smoking a
cigar and looking calmer. He called out to
Val: "Where's everybody?"

"Walter's had a call from his father," said
Val in a muffled voice from the bedroom.

"Oh. . . . Where do I put my hat?"

"In the foyer closet, silly. And be sure
from now on you hang things up. This is
going to be a co-operative joint."

Jardin chuckled, put away his hat, and
went into his bedroom to unpack.

By 5.30 their clothes were hung and
there was nothing left to be done.

"I wonder where Walter is," said Val
worriedly.

"He's only been gone a half-hour."

Val bit her lip. "He said — Let's wait in
the lobby."

"It's raining again," said Rhys, at the
closet. "Val, this isn't my camel's-hair."

"Walter took it by mistake."

Jardin put on a tweed topcoat and they

went downstairs. Val stared at the clock over the desk. It was 5.35.

She said nervously: "I'm going to call him."

"What's the matter with you, puss?" Jardin sat down near the potted palm and picked up a newspaper; but when he saw his photograph on the front page he put the newspaper down.

"Get me Solomon Spaeth's residence," said Val in a low voice. "I think it's Hillcrest 2411."

Mibs plugged in. "Hillcrest 2411. . . . Nice guy, Walter Spaeth. Lovely eyes, Miss Jardin, don't you think so? . . . Hello. Is that you, Mr. Spaeth? . . . This *is* Mr. Walter Spaeth, isn't it? I thought I recognized your voice, Mr. Spaeth. Miss Jardin's calling. . . . Take it right here, Miss Jardin."

Val snatched the telephone. "Walter! Is there any trouble? You said —"

Walter's voice sounded queerly thick in her ear. "Val. I've got no time now. Something awful — something awful —"

Val whispered: "Yes, Walter."

"Wait for me at the *La Salle*," said Walter's funny voice. "I'll be there as soon as I can." His voice sank. "Val. Please. Don't mention this call to any one. No one!"

Val whispered again: "Yes, Walter."

She heard the click; it sounded very loud. She hung up and said slowly: "Let's sit down."

At 6.30 Val said in a hoarse voice: "I can't stand it any longer. He told me not to tell — He's in trouble."

"Now, puss —" said Rhys uncomfortably.

She whispered: "Something awful. That's what Walter said. Something awful."

Her father looked at her with concern. "All right, Val. We'll go over there."

He drove up into the hills at fifty miles an hour. Val hung out of the car. Neither said a word.

The moment they swung into the road outside the gate of *Sans Souci* they knew something was wrong. The crowds which had swarmed there for weeks were gone. In their place were the running lights of many large, official-looking cars. It was growing dark.

"I told you," said Val. "Didn't I tell you? Something — something —"

The gate was opened by a policeman. There was no sign of Walewski, the night gateman, near his pillbox. But there were other policemen.

"What's happened, officer?" demanded Jardin. "I'm Rhys Jardin."

"Oh, are you? Hold it a minute." The policeman said something to another policeman, and the second man went into the pillbox; and they heard the tinkle of Walewski's telephone. Then he came out and jerked his finger.

Jardin shifted into first and drove through the gate. The second policeman hopped onto the running-board and stayed there.

Val, on the edge of her seat, was conscious of a long howling in her ears, as of winds.

At the Spaeth door they were met by three men, all in plain clothes. The three looked them over very coldly. Then one, taller than the rest, with a nose like an arrowhead, said: "Come in, please."

They were surrounded by the three and marched through the house. On the way they passed Winni Moon, who sat on the lowest step of the stairs which led to the upper floor staring with horror at her long feet while Jo-Jo chattered on her shoulder.

Solomon Spaeth's study was packed with men — men with cameras, men with flashbulbs, men with tape measures, men with bottles and brushes, men with pencils. The air was thick and blue with smoke.

And there was Walter, too. Walter was sitting behind his father's dcsk, pushed away, with a large man over him. His face was drawn and pale. And there was a crude bandage wound around his head which would have given him a rakish look if not for the ragged blob of blood which had soaked through from his left temple.

"Walter!"

Valerie tried to run to him, but the tall arrow-nosed man put his hand on her arm. Val stopped. She felt really very calm. Everything was so water-clear — the smoke was so blue and the bandage was so red, and Walter's head moved from side to side so very definitely as he looked at her.

From side to side. Like a signal. Or a warning.

The room misted over suddenly and Val leaned back against the nearest wall.

"You're Miss Jardin?" said the tall man abruptly.

"Yes," said Val. "Of course I am." Wasn't that an absurd thing to say?

"My name is Glücke — Inspector, Detective Division."

"How do you do." That was even more absurd, but it was the strangest thing. Her brain had no control over her mouth.

"Were you looking for Mr. Walter Spaeth?"

"Inspector," began Rhys. But the tall man frowned.

"Yes," said Valerie. "Yes, of course. Why not? We had an appointment for dinner. We looked for Mr. Spaeth in his apartment but he wasn't there so we thought perhaps he had gone to his father's house and so we came over —"

"I see," said Glücke, looking elsewhere with his brilliant eyes. It seemed to Val that Walter nodded the least bit in approval. It was all so queer — everything. She mustn't lose her head. It would come out soon. Glücke — that was a funny name. Until she found out what . . .

Jardin said: "That's right, Inspector. My daughter has told you. . . . May I ask what's happened?"

"Don't you know?"

"I beg your pardon."

"Well," said the tall man dryly, "they don't send for the Homicide Detail in petit larceny cases."

He stood still. Then he made a sign, a small sign with no question in it, as a man would make it who is accustomed to be instantly obeyed. A group of men crowded together before the ell beside the fireplace separated.

A dead man was sitting on the floor in the angle of thc cll, one foot doubled under him. A reddish, brownish, ragged stab-wound marred the otherwise immaculate appearance of his dove-gray gabardine jacket. As he sat there in the corner he looked like a small fat boy who has been slapped without warning; there was an expression of pure surprise on his unmoving face.

Val yelped and spun about to hide her eyes against her father's coat.

A reporter with a cigaret cached above his ear shouted into the telephone on the desk: "Benny! For the love of Mike, do I get a rewrite or not? Benny! . . . Get this. Act of God. . . . No, you dope, act of *God!* Solly Spaeth's just been murdered!"

PART
TWO

5

GENTLEMAN OR THE TIGER?

Rhys's heart was a church bell resounding, a measured gong. Val pressed her head against it.

And suddenly it skipped two whole beats.

Val pushed away and looked up into her father's face. Rhys's lips parted and framed the word: "Coat."

"Coat," said Val, almost aloud.

Coat? Her father's coat!

They stood still in the bedlam. Inspector Glücke was pinching the tip of his sharp nose and regarding Walter with absorption.

Rhys's coat, that Walter had taken from the *La Salle* by mistake. By *mistake*.

Where was it?

Walter sat stonily behind dead Solly's desk. His hat, out of shape and streaked with dirt, lay near his left fist. But he was not wearing a topcoat. The camel's-hair coat, Rhys's coat, was not on the desk. Nor was it on the back of the chair.

Val no longer feared the dead man. She

could return his round frog-eyed stare now without flinching. The coat. Rhys's coat. That was the important thing. That was the thing to be afraid of.

Casually, carefully, they both made a slow survey of the study. The coat was nowhere to be seen.

Where was it? What had Walter done with it?

The Jardins drew closer together by an inch. It was necessary to concentrate. Concentrate, thought Val desperately. This is murder. Keep your mind clear. Listen.

"Get that reporter out of here," Inspector Glücke was saying. "How you boys fixed?"

The Surveyor was already gone. The photographers, other men, dribbled off. The room began to enlarge. Then a gaunt young man swinging a black bag came in.

"There's the stiff, Doc. See what you get."

The coroner's physician knelt by Solly's squatting remains and detectives made a wall about the dead man and the living.

"Take their prints, Pappas."

"Prints?" said Rhys slowly. "Isn't that a bit premature, Inspector?"

"Any objection, Mr. Jardin?" rapped Glücke.

Rhys was silent.

The fingerprint man approached with his paraphernalia. Inspector Glücke pulled the tip of his nose again, almost in embarrassment. "It's only routine. We've got the whole room mugged. There are a lot of prints. Weeding 'em out, you understand."

"You'll probably find some of mine about," said Rhys.

"Yes?"

"I was in this room only this morning."

"Is that so? I'll take your statement in a minute. Go ahead, Pappas."

Pappas went ahead. Val watched her father's strong fingers deposit inky designs on paper. Then the man took her hands. His touch was cold, like the body of a fish; her flesh crawled. But all the while Val was saying over and over inside: Where is pop's coat? What has Walter done with pop's coat?

The coroner's physician broke through the living wall and looked around. He made for the desk.

"Anything the matter?" asked the Inspector.

The doctor spoke into the telephone. "Don't know exactly. Something queer. C.I. Lab, please. . . . Chemist. . . . Bronson? Polk. I've got something for you on the Spaeth murder. . . . Yes, as fast as you can."

He hurried back to the ell and the wall solidified about him once more.

"I think," began Glücke, when a husky voice said from the corridor doorway: "Hello."

Everybody turned around.

The bearded young man stood there looking grave; and also looking hard at the scene about him, as if he expected to be kicked out at once and wanted to memorize as many of the details as he could before his eviction.

For an instant Val's heart jumped. The bearded man was wearing a camel's-hair coat. But then she saw that there was no triangular tear below the right pocket.

"Here he is," said a detective beside him. "The guy that bought up all Jardin's stuff this afternoon."

"Out," said Glücke. "Later."

"Why not now?" asked the young man in a wheedling tone. And he advanced a step into the room, gazing intently at the bandage around Walter's head.

Glücke looked at him sharply. Walter said in a monotone: "Queen's all right, Inspector. He merely acted as my proxy in buying up the Jardin furnishings today. He can't possibly have anything to do with this."

"No?" said Glücke.

"Fact, he's a detective." Walter looked away. "Go on, Queen; I'll see you later."

"Queen, Queen," frowned the Inspector. "Any relation to Dick Queen of the New York police department?"

"His son," said Ellery, beaming. "Now may I stay?"

Inspector Glücke grunted. "I've heard about you. Who killed Solly Spaeth, Queen? You could save us a lot of trouble."

"Oh," said Ellery, and he made a face. "Sorry, Walter."

Walter said again: "It's all right, Queen. Go ahead. I'll see you later."

"He cost *me* eight hundred bucks," said Glücke. "All right, Phil, take this down. Let's go, Spaeth — for the book."

Val made fists. Oh, Walter, what happened?

Walter looked at Mr. Queen, and Mr. Queen looked away. Nevertheless, he did not stir.

"My father telephoned me at the *La Salle* about five o'clock," said Walter in a dreary tone. "He said he was home and wanted to see me."

"What for?"

"He didn't say. I drove up here in my car. I had a flat down the hill a way and that's why I took a half-hour for a ten-minute trip. Well, I parked and began to climb out. As I was stepping off backwards, something hit me on the side of the head. That's all."

"We found Spaeth unconscious just after we got here," explained the Inspector. "On the sidewalk near his car. So you never even got into the grounds?"

"I told you what happened," said Walter.

"Why'd you park around the corner from the entrance? Why didn't you drive right in?"

"The mob. I thought I'd stand a better chance of getting inside unrecognized if I went on foot. My name is Spaeth, Inspector." His lips twisted.

"There wasn't any mob. There wasn't a soul near the place late this afternoon, the night man says."

"I didn't know that."

"So you were bumped on the head around five-thirty?"

"Just about."

"Any idea who hit you?"

"The assault came as a complete surprise."

"Who do you think it was?"

"How the hell should I know?" growled Walter.

But it was remarkable how he kept looking at Val. Just looking, with the oddest wooden expression.

Val scuffed Solly's silky antique Indian rug with her toe. Walter didn't enter the grounds. He was attacked before he entered the grounds. That's what he said. That's what he wanted the police to believe.

But Val knew he *had* entered the grounds. She had spoken to him on the telephone, and he had been on the other end of the wire — Hillcrest 2411, his father's number. It had been Walter, all right; Val knew his voice better than — better than —

Walter had been in the house.

She studied the intricate floral design. In the house. In the house, for all she knew right at this very extension in the study, where his father had been murdered. . . .

He was lying. Lying.

"Come here without a coat, Spaeth?" asked Glücke absently, eying him.

"What?" mumbled Walter. "Oh, coat? No, I didn't wear a coat, Inspector."

And he glanced at Val again, and at her father, with that mute wooden expression.

I know! thought Val. He's hidden it. He hid the coat. He didn't want to get her father mixed up in it. Walter, you darling. . . .

99

But then she thought: He's lying. He lied about one thing. Now he was lying about another. Where was the coat? *What had he done with that coat?*

Rhys's hand lightly brushed her skirt. She glanced up at him; his brown face was a little pale, but his lips were compressed and he shook his head ever so lightly.

"May I sit down?" asked Val in a tight voice. "Or is this part of the celebrated third degree?"

Glücke waved an indifferent arm and Val felt a chair pushed against her. She looked around; it was that Mr. Queen, smiling sympathy and encouragement. But there was something else in his smile, something that made Valerie sit down suddenly and stare straight ahead at the fireplace. He had noticed. His eyes, which were like washed gray grapes, had noticed the interplay. They would have to be careful. Watch your step. Don't make a mistake. It's like being trapped in a cave by wild animals; the least false move . . . Valerie had never been trapped in a cave by wild animals, but she thought she knew now how it must feel.

"Any clue to Spaeth's assailant, Inspector?" asked Mr. Queen amiably.

"We found one of those rustic benches

100

up against the willow fence inside the grounds near the spot where Spaeth's car was parked. A little scraped mud on it, so it was stepped on. That looks as if whoever sloughed Spaeth came over the fence from inside. Laying for you, hey, Spaeth?"

Walter looked blank.

"He wouldn't know, of course," said Mr. Queen.

"I guess not," said Inspector Glücke. "McMahon, get Ruhig and Walewski in here."

Anatole Ruhig came in gingerly, with small arched steps, like a man walking on coals of fire. Val restrained a mad impulse to giggle; it was the first time she had ever noticed his shoes, which had built-up heels, like a cowboy's. She wondered if he wore corsets; no, she was sure of it. Oh, the coat, the coat!

As for Mr. Ruhig, his bright blue little eyes made one panorama of the room, resting for the merest instant on Mr. Queen, and then retreated behind their fat lids.

"Too bad, Walter," he said quickly. "Too bad, Mr. Jardin. Too bad, Miss Jardin." Then he added: "Too bad," in a generally regretful tone, and stopped, blinking.

You left out Solly. . . . Val bit her lip, for there was Walewski. Frightened. Every one was frightened. Walewski was an old round-backed man with a crown of grimy white hair which stood on end. He came into the room sidewise, like a crab, his red eyes sloshing about in his old face.

"We're taking this down now," said the Inspector, speaking to Ruhig but looking at Walewski.

The lawyer covered a courtroom cough. "Too, too bad. . . . I drove up to the entrance at a few minutes past six. Walewski opened the gate. I told him I had an appointment with Mr. Spaeth —"

"Did you have?"

"My dear Inspector! Well, Walewski telephoned the house from his booth —"

"Hearsay. Walewski, what did you do?"

The old man trembled. "I don't know nothing. I didn't do nothing. I didn't see nothing."

"Did you or didn't you 'phone the Spaeth house?"

"Yes, sir! I did. But there wasn't no answer. Not a bit of an answer."

"May I ask a stupid question?" said Ellery. "Where were the servants? In all this magnificence," he said mildly, "I assume servants."

"Please," said the Inspector. "Well, if you must know, Spaeth fired 'em last week, the whole bunch. Now —"

"Really? That's strange. Now why should he have done that?"

"Oh, for God's sake." The Inspector looked annoyed. "He received several threatening letters right after Ohippi went busted and complained to the police and a district dick spotted the writer in thirty minutes — Spaeth's own chauffeur, a Filipino named Quital. Spaeth was so scared he fired everybody working here and he hasn't had a servant since."

"The wages of high finance," murmured Ellery. "And where is Mr. Quital?"

"In jail," grinned Glücke, "where he's been for a week. So what happened when you got no answer, Walewski?"

"I told Mr. Ruhig. I said Mr. Spaeth must be home, I said," mumbled the old man. "He ain't been out for a week, I said. So I let Mr. Ruhig through."

"Spaeth called me this morning," said Ruhig helpfully. "Told me to come. So when he didn't answer I knew something must be wrong. Therefore I insisted Walewski accompany me. Which the good man did. And we found — Well, I notified the police at once, as you know."

103

"He was settin' down on the floor," said Walewski, wiping the spittle from his blue lips with the back of his right hand, "he was settin' and he looked so awful surprised for a minute I thought —"

"By the way, Mr. Ruhig," said Ellery with an apologetic glance at Glücke, "what was the nature of your appointment today?"

"Another change of will," said Ruhig precisely.

"Another?" Glücke glared from Ellery to Ruhig.

"Why, yes. Last Monday — yes, exactly a week ago — Mr. Spaeth had me come over with two of my assistants and I wrote out a new will, which he signed in the presence of my assistants. This will," Ruhig coughed again, "disinherited the son, Mr. Walter Spaeth."

"Oh, is that so?" said the Inspector alertly. "Did you know your old man cut you off, Spaeth?"

"We quarreled," said Walter in a weary voice, "about his abandonment of the Ohippi plants. He telephoned Ruhig while I was still here."

"Who benefited by the will he made a week ago?"

"Mr. Spaeth's protégée, Miss Moon. He

104

left her his entire estate."

"Then what about this will business today?"

Ruhig breathed on his shiny little finger-nails. "I can't say. All I know is that he wanted to change the will again. But by the time I got here," he shrugged, "it was too late."

"Then Spaeth's estate is legally Winni's," frowned the Inspector. "Nice for her that he was bumped before he could change his mind again. . . . Well, Jerry?"

"This man Frank, the day gateman. He's here."

"Bring him in."

The one-armed gateman shuffled in, his narrow features twitching nervously. "I'm Atherton F-Frank. I don't know a single blessed thing —"

"What time did you go off duty?" demanded the Inspector.

"Six o'clock he went," put in Walewski eagerly. "That's when I come on. So you see I couldn't know nothing —"

"Six o'clock," mumbled Frank. He kept looking at his misshapen shoes.

Walter was sitting forward now, staring at the one-armed man. Val noticed that Walter's hands were twitching, too, almost in rhythm with Frank's features.

Afraid, thought Val bitterly. So you're a coward, for all your brave talk. You're afraid Frank saw you. He *must* have seen you. Unless you went over the wall. Went over the wall. . . . Val closed her eyes. Now why should Walter have gone over the wall?

"Listen, Frank," said Glücke genially. "You're an important figure in this case. You know that, don't you?"

"Me?" said Frank, raising his eyes.

"Sure! There's only one entrance to *Sans Souci*, and you were on guard there all day. You were, weren't you?"

"Oh, sure I was. Certainly I was!"

"So you know every one who went in and came out this afternoon. Why, Frank old man, you might be able to clear this case up right now."

"Yeah?" said Frank.

"Think, now. Who went in and out?"

Frank drew his sparse brows together. "Well, let's see now. Let's see. Not Mr. Spaeth. I mean — him." He jerked a dirty thumb toward the ell where the coroner's physician was working. "I didn't see him all day. . . . You mean after the auction?" he asked suddenly.

"Yes."

"After the auction. . . . Well, the crowd

106

petered out. So did the cops. A little while later Miss Moon drove out. She came back about four o'clock. Shopping, I guess; I saw packages. Her aunt, Mrs. Moon, is away in Palm Springs. Did she come back yet?"

"No," said Glücke, as man to man.

Frank scraped his lean chin. "Let's see. I guess that's all. . . . No, it ain't!" Then he stopped and looked very frightened. "I mean, I guess —"

"You mean you guess what, Frank?" asked Glücke gently.

Frank darted a hungry glance at the door. Walter sat up straighter. Val held her breath. Yes? Yes?

"Well," said Frank.

"Some one else came this afternoon!" snapped the Inspector, mask off. "Who was it?" Frank backed away. "Do you want to be held as a material witness?" thundered the Inspector.

"N-no, sir," chattered Frank. "It was him. Around half-past five. Half-past five."

"Who?"

Frank pointed a knobby forefinger at Rhys Jardin.

"No!" cried Val, springing out of the chair.

107

"Why, the man's simply mad," said Rhys in an astonished voice.

"Hold your horses," said Glücke. "You'll get your chance to talk. Are you sure it was Mr. Jardin, Frank?"

The gateman twisted a button on his coat. "I — I was sitting in the booth reading the paper . . . yes, I was reading the paper. I heard footsteps on the driveway, so I jumped up and ran out and there was Mr. Jardin walking up the drive toward the Spaeth house —"

"Hold it, hold it," said Glücke. "Did you leave the gate unlocked?"

"No, sir, I did not. But Mr. Jardin had a key to the gate — everybody in *San Susie*'s got one — so that's how he must have got in."

"Was there a car outside?"

"I didn't see no car."

"This is a joke," began Rhys, very pale. The Inspector stared at him, and he stopped.

"By the way," drawled Ellery, "if you came out of your warren, Frank, and saw a man walking *away* from you, how can you be so sure it was Mr. Jardin?"

"It was Mr. Jardin, all right," said Frank stubbornly.

Glücke looked irritated. "Can't you give

me a better identification? Didn't you see his face at all?"

"I won't *stand* here —" cried Val.

"You'll stand here and like it. Well, Frank?"

"I didn't see his face," mumbled Frank, "but I knew it was him, anyway. From his coat. From his camel's-hair coat, I knew him."

Walter very slowly slumped back against his chair. Val flashed a glance of pure hatred at him and Rhys sat down, jaws working, in the chair she had vacated.

"Oh, come," said Ellery with amusement. "Every second man in Hollywood wears a camel's-hair coat. I wear one myself. Are you sure it wasn't I you saw, Frank? I'm about the same size as Mr. Jardin."

Anger shone from Frank's eyes. "But your coat ain't torn," he said shortly.

"Oh," said Ellery; and the Inspector's face cleared.

"Torn, Frank?"

"Yes, sir. This afternoon, when Mr. Jardin left after the auction, his coat caught on the handle of his car and tore. Tore a flap right down under the pocket on the right side, a big piece."

"I thought you said," remarked Ellery,

"that you saw only the man's back."

"He was walkin' slow," muttered Frank, with a malevolent glance at his tormentor, "like he was thinking about something, and he had his hands behind his back under his coat. So that was how I saw the pocket and the rip. So I knew it was Mr. Jardin."

"Q.E.D.," murmured Ellery.

"I even called out to him, I said: 'Mr. Jardin!' in a real loud voice, but he didn't turn around, he just kept walking. So I went back to the booth. Like he didn't hear me."

"I absolutely must insist —" began Val in an outraged voice, when a man came in and held up something.

"Look what I found," he said.

It was a long narrow strip of tan camel's-hair cloth tapering to a point.

"Where?" demanded Glücke, seizing it.

"On top of one of those stakes on the fence. Right over the spot where the bench was pushed."

The inspector examined it with avid fingers. "It was torn already," he mumbled, "and when he climbed over the fence the torn piece caught and ripped clean away the length of the coat from the pocket down." He turned and eyed Rhys Jardin deliberately. "Mr. Jardin," he said in a cold voice, "where's your camel's-hair coat?"

The room was drowned in a silence that crushed the eardrums.

By all the rules of romantic justice Walter should have jumped up and explained what had happened, how he had taken Rhys's coat by mistake, how — But Walter sat there like a tailor's dummy.

Val saw why with acid clarity. He could not acknowledge having worn her father's coat without admitting he had lied. He had said he never entered the grounds at all. Yet it was clear now that he *had* entered the grounds with the key he also carried, that Frank had mistaken him for Rhys Jardin because of the torn coat, and that he had gone up to his father's house and . . . And what? *And what?*

Was that — Val said it to herself in a chill small voice — was that why Walter had lied? Was that why he had hidden or thrown away the telltale coat? Was that why he sat there so dumbly now, letting the police think Rhys had gone into Spaeth's house about the time Spaeth had been skewered?

Val knew without looking at him that her father was thinking exactly the same thoughts. It would be so easy for him to say — or for her — to Glücke: "Now look here, Inspector. Walter Spaeth took that coat by mistake this afternoon, and Frank mistook him for me. I haven't even got the coat. I don't know where it is. Ask Walter."

But Rhys said nothing. Nothing. And as for Val, she could not have spoken now if her life depended on one little word. Oh, Walter, why don't you explain, explain?

"So you won't talk, eh?" said the Inspector with a wry grin. "All right, Mr. Jardin. Frank, did any one but Miss Moon and Mr. Jardin enter *Sans Souci* after the auction today?"

"N-no, sir," said Frank, half out of the room.

"Walewski, when you took over from Frank, was Mr. Ruhig the only one you admitted — and then you both found the dead body of Spaeth?"

"That is the truth, sir!"

Glücke waved his hand at the gateman with a certain grim weariness. "Let 'em go home," he said to a detective, "and get that Moon woman in here."

The thought began to pound in Val's ears now. The more she tried to shut it out the stronger it came back.

Walter, did you murder your father?

112

6

THRUST AND PARRY

Winni Moon had been weeping. She paused at the door in an attitude of pure despair, a black handkerchief to her eyes. Fast work, thought Mr. Ellery Queen admiringly; in mourning already!

It was Mr. Queen's habit to observe what generally escaped other people; and so he now detected a metamorphosis in Attorney Anatole Ruhig. Mr. Ruhig, who had been taking everything in with admirably restrained impersonality, suddenly with Miss Moon's tragic entrance became excited. He ran over to her and held her hand, whispering a sympathetic word — to her quickly suppressed astonishment, Mr. Queen also noticed; he ran back and pulled up a chair and took her shoulders — he had to reach up for them — and steered her gallantly to the chair, like an orthodox Chinese son. Then he took up his stand behind her, the picture of a man who means to defend beauty from contumely and calumny with his last breath.

Mr. Queen wondered ungraciously if

Mr. Ruhig meant, now that Solly Spaeth had gone to join the choir invisible, to assume responsibility for Miss Moon's nebulous career.

Miss Moon began to weep afresh.

"All right, all right," said Inspector Glücke hastily. "This won't take long, and then you can cry your eyes out. Who killed Solly Spaeth?"

"I know who'd *wike* to!" cried Winni, lowering her handkerchief just long enough to glare at Rhys Jardin.

"You mean Mr. Jardin?"

At this new peril Val felt her skin tighten. That insufferable clothes-horse! But she was too steeped in more pointed miseries to do more than try to electrocute the sobbing beauty with her glance.

"Yes, I do," said Miss Moon, turning off the tears at once. "He did nothing but quawwel and quawwel with poor, darling Solly. Nothing! Last week —"

"Winni," said Walter in a choked voice, "shut that trap of yours —"

Now, thought Val, *now* he was talking!

"Your own father, too!" said Winni viciously. "I will not, Walter Spaeth. You know it's twue. Last Monday morning he and Solly had a *tewwible* battle about the floods and the factowies and ev'wything!

114

And only this morning he came over again and thweatened him —"

"Threatened him," repeated Glücke with satisfaction.

"He said he ought to be *hanged,* he said! He said he ought to be cut up in little *pieces,* he said! He said he was a *cwook!* Then I didn't hear any more —"

"The woman was obviously listening at the door," said Rhys, his brown cheeks slowly turning crimson. "It's true, Inspector, that we had a quarrel. But —"

"It's also true," said the Inspector dryly, "that you quarreled because Spaeth caused the collapse of Ohippi."

"Yes," said Rhys, "and ruined me, but —"

"You lost everything, eh, Mr. Jardin?"

"Yes!"

"Solly made you a poor man, while he cleaned up a fortune."

"But he ruined thousands of others, too!"

"What's this ape trying to do, Rhys," yelled a familiar voice, "hang this killing on you?" And Pink bounced into the room, his red hair bristling.

"Oh, Pink," cried Val, and she fell into his arms.

"It's all right," said Rhys wearily to a panting detective. "He's a friend of mine."

"Listen, you," snarled Pink to Glücke, "I don't give a damn if you eat bombs for breakfast. If you say Rhys Jardin pulled this job you're just a dumb, one-cylinder, cock-eyed heel of a liar!" He patted Val's hair clumsily. "I would have come sooner, only I didn't know till I got here. Mibs told me where you went."

"All right, Pink," said Rhys in a low voice, and Pink stopped talking. Inspector Glücke regarded him speculatively for a moment. Then he shrugged.

"You're a sportsman, aren't you, Mr. Jardin?"

"If you'll make your point —"

"You've won golf championships, you're a crack pistol shot, you beat this man Pink in the California Archery Tournament last spring, you've raced your yacht against the best. You see, I know all about you."

"Please come to the point," said Rhys coldly.

"You fence, too, don't you?"

"Yes."

Glücke nodded. "It isn't generally known, but you're also one of the best amateur swordsmen in the United States."

"I see," said Rhys slowly.

"He even twied to teach Solly!" shrilled Miss Moon. "He was always twying to make him exercise!"

The Inspector beamed. "Is that so?" he said. And he turned and pointedly looked up at the puce-colored wall above the fireplace.

A collection of old weapons hung there, decorative pieces — two silver-butted dueling-pistols, a long-barreled eighteenth-century rifle, an arquebus, a group of poniards and dirks and stilettos, a dozen or more time-blackened swords: rapiers, sabers, scimitars, jeweled court swords.

High above the rest lay a heavy channeled blade such as were carried by mounted men-at-arms in the thirteenth century. It lay on the wall obliquely. A thin light streak in the puce paint crossed the medieval piece in the opposite direction, as if at one time another sword had hung there.

"It's gone!" squealed Winni, pointing at the streak.

"Uh-huh," said Glücke.

"But it was there at only four o'cwock!"

"Was that when you saw Spaeth last, Miss Moon?"

"Yes, when I came back fwom shopping. . . ."

"Is it polite to inquire," murmured Mr. Queen, "what the beauteous Miss Moon

117

was doing between four o'clock and the time Mr. Spaeth was murdered?"

"I was in my boudoir twying on new gowns!" cried Miss Moon indignantly. "How dare you!"

"And you didn't hear anything, Miss Moon?"

Ruhig glared. "If you'll tell me what right —"

"Listen, Queen," snarled Glücke. "You'll do me a big favor if you keep your nose out of this!"

"Sorry," said Ellery.

Glücke blew a little, shaking himself. "Now," he said in a calmer tone. "Let's see what that sticker was." He went to the fireplace with the air of a stage magician about to demonstrate his most baffling trick, and set a chair before it. He stepped up on the chair, craning, and loudly read the legend on a small bronze plaque set into the wall below the streak in the paint. " 'Cup-hilted Italian rapier, seventeenth century,' " he announced. And he stepped down with an air of triumph.

No one said anything. Rhys sat quietly, his muscular hands resting without movement on his knees.

"The fact is, ladies and gentlemen," said the Inspector, facing them, "that Solly

Spaeth was stabbed to death and an Italian rapier is missing. We've pretty well established that it's gone. It isn't in this house and so far my men haven't found it on the grounds. Stab-wound — sword missing. It looks as if Solly's killer took the rapier down from the wall, backed Solly into that corner there, gave him the works, and beat it with the sword."

In the stillness Mr. Queen's voice could clearly be heard. "That," he complained, "is precisely the trouble."

Inspector Glücke slowly passed his hand over his face. "Listen, you —" Then he turned to Jardin and snapped: "You weren't by any chance trying to teach Solly a few tricks with that sword this afternoon, were you?"

Rhys smiled his brief, charming smile; and Val was so proud of him she could have wept. And Walter, the beast, just sat there!

"Figure it out for yourself," said the Inspector amiably. "Frank says you were the only outsider to enter *Sans Souci* late this afternoon. We have the missing piece from your coat in substantiation, and we'll have the coat very shortly, I promise you."

"I'd like to see it myself," said Rhys lightly.

"You've admitted to at least two quarrels with the dead man, one only this morning."

"You left something out," said Jardin with another smile. "After our tiff in this room this morning, I saw Spaeth again. He walked over to my house — I mean the one I vacated today." Val started; she had not known that. "We had another little chat in my gymnasium, as a result of which I walked out on him."

"Thanks for the tip," said Glücke. "You'd better begin to think about keeping such facts to yourself. Got that, Phil? Well, you had a nice strong motive, too, Jardin — he ruined you and, from what I hear, he wouldn't do what you asked, which was to put his profits back in Ohippi and salvage the business. And last, you're a swordsman, and a sword was used to polish him off. You may even have got him off guard by pretending to show him some kind of fencing maneuver."

"And what was he doing," said Rhys, "parrying with his arm?"

They looked across the room at each other. "Tell you what, Jardin," said the Inspector. "You sign a full confession, and I'll get Van Every to guarantee a lesser plea. We could easily make it self-defense."

"How nice," smiled Rhys. "At that, I could almost take my chances with a jury, couldn't I? They'd probably thank me for having rid the world of a menace."

"Sure, sure! What do you say, Mr. Jardin?"

"Pop —" cried Val.

"I say I'm innocent, and you may go to hell."

Glücke eyed him again. "Suit yourself," he said shortly, and turned away. "Oh, Doc. You finished?"

Dr. Polk was visible now, rolling down the sleeves of his coat. The detectives were strung out around the room; and Val, looking out of one eye, saw that the heap in the corner near the fireplace was covered with newspapers.

"Pending autopsy findings," said Dr. Polk abruptly, "you may assume the following: The wound was made by a sharp-pointed instrument, the point at surface terminus of entry being roughly a half-inch wide. It just missed the heart. I should say it was made by the missing rapier, although I'd like to see the thing before making a positive statement."

"How about the time of death?" demanded Glücke.

"Checks with the watch."

Mr. Ellery Queen stirred restlessly. "The watch?"

"Yes," said the Inspector with impatience, "his arm banged against the wall as he sank to a sitting position in that corner, because we found his wrist-watch smashed and the pieces of shattered crystal on the floor beside him. The hands stopped at 5.32."

Rhys Jardin chuckled. Even Glücke seemed surprised at the pure happiness of it. It bothered him, for he kept eying Jardin sidewise.

But Valerie knew why her father laughed. A wave of such relief swept over her that for an instant she tasted salt in her mouth. She felt like laughing hysterically herself.

Solomon Spaeth had been murdered at 5.32. But at 5.32 Rhys Jardin had been entering the self-service elevator at the *La Salle* with Val, on his way from their apartment to the lobby downstairs to wait for Walter.

5.32. . . . Val's inner laughter died in a burst of panic. Rhys was all right now — nothing could touch him now, with an alibi like that. But Walter. . . . It was different in Walter's case. At 5.35, with Rhys in full view of Mibs Austin in the *La Salle* lobby,

122

Val had telephoned Walter and Mibs had spoken to Walter and even recognized his voice.

If Inspector Glücke should question the little blond telephone operator, if she should tell him about that call, where Walter was, fix the time . . .

Val caught a blurry glimpse of Walter's face as he turned away to stare out the side windows into the blackness of the grounds. There was such agony on his face that she was ready to forgive anything just to be able to take him in her arms.

He had remembered the call, too.

Walter, she cried silently, why did you lie? What are you hiding?

A tall man bustled in lugging a kit.

"Bronson!" said Dr. Polk, the wrinkles on his forehead vanishing. "Glad you're here. I want you to have a look at this."

The Bureau Chemist hurried with the coroner's physician to the ell beside the fireplace. The detectives closed in.

"Go on home," said the Inspector brusquely to Walter. "I'll talk to you again in the morning. Unless you want to stay here?"

"No," said Walter, without moving. "No, I don't."

Then he very quickly got out of the chair and groped for his hat and made for the corridor door, stumbling once over a fold in the rug. He did not look at the Jardins.

"You can go, too — Miss Moon, Mr. Ruhig. And you, there, whatever your name is."

But Pink said: "How about taking a jump in the lake?"

"Can't — can't my father and I leave, Inspector?" asked Val, staring at the doorway through which Walter had fled. Then she closed her eyes, because Mr. Ruhig was piloting the exquisite Miss Moon deferentially through the same doorway, somehow spoiling the view.

"No," said Glücke curtly.

Val sighed.

The Inspector strode over to the group near the fireplace and Mr. Queen, unable to restrain his curiosity, hurried after him and peered over his shoulder to see what was going on.

Solly Spaeth was uncovered again. The Chemist knelt over him intently studying the brownish mouth of the stab-wound. Twice he lowered his long nose to the wound and sniffed. Then he slowly shook his head, looking up at Dr. Polk.

"It's molasses, all right," he said in a wondering voice.

"That's what I thought," replied Dr. Polk. "And it's not only at the mouth of the wound, but seems to coat the sides for some way in."

"Molasses," repeated the Inspector. "That's a hell of a note. . . . Say, stop shoving me!"

Ellery rubbed his bearded cheeks. "Sorry, Inspector. Molasses? That's exciting. Did I hear you say, Doctor, the point just missed the heart?"

The doctor regarded him with curiosity. "Yes."

Ellery shouldered Glücke out of the way and pushed through the group until he was standing directly over the dead man.

"Was the stab-wound serious enough to have caused death?"

"He's dead, isn't he?" growled the Inspector.

"Undoubtedly, but I've a faint notion things aren't quite as they seem. Well, Doctor?"

"Hard to say," frowned the coroner's physician. "There wasn't much bleeding. Given an hour or so, he probably would have bled to death — that is, without medical attention. It certainly is queer."

"So queer," said Ellery, "that I'd have Mr. Bronson analyze the molasses."

"What for?" snarled Glücke.

"The molasses and its physical disposition in the wound," murmured Ellery, "suggest that it must have been smeared on the point of the blade that made the wound. Why smear molasses on a cutting edge? Well, molasses is viscid. It could be construed as the 'binder' of another substance."

"I see, I see," muttered Dr. Polk. "I hadn't thought of it just that way, but certain indications —"

"What is this?" demanded the Inspector irritably.

"It's only a suggestion, respectful and all that," said Ellery with a placative smile, "but if you'll have Mr. Bronson test that molasses for poison — some poisonous substance that comes in solid rather than liquid form — I think you'll find something."

"Poison," muttered Glücke. He stroked his nose and glanced fretfully at Ellery out of the corner of his eye.

The Chemist carefully scraped a scum of molasses from the wound and deposited it on a slide. Then he opened his kit and went to work.

Molasses. Poison. Val closed her eyes.

"Potassium cyanide," announced Bronson at last. "I'm pretty sure. Of course, I'll have to get back to my lab before I can make it official."

"Cyanide!" exclaimed Dr. Polk. "That's it."

"Comes in powder form, of course — white crystals," said the Chemist. "It was thoroughly mixed into the molasses — a good deal of it, I'd say."

"Paralyzes certain enzymes essential to cellular metabolism," muttered the doctor. "Death within a few minutes. He'd have died before complete absorption, so the tissues through which the blade passed ought to reveal traces of the poison in autopsy." He shrugged at the dead man's gray-fringed bald spot. "Well, it was a painless death, anyway."

"Isn't any one going to congratulate me?" sighed Ellery.

Glücke glared at him and turned his back. "We'll have to get busy on that cyanide," he snapped.

"I'm afraid you won't be very successful," said Bronson, packing his kit. "It's too common — used commercially in dozens of ways — film manufacture, cleaning fluids, God knows what else. And you can buy it at any drug store."

"Nuts," said the Inspector, plainly disappointed. "Well, all right, Doc, get him out of here. Let's have your report the first thing in the morning, if you can make it."

Ellery backed off as the detectives milled about and Dr. Polk superintended the removal of the body. He seemed worried about something.

"Oh, Dr. Polk," he said as the coroner's physician was about to follow Solly's remains through the doorway. "Does the condition of the body confirm the time of death as indicated by the wrist-watch?"

"Yes. The man died of cyanide poisoning, not of stabbing, and within a very short time after the blow. From the local conditions in this room and the state of the corpse, calculating roughly, he figures to have passed out around 5.30. And the watch says 5.32, which ought to be close enough for any one. . . . Smart work, Mr. Queen. Detective, eh?"

"Enough of one," sighed Ellery, "to detect traces of hostility in the official atmosphere. Thanks, Doctor." And he watched Dr. Polk and Bronson depart.

"May we go now, Inspector?" asked Val again, examining the freckle on her left ring-finger. There had been something unpleasant about Solly's quiet contour under

the morgue sheet, and there was a vast desire within her to go somewhere and con-
sume sherry frappés.

"When I'm through with you. Here,"
roared Glücke, "what are you doing now,
damn it?"

Ellery had dragged a chair over to the
fireplace and was engaged in standing on it
while he made mysterious movements with
his body. He looked, in fact, as if he meant
to emulate Dracula and climb the fireplace
wall.

"I'm trying," he said in a friendly tone,
stepping down, "to find the answer to
three questions."

"Listen, Queen —"

"First, why did your murderer employ
that particular sword for his crime?"

"How the hell should I know? Look —"

"Why," continued Ellery, going close to
the fireplace and raising his arm to the wall
above it, "why didn't he take down this
needle-bladed French dueling-sword?"

"I don't know," barked Glücke, "and
what's more I don't give a damn. If you'll
be kind enough —"

Ellery pointed. "See where that
dustmark on the wall is — where the missing rapier hung. Now, no man could possibly have reached that rapier without

standing on something. But why haul a chair over here to reach a cup-hilted Italian rapier of the seventeenth century when you have merely to stand on the floor and extend your arm and reach a nineteenth-century French dueling-sword which will do the work equally well?"

"That's an odd note in an unpremeditated crime," said Rhys Jardin, interested despite his preoccupation.

"Who asked you?" said the Inspector, exasperated.

"And who says it was unpremeditated?" said Ellery. "No, indeed, Mr. Jardin. Either the murderer took down the rapier and coated its tip with his molasses-and-cyanide concoction just before the crime; or else he had coated the point *some time before the crime* — prepared it, as it were. But in either event he had to mix the poison with the molasses before he killed Solly, which certainly rules out a crime of impulse."

The tips of Inspector Glücke's ears were burning by this time. "I'm not in the habit of running a forum," he said in a strangled voice, "on a case I'm investigating. So you'll all be good enough —"

"You smell from herring," said Pink, who had formed a violent dislike for Glücke.

"And then," said Ellery hastily, as if he might not be able to get it out before the catastrophe, "there's my second question. Which is: Why did he smear the sword with poison at all?"

"Why?" shouted Glücke, throwing up his arms. "What the hell is this — Quiz Night? To make sure he died, that's why!"

"Isn't that a little like the man who wears not only suspenders but a belt, too?" asked Ellery earnestly. "Don't you think you could kill a man very efficiently with merely a naked blade?"

Inspector Glücke had long since regretted his weakness in allowing the bearded young man to linger on the scene. The man was clearly one of those smart-aleck, theorizing amateurs whom Glücke had always despised. Moreover, he asked embarrassing questions before subordinates. Also, by sheer luck he might stumble on a solution and thus rob a hard-working professional of the prey, the publicity, and the departmental rewards of sensational success. All in all, a nuisance.

So the Inspector blew up. "I'm not going to have my investigation disrupted by a guy who writes *detective* stories!" he bellowed. "Your old man has to take it because he's got to live with you. But you're three thousand miles away from Centre Street, and I don't give a hoot in hell *what* you think about my case!"

Ellery stiffened. "Am I to understand that you'd like me better at a distance?"

"Understand your left tonsil! Scram!"

"I never thought I'd live to see the day," murmured Ellery, nettled but trying to preserve an Emily Postian *savoir faire.* "That's Hollywood hospitality for you!"

"Mac, get this nosey lunatic out of here!"

"Desist, Mac. I'll go quietly." Ellery went over to the Jardins and said in a loud voice: "The man's an idiot. And he's quite capable of having you in clink before you're an hour older, Mr. Jardin."

"Sorry you're leaving us," sighed Rhys. "I must say I prefer your company to his."

"Thanks for the first kind word Hollywood has bestowed. Miss Jardin, goodbye. . . . I'd advise both of you to talk as economically as possible. In fact, get a lawyer."

Inspector Glücke glared at him. Ellery went sedately to the door.

"Not, however," he added with a grimace, "Mr. Ruhig."

"Will you get out, you pest?" roared the Inspector.

"Oh, yes, Inspector," said Ellery. "I almost forgot to mention my third point. You remember I said there were three bothersome questions?" Mac approached grimly. "Now, now, Mac, I must warn you that I've just taken up ju-jitsu. The point is this, Inspector: Granting that your eccentric criminal stood on a chair to get a sword for which he had a much handier substitute, granting that he smeared the sword with poison when a good jab by a child could have dispatched Mr. Spaeth just as efficiently — granting all that, why in heaven's name did he take the sword away with him after the crime?"

Inspector Glücke was speechless.

"There," said Mr. Queen, waving adieu to the Jardins, "is something for that ossified organ you call your brain to wrestle with." And he went away.

7

THE CAMEL THAT WALKED
LIKE A MAN

Val could scarcely drag one foot after the other by the time they got back to the *La Salle*. Even the yearning for sherry frappés had dissipated. It was agony just to think.

"I'll tuck pop in, flop onto my bed, and *sleep*," she thought. "Maybe when I wake up tomorrow morning I'll find it never really happened at all."

After that strange Mr. Queen's departure Inspector Glücke had cleared the study and gone to work on Rhys with a grim enthusiasm that made Val vibrant with pure loathing. Pink became rebellious at the tone of the man's questions and was ejected by two of the larger detectives. They found him later, sitting on the sidewalk near the gate in the midst of a large section of the Los Angeles press, chewing his fingernails and growling at their pleas like a bear.

Even in the excitement of their own miraculous escape from that rapacious crew — Pink said they had the morals of a bulldog, and that they wouldn't have escaped at all if not for the greater lure still within the Spaeth house — Val's stomach lay six inches lower than its usual position merely recalling Glücke's baffled pertinacity.

Throughout the ordeal Rhys had maintained a calm that served only to infuriate the policeman. He was monosyllabic about most things; and about the important things he would not talk at all. The Inspector went over and over the ground: The Ohippi partnership, the holding companies, the collapse of the securities, Rhys's quarrels with Spaeth, his movements during the afternoon — oh, thought Val, to have been able to tell the truth! — his familiarity with the house, with swords. . . .

Her father could have cleared himself at any moment of the interminable, ferocious, accusing inquisition by merely stating his alibi. But he did not; and Val, sick and exhausted, knew why he did not. It was because of Walter. Walter. . . . She hardly heard Glücke's diatribe. Through the verbal storm leered Walter's face with its incomprehensible expression.

Rhys was deliberately allowing himself to be involved in a nasty crime because Walter meant something to her — Walter, who

135

had always been so boyish and naïve and blunt and was now so frighteningly drawn into himself.

"I'll fix some eats," said Pink. "You must be starved."

"I couldn't eat now," said Valerie faintly.

Rhys said: "Pink's right," but he was abstracted.

"I laid in a raft of stuff from the market this afternoon," said Pink gruffly, "on my way back from the studio. If I left it to you capitalists —"

"Oh, Pink," sighed Val, "I don't know what we'd do without you."

"You'd probably die of hunger," said Pink.

Mibs Austin's place at the switchboard was occupied by the night clerk, a fat old man in a high collar; so they went through the lobby without stopping and took the cranky elevator upstairs. Val stumbled along the red carpeting of the corridor behind the two men. She wondered dully why Rhys and Pink, who had unlocked the door of 3-C, stood so still in the foyer.

But when she reached the apartment door and looked in she saw why.

Walter was sitting in the living-room on the edge of the armchair. He was sitting in a strangely stiff attitude, his dirty hat

136

crushed on the back of his bandaged head and his eyes like two steamy pieces of glass.

They looked at Walter, and Walter looked back at them, and his head wagged from side to side as if it were too heavy for his neck.

"Stinko," said Pink, wrinkling his nose, and he went to the windows and threw them wide open.

Rhys carefully closed the corridor door and Val advanced two steps into the living-room and faltered: "Well?"

Walter's tongue licked at his lips and out of his mouth came a mumble of sounds that conveyed nothing.

"Walter. How did you get in?"

Walter placed his right forefinger to his lips. "Shh. Sh— snuck up. Sh— swiped housh-key. Deshk."

He glared up at her from the armchair in an indignant, almost a resentful way.

"Well?" said Val again. "Haven't you anything to say to me, Walter?"

" 'Bout what? Tell me that. 'Bout what?"

"You know very well," said Val in a low voice. "About — this afternoon."

"What 'bout 'sh afternoon?" said Walter belligerently, trying to rise. "You lemme 'lone!"

Val closed her eyes. "Walter, I'm giving you your chance. You must tell me. What happened today? Where's pop's coat? Why did you —" she opened her eyes and cried — "why did you lie, Walter?"

Walter's lower lip crept forward. "None o' y'r bus'ness."

Val ran over to him and slapped his cheek twice. The marks of her fingers surged up in red streaks through the pallor beneath the stubble.

He gasped and tried to rise again, but collapsed in the armchair.

"You drunken bum," said Val passionately. "Coward. Weakling. I never want to see you again!"

Val ran into her bedroom and slammed the door.

"I'll handle him," said Pink. Rhys quietly sat down on the sofa without removing his coat. He just sat there drumming on the cushion.

Pink hauled Walter out of the chair by his collar, half strangling him. Walter sawed the air feebly, trying to fight. But Pink pushed his arm aside and dragged him into Rhys's bathroom. Rhys heard the shower start hissing and a medley of gaspy human sounds.

After a while Walter lurched back into

the living-room, the shoulders of his plaid jacket drenched, his bandaged head and face dripping. Pink tossed a towel at him and went into the kitchen while Walter dropped into the armchair and tried with ineffectual swipes of the towel to dry himself.

Rhys drummed softly.

"Put this away, big shot," said Pink, returning with a tall glass. "What a man!"

Walter groped for the glass and gulped down the tomato juice and tabasco, shuddering.

Pink lit a cigaret and went back to the kitchen. Rhys heard the clangor of clashing pans.

"I think," said Rhys politely, "I'll go down to the drug store for a cigar. Excuse me, Walter."

Walter said nothing. After a moment Rhys rose and left the apartment.

Alone, Walter inhaled deeply and stared fog-eyed at the dusty tips of his suède sport shoes. Pink was slamming dish-closet doors in the kitchen, growling to himself.

Walter got up and tottered to Val's door. "Val," he said thickly.

There was no answer. Walter turned the knob and went in, shutting the door behind him.

139

Val lay, still in her hat and coat, on the bed, staring numbly at the Van Gogh on the opposite wall. Her hat, a toque, was pushed over one eye rakishly; but she did not look rakish. She looked cold and remote.

"Val."

"Go away."

Walter reached the bed by a heroic lunge and dropped. His eyes, bleared and shadowed, peered anxiously at her through a haze. He put his right hand clumsily on her slim thigh. "Know 'm drunk. Coul'n' help it, Val: Val, don' talk t'me 'at way. I love you, Val."

"Take your hand off me," said Val.

"I love you, Val."

"You've a fine way of showing it," said Val drearily.

Walter sat up with a jerk, fumbling to button his collar. "Aw right, Val. Aw right, I'll get out. 'M drunk."

He rose with an effort and stumbled toward the door.

Val lay still, watching his weaving progress across the room. . . . She jumped off the bed and flew past him to the door, setting her back against it. Walter stopped, blinking at her.

"Not yet," she said.

" 'M drunk."

"You're going to answer me. Why did you lie to Inspector Glücke? You know you were in that house at 5.35 this afternoon!"

"Yes," muttered Walter, trying to stand still.

"Walter." Val's heart sank. Her hands, spread against the door, gripped it harder. She could almost see past him through the rubbed aspen-crotch panel of her Hepplewhite bureau, where a certain automatic pistol lay hidden under a layer of chemises. She whispered: "Walter, I must know. Did you kill your father?"

Walter stopped rocking. His lower lip crept forward again in a curiously stubborn way. At the same time his bloodshot eyes shifted, almost with cunning.

"Lemme go," he muttered.

"Did you, Walter?" whispered Valerie.

"Goodbye," said Walter in a surprisingly sharp tone. He put his arm out to push her aside.

"If you didn't," cried Val, running to the bureau and digging into the drawer, "why were you carrying this?" She held up the automatic.

Walter said contemptuously: "Going through m' pockets, huh? Gimme!" Val let him take the pistol away from her. He

141

looked at it, snorted, and dropped it into his pocket. "Threat— threat'ning letters. Dozen of 'm. Son of man who ruined thousan's. So I bought a gun." His shoulders hunched and he said painfully: "I love you, but min' y'r own bus'ness."

This wasn't Walter. Not the Walter she had known for so many years. Or was it? Wasn't it always a crisis like this that showed a man up in the true ugliness of his naked self?

"You let that Inspector think my father went to *Sans Souci* this afternoon," she cried. "Why didn't you tell him that you were the one Frank saw sneaking up the drive — that you were wearing pop's coat?"

Walter blinked several times, as if he was trying to peer through a week's collection of Hollywood's evening mists.

"Gotta trus' me," he mumbled. "Don' ask questions, Val. No questions."

"Trust you! Why?" flared Val. "After the way you've acted? Haven't I the right to ask questions when your silence implicates my own father?" But then she grasped his sodden lapels and laid her head on his chest. "Oh, Walter," she sobbed, "I don't care what you've done, if you'll only be honest about it. Trust you! Why don't you trust me?"

It was queer how humble he could be one moment and how hard, how frozen hard, the next. It was as if certain questions congealed him instantly, making him impervious to warmth or reason or appeal.

He said, trying to control his lax tongue: "Mus'n' fin' out I was in father's house. If you tell 'm . . . Don' you dare tell 'm, Val, y'un'erstan' me?"

Then it was true. Pop! goes the weasel.

Val pushed away from him. Faith was all right in its place, which was usually in drippy novels. But a human being couldn't accept certain things on faith. Appearances might be deceptive in some cases, but usually they were photographic images of the truth. Real life had a way of being harshly unsubtle.

"Apparently," she said in a remote voice, "the fact that Glücke suspects my father of murder, that one word from you would clear him, doesn't mean a thing to you. Not when your own skin is in danger."

Walter was quite steady now. He opened his mouth to say something, but then he closed it without having uttered any sound whatever.

"So you'll please me," said Val, "by getting out."

He did not know, could not know, that

Rhys had an alibi for the time the crime was committed.

"Aw right," said Walter in a low tone.

And now he would never know — not through her! If she told him, how easy it would be for him to crawl out, to say he had known about her father's alibi all the time, that Rhys had never been in real danger and that it was necessary to him to protect himself. When he sobered up, he might even invent some plausible story to account for his damning actions. Walter was persuasive when he wanted to be. And in her heart Val knew she could not trust herself.

So she said again, bitterly: "Your secret, whatever it is, is safe with me. Will you get out?"

Walter plucked violently at his collar, as if he found its grip intolerable. Then he wrenched the door open, stumbled across the living-room, and zigzagged out of the apartment, leaving his hat behind.

Val picked the hat up from the living-room floor and threw it after him into the corridor.

That was that.

"Pink, I'm starved," she called out, going into the kitchen. "What's on the menu?" But then her eyes narrowed and she said:

"Pink, what is that?"

Pink was guiltily hiding something in his trouser pocket.

"Nothing," he said quickly. And he got up from the chair in the breakfast nook and made for the gas range, where several pots and pans were bubbling. "Is crackpot gone?"

"Pink, what are you hiding?" Val went over to him and pulled him around. "Show me that."

"It's nothing, I tell you!" said Pink, but his tone carried no conviction.

Val thrust her hand into his pocket. He tried to dodge, but she was too quick for him. Her hand emerged with a flat, small, hard-covered pamphlet.

"Why, it's a bankbook," she said. "Oh, Pink, I'm dreadfully sorry —" But then she stopped and little schools of goose-pimples rose to the surface of her flesh.

The name on the bankbook was Rhys Jardin.

"Pop deposited Walter's money," she began, and stopped again. "But this is a different bank, Pink. The Pacific Coastal. Spaeth's bank."

"Don't bother your head with it, squirt," muttered Pink; he began to stir beans with a ladle as if his life depended on their not sticking to the pan. "Don't look inside."

Val looked inside. There was one deposit listed, no withdrawals. But the size of the deposit made her eyes widen. It was impossible. It must be a mistake. But there were the figures.

$5,000,000.00.

She seized Pink's arm. "Where did you get this? Pink, tell me the truth!"

"It was this morning," said Pink, avoiding her eyes, "in the gym over at *San Susie*. I was packing the golf-bags. I found it hidden under a box of tees in a pocket of that old morocco bag of Rhys's."

"Oh," said Val, and she sat down in the breakfast nook and shaded her eyes with her hand. "Pink," she went on in a muffled voice, "you mustn't — well, don't say anything about this. It will look as if . . . as if what those people said about pop not really being broke is true."

Pink stirred with absorption. "I didn't know what the hell to do, Val. There was a chance some nosey, thievin' expressman might find it. I had to take that stuff Rhys gave away over to the Museum, so — well, I just put it in my pocket."

"Thanks, Pink," said Val from stiff lips. And neither said another word as the gas hissed and Pink stirred and Val sat at the table and looked at the bankbook.

The front door banged. Rhys called out: "Val?"

Neither made a sound.

Rhys came into the kitchen smoking a cigar and shaking his wet hat. "It's raining again. Pink, that smells wonderful." He stopped, struck by the silence.

The yellow-covered bankbook lay on the maple table in full view. He glanced at it, frowning, and then studied the two stony faces.

"Is it Walter?" he asked in a puzzled way. "Wouldn't he talk?"

"No," said Val.

Rhys sat down in his soggy coat, puffing at the cigar. "Don't go off half-cocked, puss. I watched him. He's concealing something, it's true, but I have the feeling it isn't what you think. Walter's always been close-mouthed — after all, he never had the benefits of a normal upbringing — he'll always depend on himself, keep things to himself. I've studied him, and I'm sure he's incapable of viciousness. I couldn't be wrong in him, darling —"

"I wonder," said Val tonelessly, "if I could be wrong in you."

"Val." He examined her with surprise. "Pink, what's the matter? Something's happened."

"Don't you know?" muttered Pink.

"I know," he said a trifle sharply, "that you're both being childishly mysterious."

Val pushed the bankbook an inch toward her father with the very tip of one fingernail.

He did not pick it up at once. He continued to look at Val and Pink. As he looked, a curious pallor spread under the brown of his flat cheeks.

He took the bankbook slowly, stared at his name on the cover, opened the book, stared at the figures, stared at the date, the cashier's initials. . . .

"What is this?" he asked in a flat voice. "Well, don't look at me like sticks! Pink, you know something about this. Where did it come from?"

"It's none of my business," shrugged Pink.

"I said where did it come from?"

Pink flung the ladle down. "Damn it, what do you want from me, Rhys? Don't put on an act for my benefit! It's a bankbook with a five-million-dollar deposit, and I found it this morning in your morocco golf-bag!"

Rhys rose, holding the bankbook in one hand and the fuming cigar in the other, and began to walk up and down the narrow kitchen. The brown wrinkles on his forehead deepened with each step. The paleness was gone now; the brownness had an angry red tinge.

"I never thought," said Pink bitterly, "you'd be that kind of a heel, Rhys."

Rhys stopped pacing.

"I can't help being angry," he said quietly, "although I don't blame either of you. It looks damned bad. But I'm not going to deny this more than once." Pink paled. "I know nothing about this deposit. I've never had an account at Spaeth's bank. This five million dollars isn't mine. Do you understand, both of you?"

Val felt a great shame. She was so tired she could have cried for sheer exhaustion. As for Pink, his pallor, too, vanished in a blush that reached to the roots of his red hair; and he leaned against the gas range biting his fingernails.

Rhys opened the book and glanced again at the stamped date of deposit. "Pink, where was I last Wednesday?" he asked in the same quiet tone.

Pink mumbled: "We ran the yacht down to Long Beach to see that guy who decided not to buy."

"We left at six in the morning and didn't get back to town until after dark — isn't that so?"

"Yeah."

Rhys tossed the bankbook on the table. "Look at the date of that deposit. It was made last Wednesday."

Pink snatched the book. He said nothing at all. But the blush turned burning scarlet. He kept looking at the date as if he could not believe his eyes. Or perhaps because it was the only way he could cover his embarrassment.

"Pop," said Val, resting her head on her arms, "I'm sorry."

There was a long silence.

"It could only have been Spaeth," said Rhys at last. "He visited me in the gym this morning, as I told Glücke. He must have slipped it into the golf-bag when my back was turned."

"But why, for the love of Mike?" cried Pink. "My God, who gives away five million bucks? I *had* to think —"

"I see it now." Rhys flung his cigar into the drip-pan. "I've never told you before, but when things began to go wrong with Ohippi I came to my senses and had a confidential accountant and investigator look into things."

"I *had* to think —" said Pink again, miserably.

Rhys began to pace again, nibbling at his lips. "I found that friend Solly, who up to a certain point had been perfectly coached by Ruhig, had gone on his own in one connection — and slipped very badly. He issued a prospectus for the further sale of stock in which he falsified the cash position of the companies. He had to make the stocks look sound, and he did — with false figures."

Val raised her head. "He was always a thief," she said wearily.

"Suppose he did?" demanded Pink.

"Using the mails to defraud is a serious offense, Pink," said Rhys. "It was the penitentiary for Spaeth if the government ever found him out."

"Why didn't you hold him up?" asked Pink hoarsely.

"At the time there was still a chance to recoup. But later, when the floods ruined the plants completely, I threatened to send him to prison if he didn't rehabilitate them." Rhys shrugged. "He made a counterthreat. He said he had something on me which would so blacken my reputation and so completely destroy public confidence that nothing would ever save the plants. This deposit must have been the answer, making it look as if I'd cleaned up, too, and was a hypocrite besides."

"But five million dollars!"

"If paying out ten percent of fifty millions in profits would keep him out of jail," said Rhys dryly, "he was a good enough business man to pay it out."

"The dirty rat," said Pink passionately. "Mixin' people up! Why the hell do they have to look for people who bump off rats like that? It ain't fair!"

"It puts me on a spot," sighed Rhys. "I can't keep the money, of course — it isn't mine. Yet if I used it to start a fund to salvage Ohippi, nobody'd believe the story. The auction, my being broke. . . . I can't keep it, and I can't give it away. I'll have to think about it."

"Yeah," muttered Pink, "we'll have to think about it."

Rhys went heavily out of the kitchen into the foyer, taking off his coat. Pink turned blindly to the range as something began to burn. Val pulled herself to her feet and said: "I don't think I'm hungry any more, Pink. I'm going to —"

Rhys said, strangling: "Good God."

Val was paralyzed by the horror in her father's voice.

"Pop!" She found her voice and her strength at the same instant. She almost capsized Pink trying to get to the foyer first.

Rhys had turned on the overhead light. The door of the foyer closet was open. He was squatting on his heels and staring into the closet.

On the floor of the closet lay two objects.

One was a long cup-handled rapier with a red-brown stain on its point.

The other, crushed into a ball, was a tan camel's-hair topcoat.

8

THE GLORY THAT WAS RHYS

"Your coat," said Val. "Your *coat.* The — the sword!"

Rhys grasped the rapier by the hilt and brought it out of the closet, turning it this way and that in his two shaking hands, as if he were too stupefied to do more than simply look at it.

It was the Italian rapier which had hung on Solly Spaeth's wall; there was no question about that. And if there had been a question, the stained point would have answered it.

"Don't handle it. Don't touch it," whispered Val. "It's — it's poisoned. You might get a scratch!"

"Put it away," mumbled Pink. "No. Here. Gimme that. We've got to get rid of it. Rhys, for God's sake!"

But Rhys kept holding the rapier and examining it as a child might examine a strange toy.

Pink reached in and snared the coat. He shook it out; it was Rhys's coat; there was no question about that, either. For from the right pocket to the hem a narrow strip of camel's-hair cloth was missing, leaving a long gap.

"Oh, look," said Val faintly, pointing.

The breast of the coat was smeared with a dirty brown liquid which had dried and crusted.

Fresh red blood turns dirty brown under the corrupting touch of the outer world.

Rhys got to his feet, still clutching the sword; his red-streaked eyeballs were bulging slightly. "How in the name of red devils did these things get here?" he croaked.

Before Val's eyes rose the unlovely vision of Mr. Walter Spaeth, grimy, slack with drink, and pugnacious, sitting on the edge of the armchair in their living-room when they had reached the apartment after Glücke's inquisition. He had stolen the house-key from the desk downstairs; he had confessed that. He had let himself in. He had — he had —

"Walter," said Val in a still small voice. "Walter!"

Rhys rubbed his left eye with his left hand and said painfully: "Don't jump to conclusions. Don't jump, Val. It's — We'll have to sit down and think this out, too." He stood there holding the rapier, holding

155

it because he did not seem to know what to do with it.

Pink said in an agonized treble: "Well, don't be a dope, Rhys, for God's sake. You can't just stand here with that thing. It's too risky. It's too —"

Just then some one pounded on the foyer door.

It was all so unreasonable, so theatrical, so ridiculous, that Val could only laugh. She began to laugh softly — more a titter than a laugh, and the laugh swelled until it was no longer soft and until tears rolled down her cheeks.

The buzzer rang. It rang again. Then some one leaned on it and forgot to remove his elbow.

Pink gripped Val's jaws in his iron fingers and shook her head furiously, as he might have shaken a recalcitrant puppy.

"Shut up!" he growled. "Rhys, if you don't put those things away — hide 'em. . . . In a minute!" he yelled at the door.

"Come on, open it," said a clipped voice from the other side. It was Inspector Glücke's voice.

Inspector Glücke!

"Pop, p-pop," stammered Val, looking around wildly. "Throw it out the window.

156

Anywhere. They can't find it here. They'll
— They mustn't —"

Sanity came back to her father's face.
"Here," he said slowly. "This won't do."

"Open up, Jardin, or I'll have the door
broken down."

"Oh, for God's sake, pop," whispered
Valerie.

"No." Rhys shook his head with mad-
dening slowness. "There's something inevitable about this. He's been tipped off.
He's bound to find it. No, Val. Pink, open
that door."

"Rhys, don't be a cluck!"

"Let them in, Pink."

Val shrank back. With a scowl of baffled
fury Pink stepped over to the door. Rhys
picked up the coat and carried it and the
rapier into the living-room and laid them
down on the sofa.

Men boiled in, headed by Glücke.

"Search warrant," he said curtly, waving
a paper. He pushed past Val and stopped
in the living-room archway.

"Is this what you want?" asked Rhys
tiredly, and he sat down in the armchair
and clasped his hands.

The Inspector pounced on the objects
on the sofa. His three companions blocked
the corridor door.

"Ah," said Glücke; he said nothing more.

"I suppose," murmured Rhys, "it won't do any good to assure you we just found those things on the floor of our foyer closet?"

The Inspector did not reply. He raised the coat and examined it curiously.

Then he turned and made a sign to his men, and two of them came forward with cotton bags and wrapping paper and began to stow away the coat and rapier, handling them as if they had been made of Ming porcelain.

"He's telling it to you straight," said Pink desperately. "Listen, Inspector, don't be a jackass. Listen to him, to me. We just found it — the three of us. He's being framed, Rhys is! You can't —"

"Well," said Glücke lightly, "there may be something in that, Mr. Pincus."

"Pink," muttered Pink.

"Western Union in downtown L.A. 'phoned a wire to Headquarters — anonymous — telling us to search this apartment right away. The telegram was 'phoned in to the Western Union office and we haven't been able to trace the call. So maybe all this is phony at that."

But he did not sound as if he meant what

he said. He sounded as if he were merely trying to make agreeable conversation.

He nodded at his men, and two of them followed him out of the apartment. The third man set his back against the open door and just stood there, shifting from one foot to another from time to time, as if he were tired.

Val cowered against her supporting wall in the foyer, unable to move, to think. Rhys got up from the chair in the living-room and turned to go into his bathroom.

"Hold it," said the detective at the door.

Rhys looked at him. Then he sat down again.

"Hullo," said a voice from the corridor.

Pink went to the door and dug his elbow into the detective's abdomen, and the detective shoved his arm angrily away. Pink saw the two other detectives leaning against the balustrade of the emergency stairway which led down to the lobby. They were no more than five feet from the door, and they returned his glance without expression.

"Hullo," said the same voice.

Pink looked through him. It was Fitzgerald, of the *Independent*.

The detective at the door said: "Nobody in."

Fitz's eyes under their bird's nest brows roved, took in Val before him, Rhys sitting motionless in the living-room. "I see they're keeping the death-watch here. Come on, Mac, this is the press."

"You heard him," said Pink, stepping up to him.

"I got a tip from some one I know at Headquarters," said Fitz. "It seems — Come on, mugg, out of the way."

The detective at the door closed his eyes. Pink said: "Get the hell out of here."

"Rhys," called Fitz. "I want to talk to you. This is serious, Rhys. Maybe I can give you a right steer —"

Pink put his broad palm on Fitz's chest and pushed, stepping through the doorway.

The man at the door did not open his eyes, and the two detectives across the hall did not move.

"Do you want a sock in the teeth," said Pink, "or will you go nice and quiet, like a good little man?"

Fitz laughed. He lashed out with his fist. Pink sidestepped and brought his left up in a short arc. Fitz grunted. He had been drinking, and droplets of alcoholic saliva sprayed Pink's face.

"Here, stop that," said one of the men

leaning against the balustrade. "Do your brawlin' outside."

Pink grabbed Fitz by the seat of his pants and ran him down the stairs.

Val trudged into the living-room and sat down on the floor by Rhys's knee. She rested her cheek on it.

"I don't think we have much time," said Rhys in a very low voice. "Val, listen to me."

"Yes, pop."

"Glücke will be back soon." He glanced cautiously at the detective in the doorway. "Maybe in five minutes, maybe in an hour. But whenever he comes back it will be with a warrant for my arrest."

Val shivered. "But he can't do that. You didn't do it. You couldn't have done it. You were right here —"

"Val, he'll hear you." Rhys bent low over her face, speaking into her ear. "That's what I wanted to talk to you about. The police — no one — must find out about that alibi."

Val felt her forehead. It was hard to think.

"I'm in no danger," whispered Rhys. "The Austin girl will testify at any time that I was in the *La Salle* lobby when

Spaeth was murdered. Don't you see?"

"Yes," said Val. "Yes."

"And there's at least one vital reason why I must let Glücke arrest me, puss. . . . No, don't make any noise, Val. That detective mustn't hear."

Val sank back, her face drawn, her eyes screwed up. They felt hot, brittle, sore; they felt like her brain.

"I don't — I can't seem to —"

"I think," whispered Rhys, "I'm in danger." He held her shoulders down. "I've just thought the whole thing through. Some one planted the sword and coat in our closet tonight, tipped the Inspector off that they were here. *Whoever did that is framing me for the murder.*"

"No," said Val. "No!"

"It must be, Val; it's the only reasonable explanation. So that means some one not only hated Spaeth, but hates me, too. He killed Spaeth and is taking his revenge on me by framing me for the crime."

"No!"

"Yes, puss. And if I produce my alibi now and the police clear me, what happens? The maniac who's doing all this, seeing that his frame-up has failed, will be more determined than ever to have his revenge. If he finds he can't get the law to kill me, he's liable to kill me himself. He committed murder once; why shouldn't he do it again?"

There's something behind this, thought Val. It's all mixed up and there's something behind it.

"I'll be safe in jail, safer than here. Don't you see?" Something. . . . "And there's another reason." Rhys paused. "It's Walter. If I introduce my alibi now, Val, he'll be directly involved in the crime." Walter. That's it. That's what's behind it. Walter. "The police will learn he was wearing my coat. He certainly had a motive of revenge against his father — being cut out of the will. They'll find out he was in that house at the time of the crime. They're bound to find it out — *if* we let them know about my alibi."

"But how — ?"

"Don't you see, puss?" he said patiently. "My alibi depends on the testimony of this Austin girl. She can place me in this lobby at the time of the crime, all right; but she also knows that it's tied up with that telephone call to the Spaeth house. *And she spoke directly to Walter.* The merest questioning on the part of the police would bring that out. We've got to see that she isn't questioned."

163

"No," said Val. "I won't let you do it. You've got to tell them about the alibi. You mustn't sacrifice yourself —"

"Walter didn't kill his father, Val. He isn't the killing kind. I'm protected, but he's not. Don't you see?"

I see. I see that I'm smaller than the smallest wiggly thing that crawls. And you're so big, so warm, so dear.

Rhys tilted her face. "Val, you've got to trust my judgment in this."

Val shivered again. Her tongue seemed tied up in knots.

"There's one other thing. I think I've got a clue that may lead somewhere. While I'm in jail covering Walter up you'll have to follow that clue, Val. Do you understand? We've got to find out who killed Spaeth before we talk!" Val turned her head slowly. "Listen, Val. Only this morning —"

"All right, Jardin," said Inspector Glücke.

Val jumped up. Rhys sat still.

The three detectives were in the room with Glücke, one of them looking hard at Pink, who was marking time, restlessly and unconsciously, with his feet, as if to inaudible music.

"So soon?" said Rhys with a faint smile.

164

"I had my fingerprint man waiting downstairs," said the Inspector. "Interested? Bloodstains on your coat. Your fingerprints, among others, on the rapier. And Bronson, who's also with me, says that the tip of the rapier is coated with blood and that molasses-and-cyanide goo. Have you anything to say, Jardin?"

"Will you get me my hat and coat, Pink, like a good fellow?" said Rhys, rising.

Pink went blindly into the foyer. Rhys put his arms about Valerie.

"See me tomorrow," he whispered into her ear. "The old code. Remember? We may not be able to talk. The clue may be important. Goodbye, Val. Talk to the Austin girl tonight."

"Goodbye," said Val, her lips feeling rusty and stiff.

"Thanks, Pink," said Rhys, turning around. "Take care of Val."

Pink made a strangled sound. Rhys kissed Val's cold cheek and stepped back. Pink helped him on with his coat, handed him his hat.

"Come on," said Inspector Glücke.

Two of the detectives grasped Rhys's elbows and marched him out of the apartment.

"You two," said the Inspector. "Keep on

ice." He nodded to the third man and they followed the others.

Pink stood still in the middle of the living-room, blinking and blinking as if the sun were in his eyes.

He didn't do it.

Val stumbled to the door and watched Rhys go down the hall toward the elevator, walking steadily in the midst of his guard.

He didn't do it! He has an alibi!

She tried to get the words out.

Prison. Some grubby cell. Fingerprints. Arraignment. Rogues' gallery. Reporters. Sob sisters. Keepers. Trial. Murder. . . .

Please. Please.

It would be Walter marching down the hall. If she spoke it would be Walter. If she didn't . . . Oh, wait, wait, please.

Walter or pop. Pop or Walter. It wasn't fair. It wasn't a choice. He didn't do it, I tell you. He has an alibi. Stop!

But nothing came out, and the elevator swallowed the marchers, leaving the corridor bleak and empty.

PART
THREE

9

LADY OF THE PRESS

Valerie did not sleep well Monday night. The apartment was dark and cold and full of whispering voices. She tossed open-eyed on her bed until the first grilles formed through the Venetian blinds; then she dozed.

Pink pounded at the door at seven, and she crept out of bed to let him in. When she reappeared later in an old tweed sports outfit he had breakfast ready. They ate together in silence. She washed the dishes and Pink, whose broad shoulders seemed to have acquired a permanent droop, went out for the morning papers.

It occurred to Val, scrubbing the pots with aluminum wool, that she had spoken her last word aloud the night before. It had been "Goodbye," and in retrospect it seemed darkly prophetic. She said to the dripping pan: "Hello," and was so startled at the sound of her voice that she almost dropped the pan.

When Pink got back with the papers he found her powdering her nose, which had a suspiciously pink tinge.

And there it was in cold print. The coarse-screen halftone of Rhys made him look like Public Enemy Number 1. Sportsman Held As Material Witness. Arrest on Murder Charge Hinted by Van Every. Spaeth Partner Refuses to Talk. . . . "Rhys Jardin, 49, ex-millionaire and prominent Hollywood society man, is in Los Angeles City Jail this morning held as a material witness in the sensational murder yesterday of Solomon Spaeth, Jardin's business partner in the ill-fated Ohippi Hydro-Electric Development. . . ."

Val pushed the paper away. "I'm not going to read it. I won't read it."

"Why don't he hire a mouthpiece?" exclaimed Pink. "It says here he won't open his trap except to say he's innocent. Is he nuts?"

The buzzer jarred and Pink opened the door. He tried to shut it immediately, but he might have been pitting his strength against the Pacific Ocean. He vanished in a wave of arms, legs, cameras, and flash bulbs.

Val fled to her bedroom and locked the door.

"Out!" yelled Pink. "Out, you skunks! Paid parasites of the capitalist press! Get the hell out of here!"

"Where's the closet where that sword was found?"

"Is this it, punk?"

"Where was the camel's-hair coat?"

"Get that homely ape out of the way!"

"Miss Ja-a-ardin! How about a statement — Daughter Flies to Defense of Father?"

"This way, Pincus my boy. Look tough!"

Pink finally got them out. He was panting as Val cautiously peeped out of her bedroom.

"This is terrible," she moaned.

"Wait a minute. I smell a rat." Pink sneaked into Rhys's bathroom and found a knight of the lens gallantly photographing Rhys's tub. When the cameraman saw Val he hastily put a new plate into his camera.

Val bounded back to her bedroom like a gazelle.

"Funny thing about me. Either I like a guy," Pink said, knocking the photographer down, "or I don't. Scram, you three-eyed gorilla!"

The photographer scrammed.

Val peered out again. "Are they *all* gone now?"

"Unless there's one hiding in the drain," growled Pink.

"I'm going," said Val hysterically, clapping on the first hat she could find. "I'm getting out of here."

"Hey — where you going?" demanded Pink, alarmed.

"I don't know!"

Val ducked down the emergency stairway, preceded Indian-wise by Pink, who flailed through the crowd in the lobby and executed a feint by loudly warning Mibs Austin, who was barricaded behind the switchboard, to keep her mouth shut or he would break her neck, and then challenging every newspaperman in Los Angeles to a fist-fight.

He won his desire, *en masse;* and while Mibs shrieked encouragement to her red-haired gladiator and the lone policeman on duty prudently backed into the elevator, Val escaped unnoticed through the side-exit of the *La Salle*.

She almost stripped the gears of Rhys's sedan getting away from the curb.

A long time later she became conscious of the fact that the sedan was bowling along the Ocean Speedway, near Malibu Beach, the spangled Pacific glittering in the sunshine to her left and the stinging breeze lifting her hair.

The taffy sand, the chunky Santa Monica Mountains, the paintbox blue of the ocean, the salt smell and white road and warming sun did something to her; and after a while she felt quieted and comfortable, like a child dozing in its mother's lap.

Back there, in the haze-covered city, Rhys gripped gray bars, the papers whooped it up in an orgiastic war-dance, Walter sat steeped in some mysterious liquid agony of his own fermentation. But here, by the sea, in the sun, one could think things out, point by point, and reach serene, reasonable conclusions.

Oxnard slipped by, the flat white miniature Mexico of Ventura, the grove-splashed orange country where occasional fruit glowed in the trees, yellow sapphires imbedded in crushed green velvet.

Valerie drew a deep breath.

At Santa Barbara she headed for the hills. And when she got to the top she stopped the car and got out and slipped into the silence and coolness of the old Mission. She was there a long time.

Later, feeling hungry, she drove down into the sunny Spanish town and consumed *enchiladas*.

When she returned to Hollywood, in the late evening, she felt regenerated. She knew exactly what she had to do.

★ ★ ★

The Wednesday morning papers bellowed news. Inspector Glücke had decided, after a long conference with District Attorney Van Every, the Chief of Police, the Chief of Staff, and the Chief of Detectives, to charge Rhys Jardin with the premeditated murder of Solomon Spaeth.

Val drove the ten miles into downtown Los Angeles and left her sedan in a parking lot on Hill Street, near First. It was only a few steps to the City Jail. But she did not go that way. Instead, she walked southeast, crossed Broadway, turned south on Spring, and stopped before a grimy building. She hesitated only a moment. Then she went in.

The elevator deposited her on the fifth floor, and she said firmly to the reception clerk: "I want to see the managing editor."

"Who wants to see him?"

"Valerie Jardin."

The clerk said: "Wait a minute, wait a minute," and babbled into the telephone. Ten seconds later the door opened and Fitzgerald said eagerly: "Come on in, Val. Come in!"

Fitz led the way with hungry strides through the city room. Inquisitive eyes followed Val's progress through the room. But Val did not care; her lips were compressed. One man, sitting over a drawing board in a far corner, got half out of his chair and then sank down again, gripping a stick of charcoal nervously and adjusting his green eyeshade. Val suppressed a start and walked on. Walter back at work! She did not glance his way again.

Fitz slammed the door of his office. "Sit down, Val. Cigaret? Drink? Tough about the old man. What's on your mind?"

"Fitz," said Val, sitting down and clasping her hands, "how much money have you?"

"Me?" The Irishman stared. "I'm busted — Ohippi. Do you need dough? Maybe I can scare up a few C's —"

"I didn't come here for that." Valerie looked him in the eye. "Fitz, I want a job."

Fitz rubbed his black jowls. "Look, Val, if you're broke, why —"

Val said with a faint smile: "I'm a special sort of person right now, isn't that so?"

"What's the point?"

"Daughter of a famous man charged with a front-page murder?"

Fitz got out of his chair and, still rubbing his face, went to the dust-streaked window. When he turned around his bird's-nest brows almost completely concealed his eyes.

"I'm listening," he said, sitting down again.

Val smiled once more. Fitz was a little transparent. A nerve near his right eye was jumping.

"I couldn't write a news story, but you've got plenty of people who can. On the other hand, I can give you information you'd never get without my help."

Fitz flipped a switch on his communicator. "Bill. I don't want to be disturbed." He sat back. "I'm still listening."

"Well, I'm the daughter of the accused. The byline alone will sell papers."

Fitz grinned. "Oh, you want a byline, too?"

"Second, I'll be able to predict the defense before it comes out in court."

"Yes," said Fitz. "You certainly will."

"Third, I'll have inside information no other paper in town could possibly dig out. Where it won't hurt my father, you'll have an exclusive story."

Fitzgerald began to play with a paper-knife.

"And last, you can play up the human-interest angle — rich gal loses all her money, goes to work in defense of accused father." Fitz leaned forward toward his communicator again. "Wait a minute, darling," said Val. "I'm no philanthropist. I'm proposing to do something that nauseates me. It's going to take a lot of money to cure that nausea."

"Oh," said the Irishman. "All right, how much?"

Val said bravely: "A thousand dollars a yarn."

"Hey!" growled Fitz.

"I need lots of money, Fitz. If you won't give it to me, some other paper will."

"Have a heart, Val — a story a day! This thing may drag on for months."

Val rose. "I know what you're thinking. They've got pop dead to rights, no sensational news angle can come out of the case, it will be cut-and-dried, the usual story of a guilty man brought to trial. If you think that, Fitz, you're a long way off."

"What d'ye mean?"

"Do you believe pop's guilty?"

"Sure not," said Fitz soothingly. "Sit down, Val."

"I tell you he isn't."

"Sure he isn't."

"I *know* he isn't!"

Val walked to the door. Fitz shot out of his chair and ran to head her off.

"Don't be so damned hasty! You mean you've got information —"

"I mean," said Val, "that I have a clue that will lead to the real criminal, Friend Scrooge."

"You have?" shouted Fitz. "Look, Val mavourneen, come here and sit down again. What is it? Tell old Fitz. After all, I'm an old friend of your father's —"

"Do I get my thousand a story?"

"Sure!"

"You'll let me work my own way?"

"Anything you want!"

"No questions asked, and I work alone?"

"That's not fair. How do I know you're not sandbagging me? How do I know —"

"Take it or leave it, Mr. Fitzgerald."

"You've got the instincts of an Apache!"

"Goodbye," said Val, turning again to go.

"For God's sake, hold it, will you? Listen, Val, you haven't any experience. You may get into trouble."

"Don't worry about that," said Val sweetly.

"Or you may ruin a great story. Let me assign one of my men to double up with you. How's that? Then I'll be protected, and so will you."

"I don't want any spies or story-stealers around," frowned Val.

"Wait a minute! I give you my word it'll

be on the level, Val. You can't gang up on me this way! A good man who knows his stuff, won't blab, and will steer you right."

Val stood thinking. In a way, Fitz was right. She had no idea where her investigation might lead. An experienced newspaperman to advise and assist and even provide physical protection in the event of danger was a wise precaution.

"All right, Fitz," she said finally.

Fitz beamed. "It's a deal! Be back here at two o'clock and I'll have my man ready. We'll give you a press card, put you on the payroll, and you'll be all set. You're sure you've got something?" he asked anxiously.

"You'll have to take your chances," said Val. Sure? She didn't even know what the clue was!

"Get out of here," groaned Fitz.

When Valerie emerged into the city room Walter was standing in the aisle, waiting.

Val tried to pass him, but he moved over to block her path.

"Please," said Val.

"I've got to talk to you," said Walter in a low voice.

"Please!"

"I've got to, Val."

179

Val eyed him coolly. "Well, if you must I suppose you must. I don't care for an audience, though, so let's go into the hall."

He took her arm and hurried her through the city room. Val studied him covertly. She was shocked by his appearance. His cheeks were sunken; there were leaden hollows under his eyes, which were inflamed. He looked ill, as if he were in pain and had not slept for days.

He backed her against the marble wall near the elevators. "I've read about Rhys's arrest," he said feverishly. "It muddles things for me, Val. You've got to give me time to think this over —"

"Who's stopping you?"

"Please have patience with me. I can't explain yet —"

"Nasty habit you have," said Val, "of not being able to explain. Please, Walter. You're hurting me."

Walter released her. "I'm sorry about Monday night. Getting drunk, I mean. The things I said. Val, if you'd only have a little faith in me . . ."

"I suppose you know," said Val, "that some one planted the rapier and pop's coat in our closet, and tipped off the police that they were there. Or don't you?"

"Do you believe *I* did that?" said

Walter in a low voice.

Val stirred restlessly. Nothing could come of this. "I'm going," she said.

"Wait —"

"Oh, yes. I've just taken a job here. Special features on the case. I'm going to do a little investigating of my own. I thought you'd like to know."

Walter grew paler under his two-day growth of beard. "Val! Why?"

"Because trials cost money and lawyers are expensive."

"But you've got that money I gave you. I mean —"

"That's another thing. Of course we can't accept that, Walter. Pop has it in a bank, but I'll have him write out a check for the full amount."

"I don't want it! Oh, damn it. Val! Don't start something that might — that might bring you —"

"Yes?" murmured Valerie.

Walter was silent, gnawing his lower lip.

"Yes?" said Val again, with the merest accent of contempt. But she could not prevent a certain pity from creeping into her voice, too.

Walter did not reply.

Val pressed the elevator-button. The door slid open after a while. She got in and turned around. The operator began to pull the door shut

Walter just stood there.

10

A STAR REPORTER IS BORN

Fitz sauntered into the reception room of Magna Studios and said to the man at the desk: "Hullo, Bob. Is Ellery Queen in?"

"Who?" said the man.

"Ellery Queen."

"Queen, Queen. Does he work here?" said the man, reaching for a directory.

"I believe he's under that impression," said Fitz.

"Oh, yes. Writer. Writers' Annex, Room 25. Just a second." He picked up his telephone.

Fitz stuck a cigar into the man's mouth, said: "Cut the clowning. What d'ye think I am, a trade-paper ad salesman?" and went through.

He strolled along the cement walk before the open-air quadrangle of executive buildings, past the bootblack stand, and into the alley marked " 'A' Street" alongside Sound Stage One. At the end of the alley cowered a long, lean, two-story building with a red-gabled roof and stained stucco walls.

Fitz mounted the steps to the open terrace and searched along the terrace until he found an open door with the number 25 on it.

It was a magnificent room, with two magnificent desks, a magnificent rug, a magnificent central fixture, magnificent draperies, and magnificent art on the walls. And it was magnificently empty.

A typewriter stood on a mahogany work-table opposite the door; a chair with polished arms magnificently etched into curlicues by some one's penknife lay over-turned on the floor before the table. From the carriage of the typewriter jutted a sheet of heavy bond paper, with words on it.

Fitz went in and read them. The words were:

"If a miracle should happen and some-body should walk into this hermit's lonely desert cell, I am currently in the office of His Holiness Seymour A. Hugger, Grand Lama of the Writers' Division of Magna Pictures, giving him a piece of what is left of my mind. For God's sake, pal, wait for me.
ELLERY QUEEN."

Fitz grinned and went out. On the way to the terrace steps he caught sight through a window of a long-legged literary person in slacks and a yellow polo shirt. The gentleman sccmed fiercely intent on a toothpaste advertisement in *Cosmopolitan.* But then Fitz saw that he was asleep.

He returned to the Administration Building and hunted through the polished corridor until he discovered a door which proclaimed the presence of Mr. Hugger.

Opening the door, he found himself in a sort of glorified cubbyhole containing three large desks at which three beautiful young women sat buffing their fingernails, and a worried-looking young man who clutched a sheaf of yellow papers marked "Sequence A" which he was reading nervously.

"Yes?" said one of the young women without looking up, but Fitz opened the door lettered "Private" and strolled into Mr. Hugger's domain without stooping to conversation.

Ensconced in a throne-like chair behind a dazzling cowhide-covered desk sat a chubby young man with thin hair and a benign demeanor. The room, the rug, the desk, the radio, the draperies, the bookcases, and the *objets d'art* were even more magnificent than their generic cousins in Room 25, Writers' Annex. Moreover, Mr.

Hugger was magnificent in his happiness. Mr. Hugger seemed to want every one to know that he was happy. Particularly the bearded, purple-visaged maniac who was waving his arms and scudding up and down the room like a Sunday yacht.

"If you'll calm down for a minute, Mr. Queen," Mr. Hugger was saying in avuncular accents as Fitz walked in.

"I'll be damned if I will!" yelled Mr. Queen. "What I want to know is — why can't I see Butcher?"

"I've told you, Mr. Queen. He's *very* temperamental, Mr. Butcher is. He takes his time. Patience. Just have patience. Nobody's rushing you —"

"That's just the bloody trouble!" shouted Mr. Queen. "I want to be rushed. I want to work day and night. I want to hear a human voice. I want to engage in debates about the weather. What did you bring me out here for, anyway?"

"Excuse me," said Fitz.

"Oh, hello," said Ellery, and he sank into a ten-foot divan and plunged his hands into his beard.

"Yes?" said Mr. Hugger with an executive look.

"Oh." Ellery waved his hand wearily. "Mr. Hugger, Mr. Fitzgerald. Fitz is man-

186

aging editor of the *Independent*."

"Newspaperman," said Mr. Hugger, becoming happy again. "Have a cigar, Mr. Fitzgerald. Would you be kind enough to wait outside for a moment? Mr. Queen and I —"

"Thanks, I'll wait here," said Fitz genially, licking the end of Mr. Hugger's cigar. "What's the trouble, MasterMind?"

"I ask you," cried Ellery, bouncing up. "They brought me out here to write for the movies. They gave me twenty-four hours to get ready in New York, and they couldn't even wait for me to get off the train. I didn't have time to take a bath. Get him right down to the studio! they told my agent. So I hurried down here, full of alkali, with a running nose and a sore throat, and they gave me the Doge's Palace to work in, a mountain of foolscap, a whole school of pencils, and the offer of a beautiful stenographer, which I refused. And what do you think happened?"

"I give up," said Fitz.

"Sick as I've been, I've hung around here and hung around and hung around, waiting to be called into conference by his Lordship, Jacques Butcher, the producer I'm supposed to go to work for. You know what? After all that haste, I've sat in that damned lamasery for two solid weeks and the man hasn't so much as telephoned me. I've called him, I've haunted his office, I've tried to waylay him — nothing. I've just sat on my rump praying for the sight of a human being and slowly going mad!"

"Mr. Queen doesn't understand the Hollywood way of doing things," explained Mr. Hugger quickly. "Mr. Butcher in his own way is a genius. He has peculiar methods —"

"Oh, he has, has he?" bellowed Ellery. "Well, let me tell you something, Your Majesty. Your genius has spent the past two weeks playing golf during the day and Romeo during the night with your ingénue star, Bonnie Stuart, so what do you know about that?"

"Come on out," said Fitz, lighting a cigar, "and I'll buy you a drink."

"Yes, go on," said Mr. Hugger hastily. "You need something to quiet your nerves. Mr. Butcher will get in touch with you very shortly, I'm sure."

"You *and* Mr. Butcher," said Ellery, impaling Mr. Hugger with a terrible glance, "are from hunger."

And he stamped out, followed by Fitz.

Over the third Scotch-and-soda at

Thyra's, across the street from the studio, Fitz remarked: "I see you've got your voice back."

"The sun fixed that, when he got around to it." Ellery seized his glass. "God," he said hollowly, and drained it.

"Sick of this racket already, hey?"

"If I didn't have a contract I'd take the first train out of the Santa Fe station!"

"How'd you like to get mixed up in some real excitement, not this synthetic lunacy?"

"Anything. Anything! Give me that bottle."

"It's right smack down your alley, too," murmured Fitz, obliging as he puffed at Mr. Hugger's perfecto.

"Oh," said Ellery. He put down the bottle of Scotch and looked at Fitz over the siphon. "The Spaeth case."

Fitz nodded. Ellery sat back. Then he said: "What's up?"

"You know Rhys Jardin's in the can charged with Spaeth's murder, don't you?"

"I read the papers. That's the only thing I've had to do, by God."

"You met his daughter, Valerie? Swell trick, eh?"

"Economically useless but otherwise a nice girl, I should say. Possibilities."

Fitz leaned on his elbows. "Well, they're

189

up against it for *dinero,* and Val came to me this morning and asked for a job. I gave it to her, too."

"Nice of you," said Ellery. He wondered what had become of Walter's money, but not aloud.

"Not at all. Rhys and I boned Lit together at Harvard and all that, but the hell with sentiment. It's a business proposition. She's got something to sell, and I'm buying."

Ellery said suddenly: "Think Jardin killed Spaeth?"

"How should I know? Anyway, the kid says she's got something hot — a clue of some kind. She won't tell me what it is, but I'm playing a hunch on this one. She's going to do byline stories for me daily and meanwhile run down the clue."

"And exactly where," said Ellery, marching his fingers along the checkered cloth, "do I come in?"

Fitz coughed. "Now don't say no till you hear me out, Queen. I admit it's a screwy idea —"

"In the present state of my emotions," said Ellery, "that's in its favor."

"I told her I'd put an experienced man on with her — show her the ropes, steer her right." Fitz refilled his glass carefully. "And you're it."

190

"How do you know she'll work with me? After all, you spilled the beans about me at *Sans Souci* Monday."

"No, she mustn't know you're a detective," said Fitz hurriedly. "She'd tighten up like a wet rawhide in the sun."

"Oh," said Ellery. "You want me to spy on her."

"Look, Queen, if I wanted to do that I'd put one of my own men on with her. But she needs somebody familiar with murder. She ought to think her partner's just a legman, though; I don't want to scare her off."

Ellery frowned. "I'm not a newspaperman, and she knows what I look like."

"She wouldn't know a newspaperman if she fell over one. And how well does she know you?"

"She's seen me twice."

"Hell," said Fitz, "we can fix that."

"What do you mean?" asked Ellery, alarmed.

"Keep your pants on. The set-up's perfect, that's why I doped this out. You told me you don't normally wear a beard. So if you shaved it off Val wouldn't recognize you, would she?"

"Shave off this beautiful thing?" said

191

Ellery in dismay, caressing it.

"Sure! It's old-fashioned, anyway. Show a clean mug, comb your hair on the side instead of straight back the way you've got it now, dress a little differently, and she'll never get wise. Even your voice will fool her — she's only heard that croak you were using Monday."

"Hmm," said Ellery. "You want me to stick to Miss Jardin, find out what she knows, and crack the case if her father's innocent?"

"Right."

"Suppose he's guilty?"

"In that case," said Fitz, taking another drink, "let your conscience be your guide."

Ellery drummed for some time on the cloth. "There are other objections. I can hardly pose as a Los Angeles reporter; I've never been here before."

"You're new from the East."

"I don't know the lingo, the habits, the hangouts —"

"Oh, my God," said Fitz. "You've been reading about reporters in your own stories. Believe it or not, newspapermen talk just like anybody else. Their habits are the same, too — maybe a little better. As far as hangouts are concerned, this is a funny town. L.A.'s the largest city in area in the

192

United States — covers four hundred and forty-two square miles. After we go to press the boys scatter to the four winds — Tujunga, Sierra Madre, Altadena, Santa Monica Canyon, Brentwood Park. Hangouts? You don't hang out anywhere when you've got to drive sixty miles to get home to the wife and kids."

"I'm convinced. How about a name?"

"Damn. That's right. Let's see. Ellery —"

"Celery. . . ."

"Pillory. . . ."

"Hilary! That's it. Hilary what? Queen —"

"King!"

"Hilary King. Ingenious."

"Then it's all set," said Fitz, rising.

"Wait a minute. Aren't you interested in the financial aspect of the deal?"

"Are you going to blackjack me, too?" growled Fitz.

Ellery grinned. "I'll take it on for nothing and expenses, you lucky dog."

Fitz looked suspicious. "Why?"

"Because I'm sick of Messrs. Butcher and Hugger. Because there are things about the Spaeth case that positively make my mouth water. Because I like the people most directly involved. And because," said Ellery, jamming on his hat, "I've got a score to settle with the High

Hocus-Pocus of the Homicide Detail!"

"An idealist, b'gorra," said Fitz. "Be in my office at two o'clock."

11

CARDS UNDER THE TABLE

When Val left the *Los Angeles Independent* building, she hunted up a shop, spent a few minutes there, hurried out, and made her way to the City Jail.

There was a great deal of concealed official emotion when she announced her identity. Val, holding her package casually, pretended not to notice.

It was all rather worse than she had imagined, but somehow things were different this morning. Lovelace's lines popped into her mind — what a fanatic Miss Prentiss had been on the subject of "recitations" in the ancient pigtail-and-governess days! "Minds innocent and quiet take That for an hermitage." No, stone walls do not a prison make, nor iron bars a cage.

A uniformed man said to her: "You'll have to empty your pockets and purse, Miss," and Val obeyed, raising her smooth brows. He seemed disappointed at finding no revolver underneath the vanity-case.

"What's in that bundle?" he asked suspiciously.

"Bombs," said Val.

He opened the package, glaring at her. "Okay," he said shortly.

Val gathered her purchases up and said with a sweet smile: "You have to be *so* careful with these desperate criminals, don't you?"

Another man, in an unpressed business suit, trailed along, as a guard conducted her to a remote cell block. Val's brows went up again.

And there he was, sitting on his pallet playing solitaire with a fuzzy, dirty old deck of cards which looked as if they had been used by four generations of prisoners. He did not notice their approach and Val studied his profile for a moment, trying to adjust her own expression. He was so calm, so unconcerned; he might have been lounging in his club.

"Here's your daughter," said the guard, unlocking the barred door.

Rhys looked around, startled. Then he bounced to his feet and held out his arms.

The keeper locked the door again and said to the shabby man who had followed Val: "Come on, Joe, let 'em alone. Man's got a right to talk private, ain't he?"

"Sure," said Joe heartily. "That's right, Grady."

It seemed to Val that both had spoken in unnecessarily loud voices. She looked up at her father and he grinned in answer. The keeper and the shabby man marched ostentatiously away.

"Don't you think," began Val, "that they —"

"Darling," said Rhys. He pulled her over to the pallet and sat her down. The greasy cards he pushed carelessly aside, and Val put her package down. "How's my puss?"

"How are you, pop? Like it here?" said Val, smiling.

"I don't know what those literary-minded convicts who write memoirs keep kicking about. A place like this is perfect for resting the tired business man."

"I thought those two —" began Val again.

Rhys said easily: "I do miss decent cards, though. These things must have come into California with Porciúncula."

"I've brought you a new deck," said Val, undoing her package again. She knew suddenly that he did not want her to discuss anything of possible interest to an eavesdropper. She glanced at him and he motioned meaningly toward the wall behind his pallet. So some one was planted in the next cell! Probably, thought Val, with a dictograph.

"Thanks, darling," said Rhys, as she handed him a new deck of cards with brilliant blue backs showing a schooner in full sail. "It's hell playing with fifty-two dishrags. And what's this — cigars!"

"I bought you the king size — they last longer, don't they?"

"You're simply wonderful." Rhys gathered up the old cards and began to pat them into a neat pile. "I was beginning to think you'd run out on me. In durance vile for thirty-six hours, and not a peep out of you!"

"I tried last night, but they wouldn't give you a telephone message."

"Nasty of them. Here, take these damned shingles and burn 'em." He handed her the old deck of cards and she furtively put it into her purse.

Rhys leaned back with a long sigh. Valerie closed her purse with a snap. "Did they — did they do anything to you that —"

He waved his hand. "They're cooking up an arraignment or indictment or whatever they call it, and I suppose I'll have to attend. There's been a good deal of questioning, of course."

"Questioning," said Val in a faint voice.

"Nothing brutal, you understand. You

really should meet Van Every — charming fellow. I must say I like him better than that ogre Glücke."

Chit-chat, inconsequentials, to deceive the man in the next cell. To deceive her, too? Val suddenly leaned over and kissed him. They were both silent for a moment.

Then Val said: "I've got something to tell you."

He shook his head in warning. But Val reassured him with a glance and went on: "I've taken a job with Fitz."

"A job?"

She told him the story of her interview with Fitzgerald. "Its — well, it's money, pop. We've got to have some." He was silent again. "And don't you think we ought to pay back — that other money we owe?"

"Yes. Of course." He knew which money she meant, but somehow neither seemed to want to mention Walter's name. "But not now. It can wait. Naturally I won't touch it."

"Naturally." Val understood. To return Walter's money now would raise all sorts of questions. Walter's sympathy with Jardin was better kept secret — for Walter's sake. For Walter's sake! Everything, everything was for Walter's sake.

"Is there anything else I can get you?" asked Val.

"No, Val. I'm really quite comfortable."

They looked deeply into each other's eyes. Val kissed him again. Then she rose and said hurriedly: "I'll see you later," and ran to the door and began shaking the bars like a young female monkey.

"Guard!" called Rhys with a curious smile, and the keeper came running. "It's a funny feeling, isn't it, puss?"

"Goodbye, darling," said Val without looking around, and she followed the man out with her head held high but seeing very little of the massive masonry and iron-work that escorted her to the very street.

Val had taken no more than twenty steps on First Street when she knew she was being followed.

To make sure, she headed for the lot where she had parked her car. There, while the attendant hunted through the rows, Val became busy examining her face in her mirror and incidentally watching the street. Yes, there was no doubt about it. A long black sedan with two men in it had inched away from the curb across the street from the Jail and had followed her walking figure at five miles an hour. Now it was waiting unobtrusively before the parking lot, as if held up by traffic. But there was very little traffic.

The attendant brought up her car and Val got in, feeling her hcart beat fast. She clutched her purse tighter and drove out of the lot with one hand.

The black sedan began to crawl again.

Val set her bag down and began to dodge in and out of traffic.

Fifteen minutes later, after a circuitous route, she found herself on Wilshire Boulevard near LaFayette Park — and the big sedan was still fifty feet behind her.

There was only one thing to do, and Val did it. She sped west on Wilshire, bound for home. North on Highland, past Third, Beverly, Melrose, Santa Monica, Sunset . . . the sedan followed grimly, maintaining its distance.

Val drove up to the *La Salle*, parked the car, snatched her purse from the seat, slipped into the lobby by the side-entrance and dodged up the stairway to 3-C. She locked her door with shaking fingers.

She flung her hat aside and sat down for a moment to catch her breath. The apartment was quiet, the Venetian blinds tipped down. She rose and went to the breakfast-room window and peered out. There, in the back street, stood the sedan; its two occupants were still sitting in it, smoking.

Val hurried back to the living-room and tore open her purse. In her nervousness the cards cascaded to the floor. She sat down cross-legged and picked them up.

She began quickly to separate the suits — clubs, diamonds, hearts, spades. When all the clubs were in one pile, she arranged them in descending order — ace on top, then king, queen, jack, down to the deuce. She repeated this curious procedure with the three other suits. When this was finished she took up the thirteen spades, then the hearts, then the diamonds, and finally the clubs.

Val turned the rearranged deck over in her hands, frowning. Something was wrong. Along both sides appeared pencil marks — dots, dashes, and on some card-edges nothing at all. It looked like a telegraph code. But that couldn't be.

Oh, she was stupid! Some cards were turned one way, the rest the other. She would have to turn each card so that its marked edge coincided with the marked edges of the cards above and below it. That was what she had had to do as a little girl, when Rhys amused her with what had then seemed a fascinating trick of secret communication.

There! The thing was done. All the marked edges lay one way, and the pencilled dots and dashes became parts of an intelligible message written in simple block letters over the tightly compressed side of the deck.

There was not enough light on the floor. Val scrambled up and ran to the breakfast-room window, careful to remain invisible to the watchers below.

She breathed a little harder as she read the clear, tiny letters. The message said:

SS PHONED AR MON AM COME OVER URGENT BETW 5–5.30 PM

Val slowly sat down on the breakfast-nook bench. SS — that stood for Solomon Spaeth. AR — Anatole Ruhig. Solomon Spaeth had telephoned Anatole Ruhig Monday morning to call at the Spaeth house *between five and five-thirty Monday afternoon* on an urgent matter!

So that was the clue. Rhys had gone over to Spaeth's house Monday morning; they had had their argument in Spaeth's study. It must have been during this visit that Spaeth had telephoned his lawyer, and Rhys had overheard.

Between five and five-thirty Monday afternoon. But Spaeth had been murdered at five-thirty!

Val clenched her hands under her chin. What had Ruhig told Glücke? Yes, that he had appeared at *Sans Souci* a few minutes past six Monday afternoon. But that must have been true, otherwise Walewski would have called him a liar. Unless Walewski . . .

Val frowned. Spaeth had commanded his lawyer to appear between five and five-thirty, and Ruhig had simply been more than a half-hour late for the appointment. That was the reasonable explanation. Besides, had Ruhig really been on time, wouldn't Frank — on duty at the gate — have seen him and reported his visit to Inspector Glücke? Unless Frank . . .

Val was so disappointed she flung the cards from her and glowered at them as they lay strewn about the kitchen floor. She could have wept for sheer chagrin.

But she did nothing of the sort. She got down on her hands and knees and picked the cards up one by one, getting a run in one stocking in the process; and when she had them together again she rose and went into her bedroom and stowed them away in the bureau under the chemises.

Then she undressed, washed her face and hands, changed her stockings, made up, put on her black silk print with the magnolia-petal design and the last expensive hat she had bought — the one that looked so fetchingly like a modernistic soup plate — transferred her vanity and key-case and money to the alligator bag, and departed, a lady with a mission.

The information about Counselor Anatole Ruhig was the only clue she had; and, for better or worse, it had to be traced to its bitter end.

At two o'clock precisely the door of Managing Editor Fitzgerald's office flew open and an apparition appeared, making Mr. Fitzgerald choke over a hooker of eighteen-year-old whisky which he was in the process of swallowing.

"Hi, Chief," said the apparition, swaggering in.

"Who the hell do you think you're impersonating," spluttered Fitz, "a burlycue comic?"

The apparition was a tall lean young man with a clean-shaven face and features just a trifle too sharp to be handsome. But Fitzgerald was examining the costume, not the face. The young man was attired in shapeless slacks of a dingy gray hue and the loudest sport coat Fitzgerald, who had seen nearly everything, had ever laid eyes on. It was a sort of disappointed terra cotta, with wide cobalt stripes slashing through an assortment of brown plaid checks. His shoes were yellow brogues. His red-and-blue plaid socks curled around his ankles. On his head he wore a tan felt hat with the fore part of the brim sticking straight up in the air. And his eyes were covered by blue-tinted sun-glasses.

"Hilary 'Scoop' King, the demon of the city room," said the apparition, leering. "Hahzit, Fitz?"

"Oh, my God," groaned Fitz, hastily shutting his door.

"What's the matter? Don't I look the part?"

"You look like a hasheesh-eater's dream of heaven," cried Fitz. "That coat — jeeze! It must have come down to you straight from Joseph."

"Protective coloration," said Ellery defensively.

"Yeah — your own father wouldn't know you in that get-up. And with the beaver gone you don't look the same man. Only for cripe's sake don't go around telling anybody you work here. I'd be laughed out of the *pueblo*."

The door opened a little and Val said timidly: "May I come in?"

"Sure," said Fitz in a hearty voice, and he glared at Ellery, who hastily got off the desk.

206

Val slipped in, and Fitz shut the door behind her. "Don't let the get-up scare you, Val. This is Hilary King, thc man I told you about. He's new to L.A. and he thinks the local men dress like a shopgirl's conception of Clark Gable relaxing. King, Miss Valerie Jardin."

"How do you do," said Val, trying not to giggle.

"Hi," said Ellery, removing his hat. But then he remembered that newspapermen in the movies never remove their hats, so he put it on again.

"I decided not to use a local man after all, Val," said Fitz, "because the boys would know him and get wise to what's going on. King's just in from — uh — Evansville; great record out there, especially on police work."

He bustled to his desk and Val eyed her new colleague sidewise. He looked like a perfect idiot. But then Fitz was smart, and appearances *weren't* always to be trusted. She also thought she had seen the creature before, but she couldn't decide when or where.

"Here are your credentials," said Fitz, "and yours, too, King."

"Does the gentleman from Evansville know what his job is?" asked Val.

"Oh, sure," said Ellery. "Fitz told me.

Keep an eye on you, give you fatherly advice. Don't worry about me — baby."

"How," said Val, "are the gentleman's morals?"

"Who, me? I'm practically sexless."

"Not," retorted Val, "that it would do you any good if you weren't. I just wanted to avoid possible unpleasantness."

"Go on, get going, both of you," said Fitz benevolently.

"I'll have my first story," said Val, "ready for the rewrite desk tonight, Fitz."

"Not in this man's trade, you won't," grinned Fitz. "We've got a daily paper to get out. Besides, it's all written."

"What!"

"Now don't fret yourself," soothed Fitz. "You don't have to pound out the grind stuff. I've got people here who can make up a better human-interest yarn out of their heads than you could out of facts. You'll get your byline and your grand just the same."

"But I don't understand."

"Part of your value to me is your name. The other part is that clue you're battin' about. Don't worry about the writing, Val. Follow up that clue, and if you pick up any special slants, 'phone 'em in. I'll take care of the rest."

"Mr. King," said Val, eying the apparition. "For whom are you working — Fitz or me?"

"The answer to a dame," said Mr. King, "is always yes."

"Hey!" shouted Fitz.

"Now that you've learned your catechism," said Val with a kindly smile, "come along, Mr. King, and learn something else."

12

THE AFFAIRS OF ANATOLE

"The first thing I crave," said Hilary "Scoop" King as they paused on the sidewalk before the *Independent* building, "is lunch. Have you eaten?"

"No, but we've got an important call to make —"

"It can wait; most everything can in this world. What would you suggest?"

Val shrugged. "If you're a stranger here, you might like the Café in El Paseo."

"That sounds hundreds of miles away, to the south."

"It's in the heart of the city," laughed Val. "We can hoof it from here."

Ellery politely took the outside position, noting that a black sedan was following them slowly. Val led him up Main Street through the old Plaza, pointing out the landmarks — Pico House, the Lugo mansion plastered with placards displaying red Chinese ideographs, Nigger Alley, Marchessault Street.

When she took him into El Paseo, it was like turning a corner into old Mexico.

Booths ran down the middle of the street displaying black-paper *cigarillos*, little clay toys and holy images, queer cactus plants, candles. The very stones underfoot were alien and fascinating. Along both sides of the narrow thoroughfare were *ramadas*, ovens of brick and wooden tables where fat Mexican women patted an endless array of *tortillas*. At the end of the street there was a forge, where a man sat pounding lumps of incandescent iron into cunning Mexican objects.

Ellery was enchanted. Val indicated their destination, La Golondrina Café, with its quaint overhanging balcony.

"What are those scarlet and yellow dishes I see the *señoritas* carrying about?"

They sat down at one of the sidewalk tables and Val ordered. She watched with a secret mischievousness as he bit innocently into an *enchilada*.

"*Muy caliente!*" he gasped, reaching for the water-jug. "Wow!"

Val laughed aloud then and felt better. She began to like him. And when they got down to the business of serious eating and he chattered on with the fluency of a retired diplomat, she liked him even more.

Before she knew it, she was talking about herself and Rhys and Pink and Winni

Moon and Walter and Solly Spaeth. He asked guileless questions, but by some wizardry of dialectic the answers always had to be factual in order to be intelligible; and before long Val had told him nearly everything she knew about the case.

It was only the important events of Monday afternoon — Rhys's alibi, Walter's taking of Rhys's coat, the fact that Walter had really been inside his father's house at the time of the crime — that Valerie held back. Consequently there were gaps in her account, gaps of which her companion seemed casually aware — too casually, thought Val; and she sprang up and said they would have to be going.

Ellery paid the check and they sauntered out of El Paseo.

"Now where?" he said.

"To see Ruhig."

"Oh, Spaeth's lawyer. What for?"

"I have reason to believe that Ruhig had an appointment with Spaeth on Monday afternoon for five or five-thirty. He told Glücke he got there after six. You won't blab!"

"Cross my heart and hope to die a pulp-writer," said Ellery. "But suppose it's true? He could merely have been late for the appointment."

"Let's hope not," said Val grimly. "Come on — it isn't far to his office."

They made their way past the fringe of Chinatown into the business district, and after a while Ellery said in a pleasant voice: "Don't be alarmed, but we're being followed."

"Oh," said Val. "A big black sedan?"

Ellery raised his brows. "I didn't think you'd noticed. All the earmarks, incidentally, of a police car."

"So that's what it is! It followed me all morning."

"Hmm. And that's not all."

"What do you mean?"

"No, no, don't look around. There's some one else, too. A man — I've caught a blurred glimpse or two. Not enough for identification. He's on our trail like a buzzard."

"What'll we do?" asked Val in panic.

"Keep right on ambling along," said Ellery with a broad smile. "I hardly think he'll attempt assassination with all these potential witnesses around."

Val walked stiffly after that, glad that she had given in to Fitzgerald, glad that Hilary "Scoop" King, leading citizen of Evansville, was by her side. When they reached the Lawyers' Trust Building she dodged

213

into the lobby with an exhalation of relief. But Mr. King contrived to pause and inspect the street. There was the black sedan, snuffling like a trained seal across the street; but the man on foot was nowhere to be seen. Either he was hiding in a doorway or had given up the chase.

Mr. Ruhig's office was like himself — small, neat, and deceptively ingenuous. It was apparent that Mr. Ruhig did not believe in pampering his clients with an atmosphere. There was a gaunt, worried-looking girl at the switchboard, several clerks and runners with flinty, unemotional faces, and a wall covered with law books which had an air of being used.

There was no difficulty getting in to see the great man. In fact, he came bustling out of his office to meet them.

"This is a pleasant surprise," he cried, bobbing and beaming. "Shocking about your father, Miss Jardin. What can I do for you? If it's advice you want, I'm completely at your service, although I'm not in the criminal end. Gratis, of course. I feel like an old friend of the family."

And all the while he eyed Ellery with a puzzled, unobtrusive interest.

"Mr. Ruhig, Mr. King," said Val crisply,

sitting down in the plain office. "I hope you don't mind Mr. King's being with me, Mr. Ruhig. He's an old college chum who's volunteered to help."

"Not at all, not at all. What are friends for?" beamed Mr. Ruhig. Apparently the Joseph's coat reassured him, for he paid no further attention to Mr. King.

"I'll come right to the point," said Val, who had no intention of doing any such thing. "I'm not here as Rhys Jardin's daughter but as an employee of the *Los Angeles Independent*."

"Well! Since when, Miss Jardin? I must say that's an unlooked-for development."

"Since this morning. My father and I need money, and it was the only way I knew of earning a great deal quickly."

"Fitzgerald," nodded Ruhig approvingly. "Great character, Fitzgerald. Heart as big as all outdoors. Hasn't stopped agitating for Mooney's release in ten years."

"Now that I've got a job, I've got to earn my keep. Has anything come up on your end, Mr. Ruhig, that might be construed as news?"

"My end?" smiled the lawyer. "Now that's putting it professionally, I'll say that. What would my end be? Oh, you mean the will. Well, of course, I've filed it for pro-

215

bate. There are certain unavoidable technicalities to go through before it's finally probated —"

"I suppose," said Valerie dryly, "Wicious Winni is simply prostrated with grief over the necessity of taking that fifty million dollars."

Ruhig clucked. "I should resent that remark, Miss Jardin."

"Why should you?"

"I mean the — ah — disparaging reference to Miss Moon." He clasped his hands over his little belly and smiled suddenly. "I'll tell you what I'll do. Suppose I start your newspaper career off with a bang, eh? Then you'll feel a little more charitable toward Anatole Ruhig."

Mr. King lounged in his chair studying Mr. Ruhig. Beneath that bland exterior he fancied he saw a considerable equipment for skulduggery. No, Mr. Ruhig was not doing anything out of pure kindness of heart.

"I was going," went on the lawyer paternally, "to call in the press this afternoon and make a general announcement, but since you're here I'll give you an exclusive story. That ought to put you in solid with Fitzgerald! You know," he coughed and paused to take a drink of water from the chipped bronze carafe on his desk, "Miss Moon on the death of Solly Spaeth lost a dear friend — a dear friend. One of the few friends she had in the world. A dear friend."

"That," said Val, "is putting it mildly."

"Now I've always admired Miss Moon from afar, as you might say — the dry man of the law worshipping at the feet of unattainable beauty, ha-ha! But with Spaeth's death attainment, so to speak, becomes possible. I'm afraid I've taken advantage of dear Winni's grief-stricken condition." He coughed again. "In a word, Miss Moon has consented to be my wife."

Val, torn between astonishment and nausea, sat silent. Spaeth not even buried, and that horrible creature already accepting the advances of another man!

"If I were you, Val darling," said Mr. King in an old-college-chummy way, "I'd pick up that telephone and relate this momentous intelligence to your editor."

"Didn't I tell you it was news?" beamed Ruhig.

"Yes, yes," said Val breathlessly. "May I use your 'phone? When are you going to be married? I mean —"

A cloud passed over Mr. Ruhig's rubicund features. "Obviously there is a certain decorum that must be preserved. We haven't thought of a — ah — a date. It will not even be a formal engagement. Merely — what shall I say? — an understanding. By all means use the 'phone."

Mr. King ruminated while Val seized the instrument. Such a public announcement now would hardly endear Mr. Ruhig, already disliked, to a citizenry whose money Mr. Ruhig was proposing to marry. Obviously, then, Mr. Ruhig in making it had an important object in mind.

What?

"Oh, damn," said Val into the telephone. "Fitz isn't in now. Give me . . ." She bit her lip. "Give me Walter Spaeth! . . . Walter? Val. . . . No. . . . Now, please. I've called Fitz but he isn't in, and you're the only other one. . . . It's a story. . . . Yes! Anatole Ruhig has just told me confidentially he and Winni Moon are going to be married, date uncertain. . . . Walter!" She jiggled the telephone, but Walter had hung up.

Mr. Ruhig breathed on his fingernails. "And now —" he said in the tone of a man who would like to prolong a delightful conversation but must regretfully terminate it.

Val sat down again. "There's something else."

"Something else?"

"I'm sort of checking up the day of the murder."

"Monday? Yes?"

"Did you say," asked Val, leaning forward, "that you got to *Sans Souci* a little past six Monday?"

Mr. Ruhig looked astonished. "My dear child! Certainly."

He was going to deny it. He had to deny it. Or perhaps it all wasn't true. Val inhaled like a diver and took the plunge. "What time did Spaeth set for your appointment with him?"

"Between five and five-thirty," said Mr. Ruhig instantly.

Ellery, quietly watching, felt a backwash of admiration. No hesitation at all. Between five and five-thirty. Just like that.

"But you just said you — you got there after six!"

"So I did."

"Then you were *late?* You didn't get there between five and five-thirty at all?"

Mr. Ruhig smiled. "But I did get there between five and five-thirty. . . . How did you know?" he asked suddenly.

Val gripped her alligator bag, trying to keep calm. As for Mr. Hilary King, he saw the point. Mr. Ruhig was an old hand at

219

questions and answers. If he was being questioned about the exact time of his arrival, then he knew Val had reason to ask the question. If she had reason, it might be based on evidence. If there was evidence, truth was safer than fiction. Mr. King's admiration for Mr. Ruhig waxed.

"Let's get this straight," said Val. "You got to *Sans Souci* when?"

"At five-fifteen, to be exact," replied Mr. Ruhig.

"Then why didn't you tell Inspector Glücke —"

"He didn't ask me when the *appointment* was for. And I merely said I drove up a bit after six, which is true. Except that it was the second time I drove up, not the first."

"A minor technicality," commented Mr. King.

"The legal training," said Mr. Ruhig with a modest downward glance. "Answer the question as asked, and don't volunteer information."

"Then you were in the house during the crime," cried Val, "and Atherton Frank lied about no one coming in but —"

"My dear child, you'll learn as you grow older never to jump at conclusions. I drove up the first time at a quarter after five, but that doesn't mean I entered the grounds."

"Oh," said Val.

"Ah," said Mr. King.

"Frank wasn't around," continued the lawyer conversationally. "You might question the one-armed gentleman, because he testified he was on duty all afternoon. But when I got there at five-fifteen the gate was locked and he wasn't in his booth, so I drove off and returned a bit after six, at which time Walewski was on duty. That's all."

"Is it?" murmured Val.

"As a matter of fact," said Ruhig, "I've been debating with myself whether to tell the Inspector about Frank's absence or not. It puts me in rather a spot. I forgot to mention it Monday night, and when I recalled it later it occurred to me that Glücke might become — uh — troublesome over my lapse of memory. However, I think now I'd better tell him."

You didn't forget anything, Mr. Ruhig, thought Mr. King. And you don't want Inspector Glücke to know even now. You're bluffing.

"No," said Val quickly. "Please don't. Just keep it to yourself for a while, Mr. Ruhig."

"But it's a criminal offense!" protested Mr. Ruhig.

"I know, but it may come in handy in the defense if — when pop goes on trial. Don't you see? They couldn't be so sure, then, that he was the *only* one —"

"You'd make a persuasive advocate," beamed Mr. Ruhig. "I'll think it over. . . . No, I shan't, either! Friendship is friendship. I won't talk until you give the word."

Well done, friend.

"Thank you," said Val, rising. "Uh . . . Hilary, let's go."

"Why not?" said Ellery-Hilary, and he uncoiled his legs from under Mr. Ruhig's uncomfortable chair.

He had scarcely got out of it when Ruhig's office door flew open and Walter Spaeth strode in, hatless and panting, as if he had run all the way from Spring Street.

"What's this," he demanded of Ruhig, "about you and Winni?"

"Ah. Walter!"

Walter's right fist smashed down on Ruhig's desk. "So that's the game," he said in a hard voice. "All right, Ruhig, I'll get into it, too."

"What are you talking about?" asked the lawyer brusquely.

"You aren't satisfied with the hundreds of thousands you collected from my father in fees in that crooked Ohippi operation.

Now that he's dead you want the big money — the millions. And you're marrying that damned empty-headed fool of a woman to get them!"

"Get out," said Ruhig. "Get out of here."

"I've been thinking it over for some time. Ruhig, there's something rotten about that will!"

"You will find," said Mr. Ruhig with a dangerous softness, "that your father had full testamentary capacity."

"I'll spike your little scheme. I'm getting a lawyer to file a protest. I'll break that will, Ruhig. You'll never live to see it probated."

"Your father," snapped Ruhig like a tormented little badger, "was entirely able to comprehend the nature and extent of his property, his relationship to the natural objects of his bounty, and the scope and effects of the contents of his will. Will you get out, or do I have to have my clerks put you out?"

Walter actually smiled. "So it's a fight, is it? By God, Ruhig, I've been itching for one."

And he strode out with no more than a passing glance at Val and Mr. King — an absent glance that sharpened momentarily and then grew absent again.

"Goodbye," said Val in a small voice.

They left Mr. Ruhig sitting still behind his desk, no longer smiling. In fact, Mr. Ruhig was immersed in thought — half-drowned in it, Mr. King would have said.

13

WINNI THE POOH ET CETERA

"There's that man again," said Ellery, as they walked down the street.

"Where?"

"Somewhere behind us. I'm psychic about these things. Where's your car parked?"

"N-near Hill."

"Head for it and I'll drop behind. Let's see if we can't bag this squirrel."

Val stepped off the curb and nervously crossed the street. She was just mounting the sidewalk on the other side when she heard an outcry behind her. She whirled about.

Mr. Hilary King was struggling with a medium-sized, broad-shouldered man whose bellow could be heard as far as City Hall.

"Stop!" cried Val, racing back across the street. She yanked Ellery's arm, which was engaged in a futile-seeming maneuver that looked like ju-jitsu, and was, and then shook the other man, who had just caught Ellery flush on the nose with his freckled fist.

"Pink!" she screamed. "Mr. King, stop! It's Pink!"

"I'm ready to call it quits," panted Mr. King, feeling his nose with his free sleeve, "if this wildcat is."

"Who is this guy?" stormed Pink. "I spotted him for a ringer right away! Did he force you, Val? I'll tear his gizzard out!"

"Don't be an ass," said Val irritably. "Come on, they'll have the riot squad out in a minute." And indeed Old Faithful, the black sedan, had stopped and its two occupants were hastily getting out.

The three of them looked at the sedan, the gaping crowd about them, the approaching detectives, and ran. They ran all the way to Hill Street, pursued, grabbed Val's car, and shot away into the late afternoon traffic.

"There's one consolation," said Mr. King, still caressing his nose, "we've lost our escort."

Pink slumped back in the rear, trying to compress himself into the smallest possible space.

"You're an idiot," snapped Val, driving furiously. "Was it you who were following us? Pink, if you don't stop wet-nursing me —"

"How should I know?" whined Pink.

"This guy looked like a phony to me. And Rhys told me to take care of you."

"That's no excuse. This is Mr. King, a — an old school chum. He's helping me on my job."

"Job!" Pink goggled.

Val told him about the events of the day, concluding with the Ruhig incident.

"Say!" exclaimed Pink. "I know why Ruhig admitted being at *San Susie* Monday at five-fifteen."

"You do?"

"I've been doin' a little snooping myself," said Pink proudly. "I got to thinking about this Ruhig menace, and I says maybe he's hiding something, so I goes up to his office this morning and I get palsy with the switchboard gal and pretty soon she spills. Ruhig and two of his gorillas left the office Monday a little past four-thirty in Ruhig's car!"

"Pink, I retract the arm-lock," said Ellery warmly. "A good job. Ruhig discovered the girl had been talking, assumed you told Valerie, and therefore came out with the truth the instant she questioned him."

"I think," murmured Val, "we've got something." She frowned, examining the road behind her in the mirror. Then she swung off the boulevard and headed the car northwest.

"Where you going now?" demanded Pink.

"To *Sans Souci*. I want to talk to Frank, and I simply must interview dear, dear Winni — the damned *Pooh!*" And she stepped viciously on the accelerator.

A detective sat dozing in the pillbox, while Frank crouched disconsolately on an empty orange-crate near the gate.

The detective opened one eye at the sound of Val's klaxon, then quickly got up and came out to the gate.

"Can't go in," he said, waving his hand. "Orders."

"Oh, dear," said Val. "Look, Lieutenant, we're not —"

"I ain't, but you can't come in."

Ellery nudged her. "Have you forgotten? You represent the massed power of the press."

"Dag my nab, yes," said Val. "Here, Captain, look at this. Press. Newspaper. Reporter."

She waggled her press card. He examined it suspiciously through the grille. "All right, you come in. But the two men stay here."

"Time," said Mr. King. "I, too, gather the news." And he exhibited his credentials. "It looks as if you're stuck, Pink."

"Not me. Where she goes, I go!"

"No, you don't," said the detective sourly; and Pink found himself back on the curb, where he had sat Monday night, glaring at the iron gate.

"Frank, come here," said Val. The one-armed gateman looked startled; the detective scowled. "Interview," said Val with a bewitching smile.

The two men were properly bewitched, and Frank followed Val some little distance from the pillbox, Ellery ambling behind lazily. But his eyes were sweeping the terrain. The place looked deserted.

"Frank," said Val sternly, when they were out of earshot of the gate, "you deliberately lied Monday night!"

The gateman paled. "Me, Miss Jardin? I didn't lie."

"Oh, didn't you? Didn't you tell Glücke no one but Miss Moon and a man wearing my father's coat entered the grounds between the time the auction ended and the time Walewski came on?"

"Sure I said that. It's the God's honest truth."

"You're a blaspheming, wicked old

229

man!" said Val. "You *weren't* at that gate all Monday afternoon, and you know it!"

The one-armed man grew even paler. "I — I wasn't?" he faltered. Then, fearing he had given himself away, he said loudly: "I was so!"

"Come, come," sneered Val. "Where were you at a quarter past five?"

The man started. He crouched a little and peered anxiously at the detective in the distance. "Not so loud, Miss Jardin. I didn't mean nothing wrong. I just —"

"Speak up," said Ellery in an authoritative voice. "Were you at that gate, or weren't you?"

"I just sneaked down the hill a ways to Jim's Diner for a cup of coffee. I was getting awful hungry — I always do late afternoons — I got something wrong with me. . . ."

"What time was this, Frank?" asked Val excitedly.

"You won't tell nobody? I went down the hill a little after five. Maybe eight, ten after. I was back just about half-past five. Just about."

"Did you leave the gate locked?" demanded Ellery.

"Yes, sir, I did, sir. I wouldn't go away and leave —"

"Twenty minutes," breathed Val, her eyes shining. "That means *any one* could have . . . Frank, not a word about this, do you understand?"

"Oh, no, ma'am, not me. I won't say anything. If the people at the bank found out I'd lose my job. I only been on it a couple of months. I'm a poor man, Miss Jardin —"

"Let's go, babe," said "Scoop" King, *bravura*. And he linked Val's arm in his and marched her up the drive toward the Spaeth house.

Val hurried along, trying to match his long stride. "That man Ruhig is a *liar*," she panted. "He got here at five-fifteen, he says, couldn't get in, went away. And came back a few minutes past six. That's simply unbelievable. If you knew Solly Spaeth. He didn't like to be kept waiting. And Spaeth had said it was urgent. Oh, Ruhig didn't go away!"

Ellery strode on, head down, silent.

"Do you know what I think?" whispered Val.

"Certainly." Ellery lit a cigaret. "You think that when Mr. Ruhig found the gate locked but unguarded, he climbed over the fence and visited Mr. Solly Spaeth per appointment."

"Yes!"

"I'm inclined," said Ellery, "to agree." And he walked on, smoking like a demon.

"In the house. In the house between five-fifteen and five-thirty!"

"That's only theory," warned Ellery.

"I'm sure he was! The car could have been parked on the other side of *Sans Souci* so that when he left, nobody — not even Frank — would have seen him. Climbed over the fence again. Got out the way he got in —" She stared at Ellery with a feverish absorption. "That means — that means —"

"Let us," murmured Mr. King, "interview the glamorous bride-to-be."

Miss Moon opened the door herself.

"So you're afraid to hire servants, too," said Val.

"What do you want?" said Miss Moon. She was flushed with anger.

"We want in, as they say," said Val, and she slipped by Miss Moon with a winning smile and skipped toward the study. Miss Moon glared at Mr. King, who spread his hands apologetically.

"After you, Miss Moon," said Mr. King. Miss Moon stamped off to the study.

"What is this, anyway?" she stormed, withering Val with one devastating look.

"Can't a lady have any pwivacy?"

"Mr. King, Miss Moon," murmured Val, unwithered and undevastated. "We won't take too much of your time."

"I don't talk to murdewews!"

"If I wasn't a woiking goil," said Val, "I'd scratch those mascaraed eyes of yours out, dearie. I'm writing for a Los Angeles newspaper, however, and I want to know: Is it true what they say about you and Anatole Ruhig?"

Winni raised her pale plump arms dramatically. "I'll go mad!" she cried. "I told that nasty little — I *told* Anatole to keep his twap shut! You're the second one; a reporter was just here fwom the *Independent!*"

"Are you going to marry Anatole?"

"I've got nothing to say — especially to you!"

"I wonder what the secret of her success is, Mr. King," sighed Val. "Would you say it was charm, or manners?"

"Miss Moon," said "Scoop" King, taking out pencil and paper and pretending to write. "What are you going to do with Solly Spaeth's fifty million dollars?"

"I'll talk to *you*," cooed Miss Moon, calming magically and fussing with her wheat-colored hair. "I'm buying and buying and *buying*. It's wonderful how the shops give you cwedit when you're an heiwess, isn't it?"

She swept Val's neat costume with a scornful glance.

"And is your aunt buying and buying and buying, too?" asked Mr. King, still scribbling doodads.

Miss Moon drew herself up. "My awnt isn't here any more. My awnt has gone away."

"When do you expect her back?"

"Nevaw! She deserted me in my hour of distwess, and now she can go lump it."

"Apparently," remarked Val, "she didn't hear about the fifty million soon enough. Well, thank you, dear Miss Moon. I hope your new pearls choke you to death."

And she went out, followed meekly by Mr. King and a female glare that had the glitter of knives in it.

Mr. King grabbed Miss Jardin's arm and pulled her stealthily into the doorway of a room off the corridor. He kept peering out and back toward the study.

"What's the idea?" whispered Valerie.

He shook his head, watching. So Val watched, too. In a few moments they saw Miss Moon flounce out of the study, lifting her beige hostess-gown and scratching her naked left thigh in an inelegant manner, and mumbling crankily to herself. She clumped up the stairs, her hips rising and falling like a watery horizon in a monsoon.

Ellery took Val by the hand and tiptoed back to the study.

"There," he said, closing the study door. "Now we can reconnoiter a bit, unknown to the Presence."

"But why?" asked Val blankly.

"Sheer nosiness. This is where the last rites were administered, isn't it? Park your pretty carcass in that chair while I snoop a bit."

"You're a funny sort of newspaperman," said Val, frowning.

"I'm beginning to think so myself. Now shut up, darling."

Val shut up and sat down, watching. What she saw puzzled her. Mr. King lay down on the floor near the ell in which Mr. Solomon Spaeth had been sitting so quietly Monday night. He nosed about like Mickey's Pluto; Val could almost hear the sniffs. Then he rose and examined the wall of the alcove. After a moment he stood off and looked up at the wall above the fireplace. Then, shaking his head, he went to Solly's desk and sat down in Solly's chair and thought and thought and thought. Once he looked at his wrist-watch.

"It's an impressive act," said Val presently, "but it conveys absolutely nothing to my primitive mind."

"How do you get the gateman's booth by telephone?" he asked in reply.

"Dial one-four."

He dialed. "This is that reporter again. It's five after six, so Walewski ought to be there. Is he?"

"So what?" rasped the detective's voice.

"Put him on. What's your name?"

"David Greenberg. Say, listen, pal, if —"

"I'll remember that, Dave. Put Walewski on." He waited, saying meanwhile: "That's the hell of these postmortem investigations. If there was any clue in this room, the police have ruined it. . . . Walewski? I'm a reporter. You remember Monday a few minutes past six, when Mr. Ruhig drove up to the gate?"

"Yes, sir, yes, sir," came Walewski's quavering voice.

"Was he alone in his car? Or were there two men with him?"

Val jumped. She ran to the desk, listening for the answer.

"No, sir," said Walewski. "He was all alone."

"Thanks."

Ellery hung up and Val stared at him.

Then he rose and said lightly: "What's out here? Ah, a terrace. Let's imbibe some fresh air."

The study wall facing the terrace was completely glass. They went out through the glass doors. The terrace was deserted, and its gaily striped awning, bright furniture, cushions, rattan, wrought-iron chairs, and pastel flagstones looked a little forlorn.

Ellery handed Val gallantly into the slide-swing and stretched himself out in a long summer chair.

"I think, my brave colleague," he said, settling himself comfortably and gazing out over the rock gardens and the empty pool below, "we have our Mr. Ruhig neatly figured."

"He was alone when he came back, Walewski says!"

"Exactly. Let's see what we have. Pink discovers that Ruhig left his office around four-thirty Monday afternoon, in his car, accompanied by two assistants. This checks with other facts — that the previous week when he drew up, and Spaeth signed, the will which cut Walter Spaeth off, Ruhig also came with two assistants, to serve, as he himself said, as witnesses to the signature."

"How do you know that?" frowned Val. "You weren't present when he told that to the Inspector Monday night."

"I — uh — I read it in the papers. Now. From Ruhig's office to *Sans Souci* is a good forty-minute drive through traffic; so Ruhig probably told the truth when he said he reached here at five-fifteen Monday. With, mind you, his two assistants. He says he couldn't get in and drove away and returned at six-five or so. Why? Obviously, if he hadn't got in at five-fifteen, then he still had to handle the change of will for Spaeth. But when he returned at six-five, presumably for this purpose, his two men weren't with him! What does that suggest?"

Val wrinkled her brow. "I can't imagine."

"Obviously *that he no longer needed them.* But why had he brought his assistants in the first place? To witness a new will. Then if he no longer needed them at six-five, it seems to me highly indicative that the assistants had already served their purpose by six-five. In other words, to reduce it to specifics, that they had witnessed a new will between five-fifteen, when Ruhig first came, and five-thirty-two, when Spaeth died."

"A new will!" cried Val. "Oh, lord. Then that means —"

"Hush! We don't want Winni hearing this. We don't know exactly what this means in terms of the will. But we can be pretty sure Spaeth signed a new will before he died, and that Ruhig and his men were in this study at approximately the murder-period."

Val sat thinking furiously. It did sound logical. And it changed everything. Any new will would have affected Winni Moon's gigantic legacy. Where did Walter enter the picture? Did he find that will? Was he — was he protecting Winni? What real part did that oily little Ruhig play?

"What's that?" asked Ellery sharply, sitting up.

"What's what?" asked Val in an absent way.

Ellery pointed. Fifty yards from where they sat, directly beyond the pool, was the rear terrace of the old Jardin house. Something was winking there, flashing prismatic colors in the rays of the sinking sun.

"I can't imagine," said Val. "That's the terrace of our old house. We didn't leave anything there except an odd piece or two of porch furniture we didn't want."

Ellery rose. "Let's go look-see."

They stole down the stone steps and made their way without noise across the

239

rock garden, around the pool, to the Jardin house. The awning still hung over the terrace, which was largely in shadow; but the sun illuminated an area several feet deep along the entire length of the terrace; and in this sunlit area stood an old wrought-iron porch table.

They saw at once what had caused the fiery flashes. A pair of battered binoculars lay on the table, its lenses facing the sun.

"Oh, shoot," said Val, disappointed. "It's just that old pair of binoculars."

"Here!" said Ellery sharply. "Don't touch that table." He was crouched over, studying its surface with narrowed eyes. "You mean you left them here when you moved?"

"Yes. One of the lenses is cracked."

"Did you leave it on this table?"

"Why, no," said Val, surprised. "It wasn't left here at that. We went over a lot of stuff — pop likes the races, and we have several pairs of binoculars — and we just threw this one out."

"Where did you leave it?"

"There's a pile of junk in the gym."

"Then what is it doing here?"

"I don't know," said Val truthfully. "But what difference does it make?"

Ellery did not reply. He indicated the

glass doors which led to the vacant study; they stood slightly ajar.

"That's funny," said Val slowly. "Those doors were locked when we left. Unless the landlord had some one come in and —"

"If you'll look closely, you'll find the lock broken," said Ellery, "indicating a basic disrespect for the rights of property."

"Oh!" cried Val, pointing to the table. "Those marks!"

She bent over the table and Ellery smiled faintly. The surface was covered with mottled dust. There seemed to be two layers of dust, deposited at different times. Val was studying two oval marks — they were more like smudges — under the upper dust-stratum. One was larger than the other, and they were separated by several inches.

"Damn those rains," said Ellery. "The table didn't get the full force of it, being under the awning, but it did get a fine spray, enough to remove any fingerprints that may have been here."

"But those marks," said Val. "They *look* like fingerprints. Like the marks of two fingers — a thumb and a little finger."

"That's what they are. They were deposited on an already dusty surface. Then more dust settled, and the rain messed things up, but they're still visible because the dust-layer is thinner where they are than on the rest of the table. However, there don't seem to be any distinguishing whorls — probably the rain."

He took out a handkerchief and carefully lifted the binoculars. Where they had lain was a slightly dusty surface, lighter than the surrounding surface. "Binoculars and fingermarks made at about the same time." He wrapped the binoculars in the folds of the handkerchief and calmly dropped the whole thing into the pocket of his sport jacket.

Val did not notice. She was striding excitedly up and down. "I've got it! It was still light at the time of the murder, and the glasses show some one stood right here on this terrace watching what was going on in Spaeth's study! He could easily see, because of the glass walls, like these here. *There was a witness to the murder!*"

"Excellently spoken," said Ellery. "I mean — you said a mouthful there, baby." But he was still studying the two finger-smudges on the table in a puzzled way.

"Then some one knows who killed Spaeth. Some one *saw!*"

"Very likely." Ellery looked around. "Did you say a lot of junk was left in the gym? Where's the gym?"

"A few doors down," said Val, hardly knowing what she was saying. Then she took a deep breath. "Here, I'll show you."

She led him along the terrace to the door of the empty gymnasium. This door, too, had been forced.

"There it is," said Val.

Ellery went over to a small pile of débris and poked it apart with his foot. But there was nothing of interest in the pile. He was about to return to the terrace when he spied a small closet set into one of the walls. The closet door was closed. He walked over and opened it. Inside, on a rack, hung a lone Indian club. He took it out, frowning, and examined it. It was cracked.

"Funny," he said. "Very funny." He weighed the club thoughtfully, glancing over at the pile of débris.

"What is it? What's the matter now?" asked Val, waking from her trance.

"This Indian club. Indian clubs come in pairs, weighted and matched. Why on earth should you have taken along the mate to this, when this cracked one was left behind?"

"The mate?" Val wrinkled her forehead. "But we didn't. We left them both here in the closed closet."

"Really?" said Ellery dryly. "Well, one of them is gone."

Val started, then shrugged. Ellery replaced the cracked club in the rack and, frowning, shut the closet door.

"And another thing," said Val, as they returned to the terrace. "Whoever it was who watched, it was somebody with only two fingers on his left hand — a two-fingered man! That *is* a left-hand marking, isn't it?"

"Yes."

"Two fingers!"

Ellery smiled the same faint smile. "By the way, I think you'd better telephone police headquarters."

"What for?"

"To tell them about this table. Shocking neglect on the part of Glücke — not examining your old house!"

"Why, the binoculars are gone!" cried Val.

"Only as far as my pocket. I'd put the table in there, too, only it won't fit comfortably. Call Glücke. He ought to send a fingerprint man down here right away on the off-chance that some prints *are* left."

They went quietly back to the Spaeth house and Ellery sat down on the terrace

244

again while Val tiptoed into the study to telephone. He heard her get her connection and ask for Inspector Glücke, but he was not listening too closely. Those marks . . .

He jumped at a choking sound from the study. He ran in and found Val staring at the telephone, her face a pale, pale gray.

"All right," she said weakly. "I'll be right down," and she replaced the instrument on its base with a thud, as if it were too heavy for her.

"What's the matter? What's happened?"

"It's Walter. Walter," said Val. It was always Walter. Whenever anything happened, it was Walter. "You know — I told you about — *him*. The one who ran into Ruhig's office —"

"Well, well?"

"Inspector Glücke just told me. . . ." She shivered suddenly and drew her coat more closely about her. "He says Walter has cleared my father. Walter's — cleared — pop!"

She began to giggle.

Ellery shook her violently. "None of that! What do you mean — cleared your father?"

Val giggled and giggled. It became a laugh, and then a shout, and finally it choked up and turned into a whisper. "He — just — confessed to Glücke that — *he* was the one — who wore my father's coat Monday afternoon . . . that he was the one — Frank saw. . . . Oh, Walter!"

And she buried her face in her hands.

Ellery pulled her hands away. "Come on," he said gruffly.

PART
FOUR

14

STORM OVER GLÜCKE

Val looked so preoccupied that Ellery took the wheel of her sedan. She sat still, staring ahead. He could not decide whether she was frozen with stupefaction or shocked stiff by the high voltage of some more personal emotion. Her body did not sag even while the sedan squealed around corners. As for Pink, having heard the news, he kept his mouth open all the way downtown.

Inside police headquarters Val broke into a trot. And in the anteroom to Inspector Glücke's office, while the police clerk spoke into his communicator, she pranced. When he nodded she flew to the Inspector's door — and slowly opened it.

Walter sat with outstretched legs beside Glücke's big desk, blowing smoke rings.

There were two others in the office — the Inspector and a thin whippy gentleman of indecipherable age who sat quietly in a corner grasping a stylish stick. Glücke looked grim and alert, as if he were set for some emergency; but the thin man was composed and his eyes had a cynical glitter.

"Hello," grinned Walter. "Val to the rescue."

"Oh, Walter," said Val, and she went to him and put her hand on his shoulder in a proud, tender way.

"What is this," said the Inspector dryly, "Old Home Week? What d'ye want, King?"

"So I've been reported by the demon sleuth team in the black sedan, curse it," said Ellery. His name was King, was it?

"Take a powder, King. No reporters here."

"It's all right with me," said Mr. King indifferently. "I was on my way to the office anyway with the dope I've turned up."

"What's that? What dope?"

"If you'd devote less time to playing follow-the-leader and more to examining *Sans Souci* you'd show a better homicide record. Come on, Pink, let's amble."

"Just a moment," said the thin man with a smile. "I think we can manage this without ruffled feelings, Glücke." He rose. "My name is Van Every. You say you've turned up something at *Sans Souci?*"

"Ah, the D.A." They examined each other politely. "I do, but I'm not spilling till I find out what friend Spaeth's been up to."

Van Every glanced at Glücke, and Glücke growled: "Okay." He drew his brows together. "Well, here she is, Spaeth."

"Wait," said Val quickly. "Walter, I want to —"

"It's no use, Val."

"Walter, *please*."

Walter shook his head. "I told you, Inspector, on Monday night that I didn't enter the *Sans Souci* grounds. That's not true. I did enter. I had a key to the gate, and Frank was in his booth reading a paper, so I let myself in and walked up the drive —"

"And he spotted you from the back and thought you were Rhys Jardin because you were wearing Jardin's torn coat. You've told me that already," said Glücke impatiently. "Answer some questions. So you weren't hit on the head as you got out of your car?"

"No, I was attacked after —"

"Walter!" Val put her palm over his mouth. He shook his head at her, but she kept her hand where it was. "Inspector, I want to talk to Mr. Spaeth."

Walter removed her hand gently. "Let me clear this damned thing up, Val."

"Walter, you zany! You darling idiot. . . . I insist on speaking to Walter alone, Inspector."

Glücke and the District Attorney exchanged glances, and Glücke waved his hand.

Val pulled Walter out of the chair and drew him off to a far corner. The Inspector's large ears twitched as he leaned forward, and Pink looked from Walter and Valerie to the Inspector and back again with a confused but hopeful air. But the thin man and Ellery did not stir.

Val linked her arms about Walter's neck, pressing her body close to him, her mouth an inch from his ear. Her back was toward them and they could not see her face; but they saw Walter's. As she whispered, the lines of his face stretched and vanished, as if a hot iron had passed over wrinkled damp cloth.

Val stopped whispering, and for a moment she remained pressed to him. He turned his head and kissed her on the mouth.

They came forward side by side. "I want to see Rhys Jardin." His voice was fresh and untroubled.

"Jardin?" The Inspector was astonished. "What for?"

"Never mind what for. I want to talk to him."

"Quit stalling and go into your dance!"

"I don't talk until I've seen Jardin."

"I've had just about enough of this playing around," rasped Glücke. "You walked in here of your own free will with a yarn that, if it's true, cracks this case wide open. Now that you're here you'll talk — and talk fast!"

"I think," said the thin man smoothly, "that Mr. Spaeth's story will keep for an hour, Inspector. If he wants to see Jardin — why not?"

Glücke opened his mouth, closed it, opened it again. His brilliant eyes suddenly became cunning. "All right. Tell you what I'll do. You go on down to the City Jail —"

Val surreptitiously jerked Walter's jacket.

"No," said Walter. "Have him brought here."

"Listen!" roared Glücke. "Are you going —"

"Here," said Walter.

Glücke looked baffled. He turned aside and again his eyes sought the District Attorney, and again the District Attorney made a small, clear sign.

The Inspector pressed a lever of his communicator. "Boley. Have Rhys Jardin brought to my office right away."

Val looked triumphant, and Walter grinned.

Rhys Jardin appeared between two detectives, blinking as if he were unaccustomed to strong light. He stopped short on seeing Valerie and Walter but gave no other sign of recognition.

"Yes?" he said to Inspector Glücke.

The two detectives left the room and Glücke said quickly: "Just a moment, please." He hurried to District Attorney Van Every and bent over him, speaking in a vehement undertone. Ellery strolled across the room, pushed his preposterous hat back on his head, and sat down behind Glücke's desk.

"Jardin," said Glücke. "Walter Spaeth has come in with a funny story, but before he talks he wants a private confab with you."

"Story?" said Rhys, looking at Walter.

"He claims that he was the man in the camel's-hair Frank identified as you Monday afternoon."

"Did he say that, now?" said Rhys.

"Now of course," continued Glücke in a friendly way, "this is important testimony and it changes a lot of things. But we don't want to put on the squeeze. So suppose you three straighten yourselves out, and then we'll all sit down like sensible people and get to the truth, once for all."

"I have literally nothing to say," said Rhys.

"Pop," said Val. He looked at her then.

"I'll tell you what," the Inspector went on, growing more friendly with every word. "We'll clear out of here and leave you folks alone. When you're ready, sing out." He nodded to Van Every and went to one of the several doors leading out of his office. "We'll be waiting in here."

Ellery produced a cigaret, lit it, and coughed out a volcano of smoke. He leaned over Glücke's desk in a spasm.

"If you don't mind," said Walter politely, "I think we'd rather talk somewhere else." And he opened another door, looked in, nodded, and beckoned Val and her father.

The Inspector's ears flamed. Nevertheless he said amiably: "All right. It doesn't make any difference."

Rhys Jardin crossed the room and the three of them entered the room Walter had selected. He shut the door very carefully.

"Would you gentlemen mind waiting outside?" said the District Attorney suddenly. "Inspector Glücke and I —"

"I get it," said Ellery. He rose. "Your mouth is open, Pink. Come on." He slouched over to the door at which the In-

255

spector was standing. Pink scratched his head and followed. They entered a small room which contained four walls, three chairs, and one desk; and Ellery loudly banged the door shut.

The next instant he was at the desk opening drawers. "Transparent as cellophane," he said gleefully. "Glücke wanted them to gabble in the big office so that he could overhear their conversation. Dictograph, of course. And since this is the room he seemed so eager to wait in . . . Ah!" Pink heard the click of a switch.

He sprang about in a left-handed fighter's crouch as Van Every's voice came out of thin air: "Can you hear anything?" And then Glücke's voice, similarly disembodied: "Not a ripple. He must have smelled a rat."

Pink looked foolish. "How the hell —"

"I saw through the trick and managed to locate the machine," chuckled Ellery. "There's a switch under his desk, and it was open. Now shut up and let's hear what *they're* saying."

"Say, you're a cute finagler," growled Pink suspiciously. But Ellery was crouched over the desk, paying no attention. So Pink sat down and listened, too.

The instrument was so clear they could

hear Glücke's footsteps as he walked up and down his office.

"I don't know what you gave me the high sign for, Van," said Glücke fretfully. "It's a funny way —"

"Don't be dense, Glücke," said Van Every. "This isn't an ordinary investigation. In fact, I'm beginning to think we've made a mistake in rushing matters."

"How come?"

"There's some secret relationship among those three," said the thin man thoughtfully, "we're not aware of. It's painted all over them. And until we know, I'm afraid —"

"Afraid what?"

"That we'll have to go slow. I won't bring Jardin to trial until I've got him tied up in knots."

The Inspector cursed impotently and for a while nothing came through the transmitter. Then they heard him say: "Damn them! They're talking so low I can't hear a word through this damn' door. Cagy punks!"

"Watch your blood-pressure. Who's this man King?"

"Legman for Fitzgerald of the *Independent*. He's new to L.A."

"Any idea what he's turned up?"

"Go on, he's bluffing to get a story."

"Let's talk to him anyway. By the way."

"Yeah?"

"This afternoon one of my men discovered a bank account of Jardin's we didn't know anything about."

"I thought he was busted!"

"So did I. The auction fooled me. But he's got five million dollars salted away in the Pacific Coastal, Spaeth's old bank. So the auction must have been a cover-up."

"Five million!"

"Deposited last Wednesday."

"But cripe, Van, that blows a hole in the motive."

"I'm not so sure. Anyway, a private dick came in today, scared as the devil. Did a confidential job for Jardin not long ago; and when Spaeth was murdered he decided that maybe he'd better talk."

"Well!"

"He claims he found out that Spaeth had monkeyed with Ohippi's cash position and had sent out a prospectus falsifying their financial standing. He reported that to Jardin early last week."

Glücke stared. "Jardin was broke, threatened to expose Spaeth, blackmailed him. Spaeth gave him the five million to shut him up. Jardin thought it wasn't enough —

258

Spaeth made ten times that. They had a couple of serious quarrels. So Jardin bumped Spaeth off to get whack. How's that?"

"It's a damn lie!" said Pink, clenching his left fist.

"Shut up," hissed Ellery.

"How's this yarn of Walter Spaeth's hit you?" mumbled the Inspector.

"I'm not sure."

"Spaeth and the girl are nuts about each other. He's screwy as hell, anyway. I wouldn't put it past that loony galoot to stick his head in a noose just to protect her old man."

"Well, let's see how they act when they come out. Our only smart course is to give them rope."

"Maybe," said the Inspector hopefully, "they'll hang one another."

"There's another angle on that five million," said the District Attorney after another pause. "Right now Jardin's a tin god to the public — it's the most popular crime this county's ever had, damn it. But they're for him only because they think he was a victim of Spaeth's rapacity, too. If we hold back the evidence of that five-million deposit until just before the trial, we'll swing public opinion against him when the swing will do us the most good."

"That's smart, Van! Hold it. Here they come."

Ellery turned the dictograph receiver off. "Finis."

Pink snarled: "The bastards!"

"Pink, did you know about that five million?"

"Found the bankbook in Rhys's golf-bag Monday morning, while I was packin' up. Hey!"

"What's the matter?" asked Ellery innocently.

"You ask too damn' many questions!"

"I'm on your side, Pink," said Ellery in a soothing voice. "What did Rhys say?"

"Well . . . Late Monday night he swore he didn't know a thing about it. And I believe him, too!"

"Of course, Pink. Of course."

"He reminded me that last Wednesday, when the deposit was made, he and I were away all day tryin' to sell the yacht to a guy down in Long Beach. The bankbook was a plant."

"Spaeth," said Ellery thoughtfully.

"That's what Rhys says, too."

"Uh — Pink, have you any idea what the Jardins and Spaeth have been talking about in there?"

"They didn't tell me anything, so it's none of my business. Or," said Pink, eying him stonily, "yours."

"But I want to help them, Pink."

Pink grabbed Ellery's red-and-blue necktie with his freckled left fist. "Listen, mugg. Lay off or I'll cripple you!"

"My, my, such muscles," murmured Ellery. "Well, let's see what the conferees have decided."

In Inspector Glücke's office the two Jardins and Walter were standing close together, like people threatened with a common peril and united in a common defense.

The inspector was saying incredulously: "*What?*"

"You heard me," said Walter.

Glücke was speechless. District Attorney Van Every rose and said sternly: "Look here, Spaeth, you can't pull a stunt like this and hope to get away with it. You said —"

"I know what I said. I was lying."

"Why?"

Walter put his right arm about Val. "Rhys Jardin happens to be my fiancée's father."

"You don't expect me to believe that

you'd deliberately say you were on the scene of a murder when you weren't — just for sentimental reasons! That happens in books."

"I'm an incurable romantic," sighed Walter.

"Well, you're not getting away with it!" shouted Glücke.

"Please," smiled Rhys. "Walter's a quixotic young fool. Naturally I can't let him sacrifice himself for me —"

"Then you admit you murdered Spaeth?" snapped the District Attorney.

"Nothing of the sort, Van Every," said Rhys coolly. "I'm not saying anything, as I've told you before. But I won't allow Walter to get himself in trouble on my account. My troubles are my own."

Van Every tapped his mouth pettishly. The Jardins, Walter, stood very still.

Then Glücke stamped to the main door. "Take Jardin back to his cell. As for you," he went on, eying Walter malevolently, "if you ever pull a stunt like this again I'll send you up for obstructing justice. Now beat it."

The two detectives closed in on Rhys and took him away. Walter and Val, who wore a demure expression, sauntered after. Pink glared from the Inspector to the retreating figures, jammed on his hat, and ran after them.

Ellery sighed and closed the door.

"What's on your mind, King?" snapped the Inspector. "Let's have that phony information of yours and then scram."

"Don't you think we ought to discuss this new development first?"

"Who's we? Say, you're one fresh jigger!"

"You won't lose anything by letting me coöperate with you," murmured Ellery.

"I'll be damned," said Glücke in amazement.

"Let the man talk," said the thin man with a smile. "I rather like the cut of his jib. How does this retraction of Spaeth's strike you, King?"

Ellery made a face.

"Oh, he lied all right," said the Inspector disgustedly.

"On the contrary," said Ellery, "he told the exact truth. He lied when he took the admission back. If you ask me, boys, you're further from a solution of this case now than you were Monday night."

"Go on," said the District Attorney, intent.

"There aren't enough facts to play with,

but I'm convinced Walter Spaeth was the man in Jardin's camel's-hair coat and furthermore that he knows enough about what went on in his father's study Monday afternoon to settle this grimy business in five minutes."

"It's all balled up," muttered the Inspector. "Jardin's attitude, how Spaeth figures, that closed corporation of theirs. By God, could they be accomplices?"

"Tell me something," said Ellery suddenly. "Did your crew search *Sans Souci* thoroughly, Inspector?"

"Sure."

"Then how is it," said Ellery, taking the handkerchief-wrapped binoculars out of his packet, "that they missed this?"

He unfolded the handkerchief. Glücke licked his lips. "Where?" he asked hoarsely.

Ellery told him. Glücke turned a deep scarlet.

"Some one," said Ellery, lighting a cigaret, "was on the Jardin terrace Monday afternoon watching Spaeth's study through these glasses. Whoever it was, he left the imprint of a thumb and a little finger on that iron table. You might have that table examined."

"Yeah. Sure," said Glücke with a stricken look.

"And the binoculars."

"And the binoculars."

"I'm beginning to fill up with notions," Ellery continued. "I snooped about the grounds yesterday and tried to locate the spot where Walter Spaeth parked his car and was slugged. Wasn't it on the south side, near a sewer?"

"Yeah."

"Was the sewer searched?"

"Was the sewer searched? Well, now —"

"If I were you — of course I'm not," murmured Ellery, "but if I were, mind you, I'd open that sewer and give it the twice-over."

"Open it," said the Inspector. "Yeah."

Ellery yawned. "Goodbye," he said, and strolled out.

Glücke sat at his desk, crushed.

"Let that," said District Attorney Van Every dryly, rising, "be a lesson to you."

15

EARTHLY DISCOURSE

Val came into Fitzgerald's office Thursday morning waving the front page of a late Wednesday night edition of the *Los Angeles Independent*.

"Who's responsible for this story?" she raged, pointing to the scarehead.

"If it's you, King," said Walter from the doorway, "you're a damned busybody!"

"Isn't anything sacred to you?" cried Val.

"Stand up and take it," growled Pink, pushing Walter aside.

"Desist," said Ellery.

"Shut the door," said Fitz.

"What are you sore about?" said Ellery.

"This story — Walter's admission, retraction . . ."

"Is it true?" said Ellery.

"Did it happen?" said Fitz.

"I resign!" cried Val.

"Put up your mitts, lug," said Pink.

"Oh, pipe down, the lot of you," said Ellery. "You're all too damned self-righteous for your own good."

Val looked at Walter, and Walter looked

at Val, and Pink looked at both of them for a clue to *his* attitude. Finally the three of them sat down.

Ellery uncoiled himself from Fitz's desk and began to stride up and down, smoking furiously.

Walter and Val hitched their chairs closer. Ellery, watching them from under his blue glasses, was reminded of their drawing together in Glücke's office the evening before. At the first hint of danger they flowed into a common meeting-place. There was mystery, secrecy, stubbornness written all over their young faces.

"I don't know what you two were up to last night," he said finally, "but I'm convinced of one thing — in a sort of inspired idiocy you're trying to solve a crime that should properly be left to trained people."

"Like you," sniffed Val.

"Like Glücke and Van Every. You are, aren't you?"

Val and Walter glanced at each other again.

"For heaven's sake," exploded Ellery, "can't you two do anything on your own? Must you have a conference before every speech?"

"What if we are trying to solve it?" said Val defiantly.

"Let him rave," said Walter. "Don't pay any attention to him, Val."

Ellery glared at them. "That's lovely. Babes in the woods! Next thing you know you'll be playing G-man with a Buck Rogers atomic pistol!"

"This is very interesting," said Walter, "but I've got work to do. Let's go, Val."

"Sit down! Where are you going? Do you know what to do? Do you know where to look? Answer me!" They were silent. Fitz beamed at the loudly dressed product of his imagination. The bewildered, sullen look was creeping over poor Pink's face again. "You don't. Well, I'll tell you. We're going after Mr. Anatole Ruhig in a big way."

"Ruhig?" frowned Val.

"We?" said Walter, raising his eyebrows.

"Do you remember what I told you yesterday about Ruhig and the will?" Val nodded despite herself. "We came to the conclusion that Ruhig had lied, that he'd got into *Sans Souci* on his first visit at five-fifteen, that it was at that time, just before Spaeth died, that Ruhig's men must have witnessed the signing of a new will."

"What's this?" exclaimed Walter.

"Oh, Walter," wailed Val, "I forgot to tell you!"

"The Moon woman is left everything,"

said Ellery softly, "and almost before your father's body is cold, Walter, Ruhig announces that he and she are going to be married. Why?"

"Any dope could figure that out," said Pink with a disgusted look. "He wants that dough she's falling into."

"Very lucidly put," drawled Ellery. "Any dope could figure out why *he* wants to marry *her*. But could any dope figure out why *she* wants to marry *him?*"

"I never thought of that," mumbled Val. "That's true. Why *should* she marry him?"

"There are three common reasons for relinquishing the sacred heritage of liberty," said Ellery dryly. "One, money. But the fifty millions are hers, not his. Two, to spite some one. Perhaps a reluctant swain is hanging around somewhere, but I question Miss Moon's dividing fifty million dollars just to make him feel sorry. Three, love, or whatever they call it in California. But you've seen friend Ruhig. Do you suppose any woman could feel romantically drawn to him?"

Walter jumped up and began to race up and down.

"I don't know about that," said Pink. "To look at me you wouldn't think a dame —"

"Shut up, Pithecanthropus," growled Fitz.

"The only reasonable explanation is that Winni knows her inheritance of that fifty million dollars *depends upon Ruhig.* If Ruhig could control her inheritance, if some action of his could either give her the millions or take them away, then Winni's willingness to marry him becomes understandable."

"That new will we were talking about!" cried Val.

"Exactly. With the other inferences we made yesterday, it's a cinch that Solly Spaeth signed a new will Monday afternoon, before his murder, which seriously reduced, or cut out completely, Winni's share in his estate. *That will Ruhig has suppressed.*"

"The dirty dog," said Walter. "The skunk!"

"Ruhig undoubtedly went to Winni and told her he had it in his power to see she didn't get a cent; but that if she'd marry him he'd destroy the latest will, and the older one giving her the fortune would remain in force."

"And he's holding that will over her head!" cried Walter. "He couldn't destroy it, or his hold over her would be gone.

Until they're married he's got to hold on to that new will!"

"And she won't marry him until the old will is probated," said Val breathlessly.

"Certain interesting questions," murmured Ellery, "arise. For instance, exactly when did Ruhig leave the Spaeth house Monday afternoon? Before Spaeth's murder or after?"

"You mean —"

"Nothing at all." Ellery shrugged. "But certainly Ruhig realizes that if he's caught with that new will now he's in the worst kind of jam. The police would interpret it as a Ruhig motive for murder. The will's hot — almost too hot to handle. Yet holding on to it means twenty-five million dollars to him. My guess is that he's taking a chance, at the same time safeguarding himself as much as he can."

"He certainly can't have that will in his actual possession," said Walter thoughtfully.

"Then how are we ever going to find it?" asked Val in dismay.

Fitz said briskly: "We've got to trick Ruhig into producing it. At the same time he mustn't suspect for a second that anybody knows the will exists."

"Otherwise," nodded Ellery, "rather than

be tagged for a murder, he'll destroy it."

"So," said Fitz, glaring at Pink, "we've got to keep this talk a deep, dark, dirty secret. I won't print a line of it, and you're not to talk about it even in your sleep."

"Obviously," said Ellery, "strategy is called for. Mr. Ruhig's vulnerable spot is the incomparable Winni. Consequently we'll work through her."

"How?"

"It all depends on how much Ruhig has told her. It seems unlikely that he actually showed her the new will. He wouldn't carry it around with him one second longer than necessary. We'll have to assume she hasn't seen it.

"Now. If we can somehow plant the proverbial bug in her ear that little Anatole was lying all the time, that such a will has never existed, that he just invented it to make her marry him and cut himself in on the fifty million, what will Winni do?"

"Demand to see the will!" cried Val.

"Right. And Ruhig will have to show it to her or risk losing everything. When he does — we pounce."

"Smart," said Walter curtly.

"And you're the man for the job, Walter. She knows you well — I think she even likes you."

"I guess so," said Walter, flushing. Val examined her fingernails.

"Meanwhile, we've got to be in a position to follow developments. That calls for a little scientific eavesdropping."

"And that's where yours truly comes in," said Fitz. "I've got connections, and I can get hold of a dictograph under cover. We plant it in the house there and lead the wires over to the empty Jardin house."

"That's a *swell* idea," said Val, her eyes shining. "And then we keep listening on the other end —"

"Lemme in on this," pleaded Pink. "Look, guys, I can do anything. I used to be an electrician once. I can get in and plant the machine and —"

They broke into an excited gabble. Ellery opened Fitz's drawer and helped himself to the Scotch. Fitz got busy writing out a note to one of his "connections," and Pink boasted that he was as good as any second-story man that ever lived, and Val coached Walter in exactly what he was to say to the unsuspecting Winni.

"Remember!"

"Don't worry, honey."

"Walter, get the hell out there and make a stab at your cartoon, will you? They'll think it's a Cabinet meeting in here."

"Where you going?"

"To see pop."

"Gimme that note!"

Finally Walter and Val and Pink were gone, each to a different place. Ellery hastily put the bottle down on Fitz's desk and ran after Val.

"Peace," said Fitz, reaching glassy-eyed for the Scotch. "It's wonderful."

16

QUEST FOR THE OP

Ellery caught up with Val on the street.

"Mind if I tag along?"

Val stopped abruptly on the busy corner of Spring and First. The crowd flowed around them. "I certainly do!"

"That's not polite."

"See here, Mr. King," snapped Val. "We — I appreciate what you're trying to do, and all that, but there are certain things . . . I mean, please don't be annoying. I want to see my father."

"My skin," said Ellery, taking her arm, "is one part rhinoceros hide and two parts armored plate."

Val helplessly permitted herself to be pulled along. If only she could get away from him! He was too quick, too smart. He knew too much already. The way he had analyzed the Ruhig situation. He might find out everything. He might find out that Walter . . .

There was no examination at the City Jail this morning. The shabby man was on hand, but he did not follow them. And the guard unlocked Rhys's cell door and departed at once.

Rhys was calmly playing solitaire and smoking a cigar. His eyes narrowed when he saw the flamboyant figure with Valerie, but he kissed her and shook hands with Hilary "Scoop" King when Val introduced them and invited him to sit down on his pallet, brushing the cards aside.

"I don't know what's the matter," he complained with a grin. "But my friends Glücke and Van Every are ignoring me completely. Do you suppose they've got cold feet?"

He patted the scattered cards into a neat stack.

"Absolutely frozen," nodded Ellery. "Keep it up, Mr. Jardin. You've got 'em buffaloed. They've never had a prisoner who's seemed so happy with his lot."

"It's the clean life I've led. Don't worry, eat three squares a day, and get plenty of exercise. That's the only thing I miss here. Otherwise, it's ideal."

"Oh, pop," said Val

"Why the long face, puss?"

Val said something perfunctory, and for a few minutes they chattered about inconsequentials. Ellery sucked on a cigaret.

There was something in the aristocracy of blood after all. It made things difficult for a seeker after truth whose success must depend upon the agglomeration and synthesis of facts. He kept his eyes dull but aware.

And very soon after Val opened her bag and took out a handkerchief and put it to her nose in a dainty, unnecessary gesture and closed her bag and opened it again; and Ellery, squatting on the end of the pallet, knew that something was happening. He rose and turned his back.

Val kissed her father and got up, too, and Rhys offered his hand to Ellery with a charming smile, and in a moment they were out in the corridor, walking.

And Ellery thought it strange that cards which had been decorated with a schooner should, between their coming and their going, have magically changed into cards decorated with a Dutch windmill.

Now why should an otherwise honest young woman palm one deck of cards and leave another in its place?

"I wish," said Val outside, "that you would make yourself extremely scarce, Mr. King."

"Don't be that way."

"You're getting me very angry. I don't know what you think you're accomplishing by following me, but I assure you you're wasting your time."

"I like you," sighed Ellery. "You send chills down my spine. Do you call that a waste of time?"

"That's not very funny. If you don't stop following me, I'll get Fitz to. I warn you!"

She walked rapidly away, heading for the parking lot. Ellery watched her for a moment. Then he hurried around the corner.

When Val drove northwest on First Street, a small green coupé was behind her, one of that breed of rented cars which overrun Los Angeles like mice. And when Val parked outside the *La Salle* and walked into the lobby, there was Hilary "Scoop" King, his elbows on the desk, waiting for her.

Val said contemptuously: "You worm!" and made for the telephone booth in the lobby.

Mibs Austin stuck her head around the switchboard and called out. Val stopped. "Yes, Mibs?"

"Mr. Spaeth left a note for you."

Val came back. The switchboard girl handed her a hotel envelope and she tore it open.

Mr. King heaved away from the desk and quickly went to the telephone booth.

"Fitzgerald . . . Fitz? King talking," he said rapidly. "I haven't time for explanations. Do me a favor."

"For you, Master-Mind — anything!"

"In five minutes call up Val Jardin at the *La Salle*."

"Why?"

"Shut up, will you? I'm in a hurry. Call her up and tell her to come down to the *Independent* office right away."

"But what for?"

"How should I know? But make the excuse stand up. I don't want her to get wise."

"Trust me, sweetheart."

Ellery hung up and stepped out of the booth. Val was gone.

He went to the desk and said to the blond girl: "Where did Miss Jardin go?"

"Who wants to know?" said Mibs with a hostile look.

"Give, sister. We work on the same rag."

"Oh. She went upstairs to her apartment."

"I'll show you my etchings some time."

He left the lobby ostentatiously and strolled alongside the building until he

279

came to the tradesmen's entrance. Then, with a swift look around, he ducked down the flight of stone steps, ran through an alley, and emerged into the back yard of the hotel. It took him a moment to locate the windows of the Jardin apartment. He jumped for the iron ladder of the fire-escape and clambered noiselessly to the third floor.

The Venetian blind in one of the living-room windows was raised an inch from the sill and he cautiously knelt and peered through the opening. Val was seated on the sofa, her hat still on, fumbling with the catch of her bag. She got it open, reached in, and took out a deck of cards — he saw the schooner on the top card clearly. She dropped her bag and began to spread the cards. But at that moment the telephone rang.

She jumped up, cards in her hand.

"But why?" Ellery heard her ask. There was a buzzing in the telephone. "No! Fitz, it's not possible! . . . Yes, yes. I'll be right down!"

She dropped the 'phone, threw the cards into the drawer of the refectory table — Ellery sighed with relief — grabbed her purse, and dashed out of sight. A second later he heard the front door slam.

He reached in, found the cord, yanked, and crawled over the sill.

Ellery took the loose deck of cards out of the refectory drawer, pulled a chair over to the table, and sat down.

Turning the deck curiously over in his hands he noticed odd, scattered little pencil markings on the long edges.

So that was it. The ancient playing-card code!

"The trick is," he mused, "to find the proper arrangement of the cards. Assuming such novices in chicanery as Valerie and her father . . . some simple arrangement . . . ascending suits in bridge rotation . . ."

He separated the cards into the four suits and built the spades up from the deuce to the ace. He saw at once that he was on the wrong track. So he built them down from the ace to the deuce. The markings sprang into significant groupings.

Ellery grinned. Child's play! He rearranged the hearts, diamonds, and clubs, put them all together, and read the message.

WORRIED CAN YOU CONTINUE
KEEP OP FROM TALKING

Ellery shuffled and reshuffled the cards, shuffled them again. He spread them, pushed them together, dropped them on the floor, picked them up. No point in arousing Valerie's suspicions. He was sure she had not had time to rearrange the cards and read the message before Fitzgerald's telephone call.

Op. Op. Queer. It might mean "operative." Operative? Private investigator. Detective. Detective! Whom did Jardin mean? Could he possibly be referring to a gentleman who called himself Hilary King? Had they seen through his shrieking sport jacket? "Keep op from talking." No that didn't gel.

He shook his head and returned the cards to the refectory drawer.

He was about to put his leg over the sill when he caught sight of a piece of white paper stuck between one of the cushions of the sofa and its back.

So he went back and pulled the paper out. It was a hotel envelope with "V. Jardin" scrawled on its face in pencil. Ellery fished under the cushion and soon found a crumpled sheet of hotel stationery.

Walter Spaeth's note to Valerie Jardin. Without a qualm, and with relish, Ellery read it.

Button-Nose: Pink got the dicto. and we're going over to Souci to plant it. Over the wall, of course — we won't let any one see us. If we're caught by the gendarmes, Godelpus.

Darling, I love you. I LOVE you. I love You. Damn it, I do.

The note was signed "Walter" and at the bottom of the sheet there was a gargantuan "X" which Ellery, who knew everything, recognized as the universal lover's shibboleth for "kiss." He had the grace to feel ashamed of himself.

But only for a moment. He replaced the sheet and envelope exactly, climbed out the window, reached in and pulled the cord and lowered the Venetian blind to its precise position before his illegal entry, and thoughtfully went down the fire-escape.

Valerie trudged into the lobby of the *La Salle* a long time later.

"What was it, Miss Jardin?" asked Mibs Austin eagerly.

"Mibs, you listened in!" Val sighed. "It wasn't anything. Mr. Fitzgerald heard a rumor that my father was about to be released. But when I got downtown I found

283

out nobody knew anything about it."

Ellery, hidden in the music-room off the lobby, chuckled to himself. Rather a dirty trick. But then Fitz was remorseless, with the efficiency and moral temperament of a Japanese war-lord.

He kept himself hidden while Val went to the elevator. He timed her movements. Now she was getting out at the third floor. Now she was at the door of 3-C. Now she was locking it from inside. Now she was at the refectory table. Now she was arranging the cards. Now she was reading the message. . . .

The switchboard buzzed. Ellery hid behind a drape, listening.

"What?" he heard Mibs Austin say. "Okay, Miss Jardin. I'll be right up."

There was a scrambled noise and then the blond girl called: "Mr. Max! Take the board a minute, will you? I'll be right back."

And a moment later Mibs Austin passed the doorway of the music-room bound for the elevator.

Op . . . Operator. Telephone operator. Mibs Austin!

So it was imperative to continue to keep Mibs Austin from talking, was it?

Ellery lit a cigaret and quietly went

through the lobby to the street. He was about to step into his green coupé when another coupé darted into the curb and Walter Spaeth jumped out.

"Hullo!" Walter's lean face was flushed with excitement. "King, we've pulled it off!"

"Good for you."

"It was easy. There's only one detective on duty at *Sans Souci* and Pink and I got in without being spotted. Winni was out, so we had a clear field."

"You planted the dictograph?"

"It's all set. We took along a couple of spare transmitters, just to be on the safe side. We've got one hidden in the study, one in Winni's quarters upstairs, and one in the living-room. And we led the wires over to the empty Jardin house."

"Where's Pink?"

"In the Jardin house stripped for action."

"When are you going to tackle Winni?"

"Tonight."

"Make it eight o'clock and I'll be there to listen in."

"Right." And Walter raced into the *La Salle*.

17

ALARUMS AND DISCURSIONS

Ellery shut Fitz's door and made for one of the five telephones on Fitz's desk. "Get me Inspector Glücke at headquarters, please."

"What's doing?" asked Fitz eagerly.

"Glücke? This is Hilary King of the *Independent*."

"What's on your mind?"

"Plenty. Can you take a friendly tip and keep your mouth shut?"

"Try me," said the Inspector.

"Investigate the telephone records of all calls from the *La Salle* switchboard on Monday afternoon, starting around five o'clock."

"What's up?"

"That's what I'm trying to find out. Work through the manager and warn him to keep it under his hat. It's especially important not to tip off the switchboard operator, a girl named Austin. She mustn't know the records are being inspected."

"I get you," said the Inspector slowly.

"Any luck with that fingerprint investigation of the iron table and the binoculars?"

"The rain spoiled the prints. Well, thanks for the tip, King."

"I'll be around to collect 'em in person."

Ellery hung up and sat down in Fitz's best chair, rubbing his chin. Fitz opened a drawer and produced a bottle and two glasses. They drank two quick ones.

"Well, Fitz," said Ellery, "your little white-haired figment of the imagination is beginning to smell a large rodent."

"You're worse than the State Department! What's on the fire, for the love of Mike?"

Ellery tipped his absurd hat over his tinted glasses. "Let me think a while."

"I want news, not ratiocination," growled Fitz. "You're beginning to get my goat."

"Ah, that reminds me," said Ellery. He reached for one of Fitz's 'phones again. "Get me the Magna Studios — Mr. Jacques Butcher."

"What's Butcher got to do with this?"

"Nothing. Hello! Butcher? . . . I don't *want* his secretary, damn it all! I want Butcher himself, in the flesh, Little Napoleon, the Genius. . . ." Ellery sat up excitedly. "My dear young lady, you haven't *heard* any language. I'm reserving my choicest words for that vanishing American

287

you work for. Goodbye!"

He sat back, snorting, and tipped his hat over his eyes again. Fitz looked disgusted and took another drink.

When Ellery left the *Independent* building Fitz was with him, grumbling that he'd get some news if he had to leg it all over the *pueblo* himself.

They found Inspector Glücke communing darkly with his thoughts. He jumped up when he saw Ellery.

"What's behind this, King?" he exclaimed. "Oh, Fitzgerald." He scowled.

"You take a flying leap at the moon," snarled Fitz, planting himself in the best chair.

"Peace," said Ellery. "What did you turn up, Inspector?"

"The *La Salle* telephone records show that a call was made Monday *at five-thirty-five* to Hillcrest 2411!"

"The Spaeth number," said Fitz with awe. He got up and sat down again.

"To whom was the call charged?"

"3-C — the Jardins."

"So what?" asked Fitz after a moment.

"That," said Glücke, "is what *I'd* like to know."

But Ellery did not seem disturbed. In fact, he began to beam. "Inspector, are you game to play a long shot?"

"What's this — something else I missed?" grumbled Glücke.

"Call in Rhys Jardin and tell him the charges against him are being withdrawn."

"What!" exploded Glücke. "Do you think I'm crazy?"

Fitz stayed up this time. "Go ahead, Glücke — see what this screwball's got!"

"You don't have to mean it," said Ellery soothingly. "Just to see how he reacts. What do you say?"

"Aw, nuts," said the Inspector with bitterness, and he barked an order into his communicator.

Twenty minutes later Rhys Jardin was brought into Inspector Glücke's office. The Inspector was alone.

"I've got news for you, Jardin," said Glücke abruptly.

"Anything would be better than the Coventry I've been subjected to," said Jardin with an amiable smile.

"Van Every and I have been talking your case over and we think we've pulled a boner."

"A boner?" Glücke was astounded to see that, far from receiving the news joyfully, Jardin seemed positively depressed.

"We've just about decided to withdraw

the murder charge and let you go." Jardin half-raised his hand. "As soon as the formalities —"

"Inspector — I'm going to make an unusual request."

"What?"

"Don't withdraw the charge."

"You mean you *want* to stay in the can?" asked Glücke in amazement.

"I can't explain. But there are certain reasons —"

The Inspector gaped. Then he shook his head and opened the door. The two detectives came in and Jardin's features relaxed into their usual pleasant lines.

"Thanks a lot," he said earnestly, and marched off as another man would have marched to freedom.

The Inspector closed the door and Ellery and Fitzgerald came out of one of the adjoining rooms. "Can you tie that!"

"Give," said Fitz impatiently, his thick stubby nostrils vibrating in Ellery's direction.

Glücke wagged his head. "I swear it's the first time I ever heard of a man *asking* to be kept in jail for murder!"

"This copper-rivets it," said Ellery with satisfaction. "That's all I wanted to know. The five-thirty-five telephone call Monday from the *La Salle* plus Jardin's conduct just now tell a plain story."

"It's Greek to mc."

"Why should Jardin be so anxious to remain in jail? Why should he *ask* to be held on the murder count?"

Understanding leaped into Fitz's eyes. "My God!" he shouted. "He's got an out!"

The Inspector paled. "An out?" he echoed feebly.

"Certainly," said Ellery. "It's probably an ironclad alibi. I've discovered that Jardin warned his daughter to make sure Mibs Austin kept her mouth shut. Now if that five-thirty-five call Monday was made either by Jardin himself or, as seems more likely from the facts, by Val Jardin with Jardin at her side near the switchboard in sight of the Austin girl, then the whole thing becomes clear."

"Jardin would have an alibi for almost the exact moment of the murder," cried Fitz. "And if the Austin wench testified in court . . . zowie!"

Glücke looked ill. "If that's true," he muttered, "he doesn't want the alibi spilled now, so he warns his daughter to keep the Austin girl quiet. This is wonderful." But there was no appreciation on his face.

"Why the hell should he want to keep the alibi secret?" asked Fitz, frowning. "That doesn't make sense."

"It does," drawled Ellery, "if he's trying to protect some one." The two men stared at him. "Don't you see that that's the exact point? He's keeping the heat on himself while the one he's shielding remains unsuspected. He's protecting Walter Spaeth."

"Spaeth!" exclaimed the Inspector.

"Of course. Didn't Walter admit last night he was the man Frank saw wearing Jardin's coat? He was all ready to talk when Val Jardin shut him up; and after the three of them had their council of war he retracted his admission. That can only mean that Walter didn't know about Jardin's alibi until the Jardins told him about it in this office last night. He didn't know Jardin had an out. So up to last night he was protecting Jardin — at least, he thought he was."

"From what?" demanded Fitz.

"I don't know." Ellery frowned, shrugged. "And now that they've all shut up in concert, it's evident that the Jardins are protecting Walter."

"From what?" asked Fitz doggedly.

"God only knows, and I'm not His confidant. If they'd only talk, the tight-mouthed idiots! One thing is sure, though — while Jardin has his alibi to protect him, Walter Spaeth is in no such enviable position. They seem to think he's in a tough spot. Otherwise Jardin wouldn't be acting so contrary to common sense."

"Spaeth, huh," said Glücke in a savage mumble. Fitz drew his bushy brows together, shaking his head a little.

"Yes, Spaeth," snapped Ellery. "Have you stopped to ask yourself whom Valerie Jardin could have been telephoning when she called the Spaeth house Monday afternoon?"

"Cripe! If it could have been young Spaeth himself —"

"Who else? I think Walter was in his father's house at five-thirty-five and that the Jardins have known it all along!"

"If he was," cried the Inspector, "it puts him in the murder room three minutes after the killing! Well, maybe not in the room, but we could track that down. But it's a cinch now that he, not Jardin, was the only outsider to enter the grounds during the crime period. He was wearing Jardin's coat, and we've got that coat — stained with human blood." He looked sly. "And another thing — if he killed his old man, then he also tried to frame Jardin for the crime."

"Horse manure," said Fitz.

"Didn't I let him go Monday night *before* the Jardins? Couldn't he have beat it back to the *La Salle* and planted the coat and sword in Jardin's closet? Besides — I never released this — Walter Spaeth's finger-prints were found on the rapier as well as Jardin's. Prints on the weapon!"

"What!" said Ellery in a shocked voice.

"I didn't see any point," said Glücke sheepishly, "in sort of confusing the Jardin issue —"

"Walter's prints on the rapier," muttered Ellery.

"Anyway, the motive still stands — dis-inherited, wasn't he? And always scrapping with his old man, too." The Inspector rubbed his hands. "It's a case, boys. It's got the makings of a case. All I need for Van Every is a couple of witnesses in the right places —"

"Excuse me," said Fitz, making for the door.

Ellery pounced on him. "Where are you going?"

"To make newspaper history, my fine-feathered friend," said Fitz gleefully. "My God, this yarn will sell a million papers!"

"Fitz," said Ellery in a ferocious voice, "if you dare print one syllable of what you've just heard —" He whispered the rest in Fitz's ear.

Fitz looked pugnacious. Then he looked surprised. Then he began to grin.

Ellery dragged him back to Glücke's desk.

At eight o'clock that night ghosts walked in the Jardin house at *Sans Souci.*

They were ponderable and fleshly ghosts with the air of conspirators, moving restlessly about in the room off the terrace which had served as Rhys Jardin's study. An electric-battery lantern on the floor threw long shadows to the bare walls; no light escaped through the glass wall to the terrace, for the lantern was shielded.

The chief spectre was Pink, crouched Indian-fashion on his hams with a pair of receivers over his ears, tinkering with a small apparatus before him in the light of the lantern. A pile of cans variously labeled "Soup," "Corn," and "Minced Ham" lay beside him, several open and empty.

A tall thin wraith named Queen trod the boards at one side of the room, and a large square one named Fitzgerald patrolled the other. Kneeling beside Pink was a female ghost in riding breeches — queer note in ghostly fashions — with a long tear along one thigh, as if a leg had caught on a sharp stake at the top of a fence.

"Shhh!" hissed Pink suddenly. "Here they come!"

Ellery and Fitz skittered forward. But Val was quicker. The two men fought over the last pair of earphones. Ellery won, leaving Fitz to glare and press his beefy face close to Val's ear.

Through the membranes came the sound of a door closing and Winni Moon's voice, half-frightened and half-seductive. "In here, Wally darling. We're alone here."

"Winni the Glut," whispered Val vindictively.

"Are you sure there's nobody around to overhear?" said Walter's voice.

Winni's voice was no longer frightened and altogether seductive. "Not a soul, darling. Nobody comes near me. I'm weally the loneliest person —"

"I can't stay long, Winni. No one must know I came here. So I'll have to say it fast."

"Say what, Walter?" She was frightened again.

"Do you think I'm your friend?"

They could almost see her pout. "I've twied awfully hard to *get* you to be, but you never weally showed that —"

"I'm enough of a friend of yours to come

out in the open, instead of skulking around in the dark like a rat!"

"I don't know what you *mean*," complained Winni.

"I've been doing some spying on my own. And I know," said Walter, accenting each word, "all about that little business arrangement between you and Ruhig."

"Oh!" said Winni. The gasp smashed against the receivers.

"I know that Ruhig told you there was a later will in existence. I know he told you that, unless you married him, he'd produce that will and you'd see those fifty millions pulled right out of your lap!"

"Walter. . . . How — how did you know that?"

The listeners let out their breaths.

"Jeeze," said Pink.

"He's wonderful," moaned Val.

"Shut up," howled Fitz. "Let's get this!"

"Please," groaned Ellery.

"— mind how I know. Well, I hate Ruhig's guts. I know you do, too. Winni, he's making a jackass out of you!"

She was silent.

"He's lying, Winni," said Walter gently. "There never was such a will. He's just trying to scare you into marrying him and sharing the fifty millions with him."

Her voice came through strangely distorted. "Walter, do you mean to tell me it was all — it was all —"

"He invented the whole thing," said Walter in an earnest, friendly way. "You never saw that will he spoke about, did you?"

"N-no."

"There! Doesn't that prove it? Listen, Winni. Forget that fellow; tell him to go to the devil. You and I might make some other arrangement — a settlement. Or maybe even . . ."

His voice trailed off into a mumble, as if he were whispering intimately into her ear.

Val bit a hole in the corner of her handkerchief.

The rest for the most part was inaudible. Within a short time Walter said something about having to get away, and they heard the click of the door, receding footsteps.

"Whee!" cried Val, jumping up.

"I'll be a cockeyed dinglehoofer," said Pink slowly. "It worked."

"Quiet," urged Ellery. "Let's see what happens. If I've got that blond baby figured right, she'll make straight for the telephone."

They listened eagerly. Two minutes passed. They heard the sound of a door closing again. Whether it was the study door or some other they could not tell. There were more footsteps, quick nervous ones, for five long minutes. And then suddenly the sound of some one running and another click.

"Opewator!" It was Winni's voice, hard and angry.

"I'll be damned," said Fitz. He took a flask out of his hip pocket and drank thirstily.

"Wuhig? Anatole Wuhig! . . . Wuhig! This is Winni. . . . Never mind that gweasy line! Listen to me, you. I've been thinking things over and I think you're taking me for a wide. . . . Yes, a wide! Why should I split all that money with you? I'm not going to mawwy you, and that's final!"

There was another long silence, as if Ruhig was talking slowly, voluminously, and persuasively.

"Don't give me that will stuff! I don't think there ever *was* another will! . . . I will so discuss it. Yes, and wight this minute! You're a faker and a liar! . . . Oh, you're still twying to pull the wool over my eyes, are you? Well, if there *is* a will and you've got it, why didn't you show it to me? . . . Yes, *show* it to me! And none of your fakes, either! I know Solly's handwiting.

And I don't want any what-you-call-'ems — photostatic copies. You bwing the weal thing over this second! . . . I know you don't cawwy it awound in your pocket. . . . All wight, pick your own time. *I* don't care. There's no such will, anyway. I'm fwom Missouwi, Mister Wuhig. . . . Thwee o'cwock tomowwow afternoon? In this house. . . . Yes!"

Thunder crashed — the receiver being restored to its place.

"Just goes to show," sighed Ellery. "I guess I'm a remarkable fellow."

"Do you think Ruhig's bluffing?" asked Val anxiously.

"Not at all. It's evening, which explains why he can't bring the will over now. He would if he could."

"How's that?" demanded Fitz.

"Obviously it's in a safe-deposit vault — he'll have to wait until tomorrow to get his hands on it. And he's giving himself plenty of time tomorrow to think the situation over. However, I believe Counselor Ruhig will be here per schedule."

They all started. For out of the earphones burbled a snarl scarcely recognizable as Miss Winni Moon's voice.

"Filthy little cwook!"

18

RAPE OF THE AWNING

Val awoke Friday morning with a buzzing in her ears, which quickly turned out to be the front-door bell.

She scrambled out of bed and ran through the living room, pulling a negligée on hastily. It might be Walter. She hoped it *was* Walter. They had sat up half the night making love and drinking sherry. There had hardly been time, between sips and kisses, to talk. As she ran, Val wondered if she oughtn't to go back and fix herself up. But then she thought he might just as well get used to seeing her fresh out of bed, with tousled hair and sleepy eyes and no powder or lipstick. Besides, she looked prettier that way. Rhys always said so. Rhys always said that she looked nicer with cold cream on her face and a tissue in her hand than most other women looked ready for presentation at the Court of St. James's. Rhys always said —

"In a minute," she called gaily, fumbling with the latch. She got the door open and smiled her most ravishing smile.

"Oh," said Val. "Oh. Mibs. Why, what's the trouble?"

Mibs leaped past her into the foyer and leaned against the wall, pressing her hand to her heart.

"Shut the door," she gasped. "Oh, shut it!"

Val shut it. "What's the matter, Mibs?"

"Wait — till — I get my breath!"

"You poor thing. Come in here and sit down. Why, you're shaking!"

The blond girl sank into Rhys's armchair, licking her pale lips. "Miss Jardin, I — I'm scared to death."

"Nonsense," said Val, sitting down on the arm of the chair. "Why should you be? Let me get you something."

"No. No, I'll be all right. It's just that —" She looked at Val piteously. "Miss Jardin, I'm being . . . followed."

"Oh," said Val, and she got up and went to the sofa and sat down herself.

"I wish Pink were here," whimpered the girl. "He'd know what to do. Where is he? Why hasn't he been —"

"Pink's off on a special sort of job," said Val slowly. "Tell me all about it, Mibs."

Mibs drew a quavery breath. "I've been nervous ever since you spoke to me Monday night about — about your father and my seeing him Monday afternoon and

302

speaking to Mr. Spaeth. . . . I went out to the drug store yesterday for a soda and — and I thought somebody was following me. On the way back, too. Some Hollywood wisenheimer, I thought. I didn't see him. But last night, too. When I went home. The same thing. And now, this morning, on my way to work . . . Somebody's after me, Miss Jardin!"

Val sat still, thinking. She tried to look unconcerned, but her own heart was pounding. If Mibs was being followed, that might mean . . . Could somebody actually be . . .

"We'll have to be careful, Mibs," she said in a tone she tried to make light.

"I'm so scared I — I . . ." The girl was almost hysterical.

Val went to her again and put her arms about the girl. "Have you a family, Mibs?"

Mibs was crying. "N-no. I'm all alone. I've only got Pink. I come from St. Lou, and I've been here two years and Pink's been my only f-friend. . . ."

"Hush. You don't think we'd let anybody harm you, Mibs!" The girl sobbed. "I'll tell you what we'll do, honey," said Val in a bright voice. "Suppose you stay with me for a few days until this blows over. I mean — I'm alone here, and you can sleep in my father's bed, or with me if you'd like that better —"

"Oh, could I?" cried Mibs, raising a streaked face.

"Of course, silly. It will be lots of fun. You don't even have to go back to your own place for your things. I've got heaps of underwear and stockings and things —"

"Can I have my meals here, too?"

"Certainly. Here, here's an extra key. Now dry your eyes and fix yourself up and go downstairs as if nothing happened."

"Yes," sniffled Mibs.

"I may have to go out later, but I'm sure no one's going to do anything to you in your own lobby!"

"No. That's right," said Mibs, smiling faintly.

"There! Isn't that better? Now go wash your face." And Val led the blond girl to her bathroom with a reassuring laugh and a stomach that felt like one vast, painful vacuum.

"Tell you why I called you," said Inspector Glücke to Ellery. He stooped over a small safe in his office.

"Nothing's happened?" began Ellery quickly.

"No, no, we're in the clear. It's this."

The Inspector opened his safe and brought out something wrapped in tissue paper, something with the shape of a large bottle. "It was on your tip that we found it," he said gruffly, "so you're entitled to get in on it, King. I guess we owe you a lot."

"What is it?" asked Ellery in an avid voice.

Glücke began carefully removing the folds of tissue. "We had quite a time searching that sewer outside *Sans Souci*, but we finally fished this out of the muck. It got stuck near the bottom of the sewer."

It was an Indian club, soiled and evil-smelling. A red-brown clot adhered to part of the bulging end.

"Is that," frowned Ellery, "blood?" He flicked the clot with one fingernail.

"Nothing else but."

"Any prints?"

"Some very old ones — just traces of 'em. Jardin's, the girl's."

Ellery nodded, sucking his lower lip.

"What made you tell me to search the sewer?" asked the Inspector slowly.

"Eh? Oh — a minor reasoning process. By the way, did you find anything else of interest in the sewer?"

"Not a thing."

Ellery shook his head.

He parked his coupé outside the gate at *Sans Souci*, much to Atherton Frank's surprise. Indeed, he was even assisted by the detective on duty, who seemed oddly friendly. Frank scratched his head, swinging his half-arm in an interrogatory manner.

But no one enlightened him, and Ellery sauntered up the drive toward the Spaeth house. A sense of desolation smote him. It was like coming into the main street of a ghost-city.

But he shook his head in impatience at himself and applied his mind to the problem at hand. It was a knotty one; something told him that the key-knot was missing, the discovery of which would unravel the whole puzzle fabric.

He avoided the porte-cochère and circled the Spaeth house, trudging along under the geometric row of royal palms and wrestling with thoughts that persisted in slipping through the fingers of his brain.

He mounted the terrace steps and sat down almost against the wall in Solly Spaeth's most elaborate summer chair, putting his elbows on his knees and his chin on his palms.

A hiss brought his head up. Across the

rock garden the head of Valerie Jardin protruded from the doorway of the empty Jardin study. She motioned angrily, but he shook his head, smiling. After a moment she slipped down the Jardin terrace steps and ran across to the Spaeth house.

"She'll see you!" she whispered, darting up under the protection of the terrace awning. "Are you mad?"

"Never saner," said Ellery. "Winni the Moocher is out stuffing her gullet. It seems she's sick of preparing her own meals. At least that's what the detective on duty says."

"Did you come in through the *gate?*" asked Val, horrified.

"Why not?" said Ellery innocently. "Didn't you?"

Val gazed ruefully at her ripped riding-habit. "Over the fence again. At that, Mr. King, you took an awful chance. If Ruhig should be watching —"

"He isn't."

"How do you know that?" asked Val suspiciously.

"Silence. I'm trying to concentrate."

Val looked at him in a dubious way but he merely lay back in the chair, resting his neck against the back. He folded his hands across his chest. Val experienced a twinge of bafflement. He certainly was the queerest man. Concentrate? He was just snoozing!

"Better come away from here," she said, taking a tentative step toward the stairs. "If you want to sleep, you can join Pink. He's taking a nap back there. At least Winni won't come back and find you."

"Leave this comfortable chair?" murmured Ellery. "Not on your life." He opened one eye.

"You are by all odds the most —" Val stopped, watching him in bewilderment.

The single eye, naturally invisible to her behind the tinted glasses, nevertheless contrived to communicate a certain fixity, a surface tension, to his figure. He sat up abruptly, his shoes thumping on the flagged floor.

"What's the *matter* with you?" said Val, puzzled.

It was noon, and the sun poised high. Ellery rose, looking up at the awning overhead, his Adam's apple quivering delicately. His gaze was directed toward a sliver of blinding light in the awning. He stepped on the chair and raised the blue glasses to his forehead, examining the rupture closely.

"What's wonderful about that?" demanded Val. "You're the oddest creature!

It's only a rip in the awning."

He slipped the glasses back over his eyes and stepped down, smiling. "I'm sensitive to sudden flashes of light. Go away, will you, darling?"

He settled back in the chair again. Val threw up her hands and descended to the garden. He watched her from under the glasses. She darted off on a tangent bound for the far boundary of *Sans Souci*, where the bushes and trees were thick and the fence could be climbed without benefit of witness. After a moment her slender figure, boyish in the jodhpurs, disappeared beneath the palms.

Ellery lay quiet for some time, watching the palms, the terrace of the Jardin house. Cicadas sawed away somewhere; the garden before him crawled and hummed with bees. There was no sign of human life anywhere.

So he got out of the chair again and stepped up on it and once more examined the slit in the awning overhead.

The colored stripes ran from top to bottom of the awning, the slit lying neatly parallel between a yellow stripe and a green one.

"Tear roughly a half-inch long," he mumbled to himself. "Well, well," and he took a penknife out of his pocket and was about to employ surgery on the awning when he caught sight of something else, and he stopped.

On the stone wall of the house proper, not three feet to the side of the glassed area which served as the fourth and outer wall of the study, there was a sharp, clean, fresh-looking nick. Something with a keen point had chipped away a fragment of stone. He looked at the nick in the stone, and he looked at the tear in the canvas. The nick was high on the wall, and the tear was high on the awning. Tall as he was, and standing on the chair, he still had to crane directly upwards to see them closely. Yes, the tear was a little higher than the nick, and directly in front of it, judging it by the eye with the flagged floor as a base. And tear and nick were a mere four inches apart. Four inches!

Muttering excitedly to himself, he proceeded to mutilate the unoffending awning. He slashed ruthlessly away in a rough rectangle with the penknife until he was able to pull a piece about five inches square out of the awning.

He dropped to the flags, holding the canvas scrap gingerly. In the stronger light near the edge of the terrace he thought he detected a faint brown stain on the upper edges of the slit.

Golden-brown. Molasses-brown. Molasses. Molasses and potassium cyanide?

And what would an Italian rapier be doing sticking its smeared nose through a nice, clean, summery awning?

That, said Mr. Hilary-Ellery King-Queen to himself as he rolled up the canvas square with cautious fingers, was the Question.

He wrapped the roll in a handkerchief and, holding the tubular result like a twist of diamonds under his coat, he made his way from the terrace along the row of palms to the gate, trying to look unconcerned but not succeeding.

"Well, Bronson?" said Ellery, leaning over the laboratory table.

The Chemist nodded. "Molasses and cyanide, all right. Say, I've heard about you, King, around headquarters here. Where did you get hold of this piece of canvas?"

"If you're thinking of 'phoning Glücke," said Ellery hastily, rewrapping the scrap of awning with fingers that trembled a little, "don't bother. I'll be seeing him soon myself."

"But look here —" began Bronson.

"Goodbye. Oh, isn't it a lovely day?" said Ellery, hurrying out.

19

BLONDE IN THE WOODPILE

Valerie crossed the *La Salle* lobby, vaguely noticing that the manager of the hotel, a small dark man, was seated before the switchboard with Mibs Austin's earphones clamped about his head.

She supposed the telephone girl was upstairs and made her way to the elevator, sighing. The poor thing had been so terrified. If she only knew what really hung over her!

She unlocked the door of 3-C. "Mibs, are you here?"

The door swung to and the slam echoed. There was no other sound.

"Mibs?" Val stepped into the living-room. It was empty.

"Mibs!"

The color drained out of her cheeks. She ran into her bedroom, into Rhys's room, the bathrooms, the kitchen. . . .

Mibs was not there.

She clawed at the front door and flew down the emergency stairway to the lobby.

"Where's Miss Austin?" she cried shrilly.

The manager removed the earphones. "Why, I thought —"

"Where is she?"

"Don't you know?" asked the manager, surprised.

Val was furious in her panic. "You fool, if I knew would I ask you? Where is she?"

The man looked annoyed. "Didn't you call her up an hour or so ago? I'll have to give her a talking to. She can't make excuses like that to take time off."

"Say that again," said Val, speaking with distinctness. "She told you I telephoned her?"

"That's what the snip said. She said you called her and asked her to meet you right away at the corner of Cahuenga and Sunset on an important matter. So naturally —"

Val groped for the support of the desk. "Oh, yes," she said faintly. "Thank you." And she went over to a divan and sat down under the dwarf palm, her thighs quivery with weakness.

Call. . . . She hadn't made any call. Some one had telephoned Mibs, using her name. An appointment!

The manager went back to the switchboard, looking angry. Val felt like laughing. Angry! Oh, Mibs, you fool. . . . Val managed to get out of the divan and go to the

314

telephone booth. It took her a long time to fish out the coins from her purse; her fingers seemcd incapable of holding on to anything.

"Walter Spaeth," she said, when she was connected with the *Independent*. It was supposed to be a calm, unconcerned alto; but somehow it came out a dry croak.

"Spaeth talking," said Walter's blessed voice.

"Walter. Something terrible's happened."

"Darling! What's the matter? Has Winni — Ruhig —"

"It's — it's Mibs. Mibs Austin." Val clung to the telephone. "Walter . . . she's *gone*."

Walter made a funny little sound at the other end of the wire. "Gone? I thought you said she'd agreed not to — I mean, that she wasn't to leave —"

"You don't understand, Walter," said Val stiffly. "Somebody . . . somebody telephoned her an hour ago using my name and telling her to meet me at Cahuenga and Sunset. But — I — didn't — 'phone her!"

"Oh," said Walter. Then he said: "Hold tight, funny-face. I'll be right down."

Val hung up and stood in the hot booth

for a moment. Then she went out and toiled upstairs to wait for Walter. She felt like an old, old woman.

Walter was there in thirty minutes, and she let him in and bolted the door behind him. They went into the living-room and Walter sat down. Val went to the windows mechanically and let down the Venetian blinds. That done, she moved the Chinese vase a half-inch to the left on the refectory table. Then she moved it back again.

Walter sat silently, the flesh over his eyes bunched into little knots. His fist was pounding up and down on his knee.

"Do you think," said Val in a tight voice, "do you think she's —"

Walter got up and tramped around the room, red in the face. "What I can't understand is how the little fool ever let a trick like that take her in," he muttered. "Good lord, doesn't she know your voice?"

"I haven't had much to do with her, Walter," replied Val listlessly.

"The damned fool!"

"Walter." Val twisted her fingers. "She may be — she might be . . ." It was hard to say. It was impossible to say.

Walter sat down again and buried his face in his hands. "We're up against it, Val.

For fair, this time." Val nodded wordlessly. How well she knew! "Now we've got blood on our hands."

"Walter," she moaned.

But it was true. Their scheming, their crazy impetuous scheming, their frantic effort to stave off the inevitable — Walter, Walter's predicament, Walter in the shadow of a tall gaunt thing made of wood. . . . It had cost the life of an innocent person.

Val said with a faint nausea: "Do you think she's —" But she could not get the word out.

Walter rubbed his palms together in a meaningless sort of way. "Whoever's behind this, hon, won't stop at anything. Somehow he found out about your father's alibi, and he's put the Austin kid out of the way to destroy it." His voice rose. "I can't, I simply can't understand such damned brutality, such savagery! How could any one hate another man so much?"

"It's our fault, Walter," whispered Val.

His face softened and he went over to her and pulled her to him. "Look, Val." He cupped her chin and made her look up at him. "Let's finish this mess here and now. We're miserable failures at this thing — we're wriggling like worms trying to get away from something that's bound to get us in the end."

"Not us," cried Val. "You!"

"You've done too much for me already, you and Rhys. And meanwhile we've done something to an innocent person we'll never be able to undo."

Val, thinking of the blond girl, began to cry. "How could we have let her take such chances —"

"Stop crying, Val," he said gently. "The first thing we've got to do is report her disappearance to the police." Val nodded, sobbing. "Maybe it isn't too late," he said encouragingly. "Maybe she's still alive. If she is, we can't waste a second."

"But we'll have to tell them all about — all about you —"

"High time, too!" And he grinned a little.

"No, Walter." She pressed her face against his coat.

"If I don't — what about your father?" he said in the same gentle voice. "Remember, with Mibs's disappearance he has no alibi. No alibi, Val."

"Oh, Walter, what an awful, awful mess!"

"Now let's go downtown and tell Glücke the truth."

She raised her head, agonized. "But if you do, Walter, they'll arrest you! They'll say you murdered your father!"

He kissed the tip of her nose. "Did I ever tell you you're beautiful?"

"I can't let you do it!"

"And that I've dreamed about you every night for a year?"

Walter or Rhys. Rhys or Walter. It went round and round in her head like a phonograph record. It might slide off to some other place, but it always came back to the same place. . . . She dropped her arms helplessly.

PART
FIVE

20

EVERYTHING BUT THE TRUTH

Walter went to the telephone and called police headquarters. He waited patiently, his back to Valerie. His tall figure shimmered; and Val sat down, rubbing her eyes. She wished she could go to bed and sleep and sleep for months, years.

He spoke to Inspector Glücke in a rather listless tone, telling him about the disappearance of Mibs Austin and the false telephone call, the appointment for the corner of Cahuenga and Sunset. . . . Everything had drained out, Valerie felt. What was the use of fighting?

"Let's go, Val."

"All right, Walter."

Neither spoke on the journey downtown. There didn't seem to be anything to say. The saucy child-face of Mibs Austin with its dip and crown of blondness danced before Val, obscuring the streets. She closed her eyes, but Mibs remained there like a face on a bobbing balloon.

Glücke received them in state, with two police stenographers occupying chairs beside his desk and District Attorney Van Every enthroned to one side, all silence and alertness.

"Did you find out anything?" asked Walter abruptly.

"We're working on it now," said the Inspector. "What makes you think the girl was snatched?"

"Because she had certain information which the murderer of my father didn't want known."

Glücke laughed. "Sit down, Miss Jardin. Is this another of your fairy stories, Spaeth? If you've got anything to tell me, say it now. And make it stick this time."

"I see," said Walter, "you're all ready for me." Val looked down at her hands, and they stopped twisting. "All right. I'm glad to get this off my chest. What I said —"

A scuffling sound from an adjoining room stopped him. One of the doors burst open and Rhys Jardin appeared, struggling in the arms of a detective.

"Walter!" he cried. "It's a trick! The girl wasn't abducted at all! Glücke had her —"

"Stubborn to the end," remarked the District Attorney wryly. "Too bad, Glücke."

"Pop!" Val flew to him. The detective released Jardin, puffing.

"Do you mean to say," growled Walter, "that you cooked this up, damn you?"

The Inspector made a furious sign and the detective went back into the room and came out with Mibs Austin. The girl's eyes were red and swollen, and she kept them averted, refusing to look at the Jardins, at Walter. And suddenly she began to weep.

Rhys Jardin said curtly: "It was just a trick to make you talk, Walter. That newspaperman, King, found out about my alibi —"

"King?" cried Val. "The beast! I *knew* he'd spoil everything!"

"He told Glücke and Glücke arranged for the 'abduction' of Miss Austin. He wanted to scare Walter into talking."

"Can the chatter," said the Inspector harshly. "All right, it didn't work. But I've got this girl, and she's talked plenty. Want to hear what she said, Spaeth?"

"Oh, Miss Jardin," sobbed Mibs, "I couldn't help it. They got a police matron or — or somebody to call me, and I thought you were in trouble and went down to — to —"

"It's all right, Mibs," said Val steadily. "I'm glad you're safe."

"And they brought me up here and — and made me tell. I was so frightened I didn't know what to do. They made me tell —"

"Just a minute," said Walter. "If you know about Rhys Jardin's alibi, Inspector, then you know he's innocent."

Rhys said simply: "I'm a free man, Walter."

"That," said Walter, "is a different story."

"Miss Austin says," snapped Glücke, "that she spoke to you on the 'phone at five-thirty-five Monday afternoon, and that you were talking from your father's house. That's three minutes after the murder!"

"My advice to you, young fellow," said Van Every soberly from his corner, "is to come clean."

Walter stood facing them, hands jammed in his pockets. He wore a faint grin. The stenographers poised their pencils.

But just then the door opened and Mr. Hilary King appeared, breathing hard, as if he had been running. He was carrying a long object wrapped in brown paper which had a rather curious shape.

He stopped short on the threshold, taking in the situation at a glance. "Looks like Scene Two, Act Three," he grunted. "Well, who's said what?"

"It won't be long now," announced the

Inspector triumphantly. "Spaeth's ready to talk."

"Oh," said Ellery. "Is he?"

"Am I?" murmured Walter. "And the answer is: no."

"What?" yelled Glücke. "Again?"

"I kept my mouth shut before because I didn't know about Rhys's alibi and thought I had to protect him —"

"Not knowing about his alibi," murmured Ellery, "what information did you possess which made you think Jardin killed your father?"

Walter ignored him. "Today, when I thought Miss Austin was in danger, I felt I had to talk. But now? Nuts to all of you." And he grinned.

"That's final?" demanded the Inspector.

Walter said lightly: "You'll have to speak to my lawyer."

Ellery grimaced. "You're making me do a lot of unnecessary work, Walter. Glücke, time's a-wastin'. It's two o'clock."

Glücke scowled at him. The District Attorney drew him off to a corner and they conferred earnestly. Ellery joined them, waving his package as if he were arguing.

"All right," grumbled Glücke at last. "I suppose there's plenty of time to attend to Spaeth. We'll look this Ruhig bird over and see where he fits in."

"Ruhig," said Val intensely. "You've told them!" Ellery looked guilty. "You know what you are? You're a filthy *traitor!*"

Glücke nodded to two men, and they took places on each side of Walter. "It's between you and Ruhig, Spaeth. I warn you right now, I've got two warrants in my pocket. One for you and one for Ruhig. My own hunch is you, but King seems to think we ought to give Ruhig the once-over first."

"Come on," said Ellery impatiently. "You're keeping fifty million dollars waiting."

Inspector Glücke engineered their entry into *Sans Souci* with artistic efficiency. Mr. Anatole Ruhig, who had been under secret police observation, had not yet made his unsuspecting appearance; but it was necessary to keep Miss Winni Moon, who was on the premises, in darkness. A hole had been hacked in the willow fence in a remote corner of the grounds; they crept through, constantly admonished to make no noise, and were led to the empty Jardin house from the far side, out of sight of the Spaeth house.

They caught Pink, purple-eyed and haggard from lack of sleep, completely by surprise. He jumped up with a foolish, trapped look, ready to fight; but when everybody ignored him and Glücke seized the earphones, he scratched his head and lit a cigaret and wandered about asking questions which no one bothered to answer. He did not see Rhys Jardin at first. When he did, the cigaret fell out of his mouth and Rhys stepped on it and punched his shoulder. After that Pink stayed close to Jardin with a pathetic tenacity.

Glücke's men vanished, apparently preinstructed. There was nothing to do but wait.

Val and Walter sat down on the floor and talked to each other in undertones, ignoring the others. Ellery paced up and down, smoking tasteless cigarets. Rhys Jardin leaned against a wall, and Pink helped him lean. No one said anything.

Glücke kept looking at his watch. Two-fifty. Fifty-five. Three o'clock. The earphones were dead. He glanced at Ellery with an interrogatory scowl. Three-five. . . .

"Here he comes!"

They scrambled toward him then, listening intently.

The closing of a door.

"They're in Spaeth's study," muttered Ellery, peering through the glass wall.

Mr. Anatole Ruhig's voice grumbled through the receiver. "I'm taking a terrible chance, Winni."

"You don't fool me, Anatole Wuhig!" said Winni coldly. "If there's a will, show it to me."

"You're a fool."

"How do I know what you told me was twue? You said you got into the gwounds over the fence when you couldn't find that man Fwank — I don't even believe that. You going over a wall!"

"What's come over you?" asked the lawyer irritably. "I thought we had this all straightened out. My two assistants were with me that first time, at five-fifteen; I knew Spaeth didn't like to be kept waiting, so they boosted me over the wall and followed. I saw Spaeth, and he signed the new will and it was properly witnessed. Then we left."

"Yes," said Winni in an excited voice. "And if that's twue, maybe you and your gangsters killed him!"

"Don't get notions now," said Ruhig with a dangerous softness. "I wasn't in there more than five minutes. He had the

330

will all made out. I was outside *Sans Souci* before five-thirty — had to go back over the wall, blast it; the gate was locked. When I left, Spaeth was very much alive."

"Then why did you come back? You came back after six."

"Spaeth told me to. There was other business he wanted to go over, and he said he expected Walter right away and wanted to talk to him alone. . . ."

Glücke glanced up at Walter with a twisted smile. Val gripped Walter's arm convulsively, and Walter went pale.

"Well, I think it's a pack of lies," sniffed Winni.

"Oh, for God's sake. I swiped the will right out of Spaeth's drawer when that fool Walewski and I found the body. I did it under his nose and he never knew the difference!"

"Well, show it to me, if you're so smart. Don't talk — just show it to me."

"One moment," said Ruhig's voice, and there was a snarling quality in it that brought a queer exclamation from the invisible Winni. "What made you think I was lying to you?"

"Keep away from me. My own mind, that's what."

"Your mind?" said the lawyer. "Isn't that

a little boastful?" There was a silence, as if he were backing away, looking around. "I'm a gullible cluck. Come on, tell me! This wasn't your idea, you dumb Swede!"

"If you must know," said Winni in a frightened yet defiant little rush, "Walter Spaeth warned me!"

"It's a plant!" yelled Ruhig.

And then everything happened at once. The receivers scratched and squealed, and there were confused sounds of toppling furniture, men's hoarse exclamations, scuffling.

"Let's go!" shouted Glücke, tearing the receivers from his ears. But Ellery was already sprinting around the pool in a dash for the Spaeth terrace, the long package clamped under his arm.

The Inspector scrambled after him and the others, after a stunned moment, streamed along behind.

They found Counselor Ruhig, very pallid and pasty-faced, standing lax in the grip of two detectives; and Winni lying in a faint over Solly Spaeth's most beautifully brocaded chair.

Another detective was waving a piece of folded foolscap exultantly. "Got him with his pants down. It's the will!"

"Tried to tear it up," said one of the men holding Ruhig, "but we stopped that." He shook the little man ungently.

Glücke grabbed the paper. As he was reading it, District Attorney Van Every hurried in. "Everything under control? Ah, Ruhig. Does my heart good to see you looking so gay. Let's see that, Inspector."

He read the paper very carefully. "Chalk up one more for Mr. King. This is getting monotonous. I'm afraid, Spaeth, this will comes a little too late to do you any good."

"Is it —" began Val, but she could not go on.

"It's a will properly dated, signed, and witnessed, revoking all previous wills and leaving the entire estate to Walter Spaeth."

Winni popped out of her faint. "It's a lie!" she screamed. "Solly left it to *me!*"

"I'm afraid you're out of luck, Miss Moon."

"But I owe *thousands* to dwess shops!" she wailed, jumping up and down. She glared spitefully at Val. "Now she'll get it — that sawed-off, pinky little wunt!" And she collapsed in the chair again in another faint.

Van Every shrugged, and Glücke said with a smack of his lips: "This gives us about all we need, Van. Motive's all clear now. And Ruhig's testimony that Spaeth told him he was expecting his son jibes perfectly —"

"I'll make a deal," jabbered Ruhig. "Forget this business and I'll testify I saw Spaeth —"

"Spaeth came," said Glücke, ignoring him " — we know he was in this house through Miss Austin's statement — his father showed him the new will, tried to make friends. But the skunk bumped his father off to get that dough."

"No!" shrieked Val, holding on to Walter.

"Inspector," pleaded Rhys, "for heaven's sake don't go off half-cocked. This boy wouldn't kill his own father. Walter, tell him what happened. He'll believe you. He's got to believe you!"

"He can talk all he wants when I get through," Glücke said coldly. "We've got his prints on the rapier, his own confession that he wore your coat, Jardin — which has human blood on it — and he had opportunity to plant the coat and sword in your closet at the *La Salle*."

Winni opened one eye, saw that nobody was paying any attention to her, and tried to creep out unobserved. But a detective forced her into a chair and she sat there whimpering.

Walter made a helpless gesture; the flesh around his lips was oyster-white. "I suppose it won't do any good to deny I murdered my father. But I warn you, Inspector — and you, Van Every — you're heading for trouble. You don't know a quarter of what really happened in this room last Monday afternoon. You don't even know the truth about —"

"No, you don't," said a peevish voice; and they all looked around to find Ellery glaring at them. "After all the trouble you've put me to, my dear Galahad, and all the blankets of silence you've wrapped yourself up in, you're not going to rob me of the little glory I've earned."

"King, are you crazy? Keep out of this!" barked Glücke.

"And that," said Mr. King in the same peevish tone, "goes for you two as well." And he glared at Rhys and Valerie.

"King —" spluttered the Inspector threateningly.

"Relax. Walter, do you know who killed your father?" Walter shrugged. "Do you know who killed Spaeth, Jardin? You, Val?"

"I'm not speaking to you — turncoat!"

Ellery looked whimsically at the long, brown-papered object in his hands. Then he turned and went to the glass door, opened it, stepped out on the terrace.

"Come out here," he said.

21

THE SPORT OF KING

There was such a majestic confidence in his voice that District Attorney Van Every whispered in Glücke's ear, and Glücke nodded glumly and motioned everybody out.

Ellery stood off to one side, the package tucked under one arm, waited patiently. They took positions about the terrace, some perched on the low terrace railing, others standing against the wall. Curiosity was reflected from each face — the anxious, hopeful ones of Val and Rhys; the gaping ones of the detectives, Winni, Pink; the watchful ones of Glücke and Van Every; the bitter ones of Ruhig and Walter.

The sky was blue, the garden sizzled with bees, a red hydroplane droned past high overhead. There was a strange otherworld overtone to everything, as if time had stopped still and something splendid and dreadful was about to happen.

And Ellery took a tubular object from his breast pocket and unwrapped it and said in a dreamy, mood-preserving voice:

"I have here a fragment of canvas which I cut out of this awning only today." He nodded toward the rectangle of light in the awning overhead.

"In this fragment you will find a slit, or tear, or rip, or whatever you choose to call it. It is a clean sharp incision and it runs — as you can see — parallel with the green and yellow stripes. The upper edges of the rip — that is to say the edges on the side which lay exposed to the sun — are slightly stained molasses-brown."

Glücke and Van Every ran toward him.

"No," said Ellery dryly, "don't touch it. This thing is a little like Medusa's head — one careless exposure and it turns you to clay. I had Bronson — charming fellow — analyze the stain only a couple of hours ago, and he says it is composed of thoroughly mixed molasses and potassium cyanide."

"Let's see that," said Glücke excitedly, bending over the square of canvas. "That slit — it looks —"

"About a half-inch long."

"So was the incision the sword made in Spaeth's chest!"

"And the same poison —" muttered the District Attorney.

"Then this cut in the awning was made

338

by the same rapier that killed Spaeth," exclaimed the Inspector. He looked up. He dragged a chair over and stood on it and put his nose as close to the hole in the canvas as he could get it. Then he stepped down, looking frustrated. "But how the dickens could a sword have got up there? If the stain's on top of the canvas, that means the sword came in *through* the canvas from above. That's screwy."

"It's not only screwy," said Ellery. "It didn't happen."

"Wait." Glücke jumped down the terrace steps and stared up at the house. "It could have been dropped out of one of the upper windows!"

Ellery sighed. "Come here, Inspector." Glücke came back. Ellery stood on the chair and fitted the fragment into the empty space. "See where this places the rip on the awning? Now look at the wall here. Do you notice this fresh nick in the stone? Curious place for a nick, isn't it — away over the tallest man's head? Could hardly have got there by accident, could it?"

"Well? Well?" Glücke craned with the others.

"Now observe the relative positions of the nick in the wall and the tear in the awning. About four inches apart. And the

339

tear is slightly — not much — higher from the floor than the nick. Line up nick and tear and what have you? A sharp object with a blade width of about a half-inch which went through the awning from above and struck the wall four inches inside the awning, causing the nick.

"If the sword had been dropped from a window, it would have naturally come down in a vertical position. But since the line between the rip and the nick is almost parallel with the terrace floor, it's obvious that the sharp object pierced the awning almost horizontally in relation to the floor."

He jumped down, wrapped the fragment of cloth carefully, and handed it to the Inspector, who did not seem to know what to do with it.

"I don't get this at all, King," he complained.

"Use your head, brother. Did some one stand or lie on top of the awning and stick a sword through the awning almost where it meets the wall, just for the purpose of making a nick in the stone there?"

"That's nonsense," said Van Every slowly.

"Agreed; sheer nonsense. So let's wander on. The stripes of the awning run from top to bottom; the rip is parallel with the stripes; the nick is a little lower but directly behind the rip. Therefore from what direction did the weapon come?"

"Through the air," muttered Van Every, "from a point directly facing this terrace."

"A rapier?" asked Ellery, raising his brows. "Through the air?"

"No," mumbled Glücke. "That can't be. Say — a knife! Somebody threw a knife!"

"At least," smiled Ellery, "not the rapier. We're in agreement that it's absurd to suppose somebody stood on the ground out there and hurled a sword at the awning? Very well. Then it wasn't a sword that pierced the awning. But whatever it was, it had all the characteristics of the wound in Spaeth's chest — a sharp cutting edge about a half-inch wide and coated with the same poisonous concoction that killed him."

"You mean," cried Glücke, "that Spaeth wasn't killed with that rapier at all?"

"How eloquently you put it, Inspector."

The Inspector opened his mouth wide. The others watched with a sort of horrible fascination.

"Now," said Ellery briskly, "we know one more important fact — that whatever the weapon was, it came from a point, as

341

the District Attorney says, directly facing this terrace. What directly faces this terrace?"

"The rock garden," said Pink eagerly.

"The pool," said the Inspector.

"And beyond the pool?"

"The old Jardin house."

"Or, to be precise, the terrace of the old Jardin house, which is exactly opposite this one."

Fitzgerald came puffing around the Spaeth house. "Hey! Wait for baby! What's happened? Did Ruhig —"

"Ah, Fitz. Glad you made it. You're just in time for a little demonstration. Inspector, would you mind clearing the terrace?"

"Clear it?"

"C-l-e-a-r," said Ellery sympathetically. "A five-letter word meaning get the hell out of the way. Pink, I need you."

Pink stumbled forward with that expression of bewilderment which seemed chronic with him whenever Ellery spoke. Ellery took a leather-covered pillow from a chair and propped it up against the rear wall, resting on an iron table. Then, holding the oddly shaped package in one hand, he grasped Pink's elbow with the other and led him off the terrace, speaking earnestly. Pink ambled along, nodding. They skirted the pool and made their way toward the Jardin terrace.

"Hey!" shouted Ellery across the garden. "Didn't you hear me? Get off that terrace!"

They moved, then, leaving the terrace hurriedly. And finally they were on the ground, at the side of the house, staring out across the pool toward the two men on the opposite terrace.

Ellery unwrapped the package, still talking to Pink, who was scratching his head. Ellery turned and waved them still farther to one side.

They saw Pink pick up the thing from the package with his right hand and fit something into it and draw back his left arm. There was a queer *cwang!* and something slender flashed through the air over the Jardin rock garden, over the pool, over the nearer garden, and plunked into the leather pillow on the Spaeth terrace, striking the stone wall beyond with a vicious ping.

"Creepers," said the Inspector hoarsely.

Pink grinned as Ellery clapped him on the shoulder, and then the two of them came trotting back, Pink lugging the bow and a sheaf of arrows proudly.

Ellery ran up on the terrace and tore the arrow from the pillow. "Good shot, Pink! Damsite better than the one that hit the awning Monday afternoon."

They scurried back to the terrace again. "An *arrow?*" said Van Every incredulously.

"It was the only possible answer. Because it was the only answer which explained why the murderer of Spaeth should have smeared the point of his weapon with poison."

Ellery lit a cigaret.

"If the weapon were the rapier *in veritate,* using poison on the tip was absurd. The only purpose in poisoning the tip could have been *to make sure* Spaeth died. With the weapon an arrow, and the archer fifty yards away, the situation clarifies: while an expert archer could be pretty sure of hitting his victim at fifty yards, he couldn't be positive of striking a vital spot. But with poison on the tip of the arrow even a superficial scratch would have caused death.

"No, Spaeth wasn't killed by that rapier at all. Nor was he killed in the study. He was standing out here on the terrace and his murderer shot two poisoned arrows from the Jardin terrace across the way. The first went too high and struck the top of the awning. The second hit Spaeth

344

squarely in the heart."

"But how can you be sure it was an arrow?" asked Van Every stubbornly. "There's something in what Glücke said about a knife. The killer could have been standing in the garden and thrown two knives. Such a theory would fill the bill just as satisfactorily as yours."

"Not by a long shot. Spaeth was killed by an archer, not a knife-thrower, and I can prove it. Pink, let me have that glove."

Pink stripped something leathery off his left hand. "I had quite a job hunting up a bow and arrows this afternoon," chuckled Ellery, "but when I located 'em — lo! the salesman brought out this glove. Look at it."

He tossed it to Glücke. It was a queer-looking glove. It had only three leather fingers — the middle three, providing no protection for the thumb and little finger. There was a strap which fastened about the wrist to hold the glove tight.

"Remember those two prints on the iron table of the Jardin terrace? A thumb and little finger. A person doesn't usually lean on just his thumb and little finger. Miss Jardin thought the two prints indicated a two-fingered man. But when you postulate an archer, the prints can only mean that they were made by some one wearing an archer's shooting glove, as it's called, the leather preventing the middle fingers from leaving an impression.

"Somebody wearing an archer's shooting glove was on the Jardin terrace. So the weapon must have been an arrow."

"That's absolutely uncanny," muttered Walter.

"Uncanny?" roared Fitzgerald. "It's colossal! Keep talking, King!"

"I'm afraid that from now on," replied Ellery with a certain grimness, "my conversation may take on a deadly tone, Fitz." There was an answering silence then of no superficial extent. "Walter."

Walter looked intensely at him, and Val felt a great shame.

"When you entered the study Monday afternoon dressed in Jardin's coat, you didn't find your father stabbed to death in that room; you found him with an arrow in his chest on this terrace. There was another arrow hanging from the tear in the awning up there.

"You removed the arrow from your father's body, you removed the arrow hanging from the awning. Then you dragged the body into the study and sat it down in the corner near the fireplace, where it was later found. The wrist-watch had probably smashed on this stone floor when your father fell dead; you swept up the fragments and deposited them near him in the study. Is that a reasonable reconstruction?"

Walter nodded wordlessly.

"You wanted it to look as if your father had been murdered with a sword. So you needed a sword with a blade-point approximately the same size and shape as the arrowhead. The only one that matched, judging by the eye, was the Italian rapier. So you ignored all the other swords and took down the rapier from the collection hanging over the fireplace.

"You took the arrows away with you, and the sword too — you knew it would be missed, and that the police would assume it had been the murder weapon; you couldn't leave it behind because you were afraid an expert comparison of the width of its blade with the width of the wound might show a discrepancy.

"And all the time you were doing this, the archer across the way was watching through the binoculars. He could even see what you were doing in the study, because of the glass wall."

Walter could not tear his gaze away.

"Why did you want it to look as if your

father had been murdered with a sword? For the simplest reason imaginable: because you didn't want it known that he had been killed with an arrow! But what was so damning about an arrow?

"There can be only one answer. The arrows implicated some one you wanted to protect. And whom have you been trying to protect since Monday? Your future father-in-law." Jardin's brown face twitched. "Then those two arrows must have been identifiable as Jardin's, and you knew it. I remembered the auction catalogue, the collection of medieval arrowheads which had been withdrawn from the sale and presented to the Museum. They were museum pieces, then; as such, undoubtedly known to collectors and therefore traceable directly to their owner, Jardin.

"So you took the arrows away and tried to make it look like a sword crime because you thought Jardin had killed your father. They were his arrows and he is an expert archer. Didn't he win an archery tournament in California last spring?"

"Why should he cover up his old man's murderer?" asked Glücke plaintively. "That doesn't wash, King."

"It does," said Ellery, "if you remember that his old man ruined thousands of people, including Jardin, and that his old man's murderer is the father of the girl he wants to marry."

"You mean," frowned Van Every, "that Jardin actually —"

"I'm only telling you what Walter was thinking," said Ellery, as if that were a simple matter, "since he didn't want to tell you himself. Well, Walter, am I right?"

"Yes," muttered Walter; he looked dazed. "I recognized them as two arrowheads from Rhys's collection. Of course, whoever stole them had fitted them into modern shafts; but the arrowheads couldn't be mistaken."

"They were two identical arrowheads of polished steel," said Rhys steadily. "Japanese, dating from the fourteenth century. Like many medieval Japanese arrowheads these had decorative designs in the steel which would have identified them as mine beyond question. Walter's told me about it since. Whoever the maniac was, he stole them because he wanted to frame me for Spaeth's murder." He paused, and then said lightly: "I'd like to get my hands on his throat."

"I couldn't talk," said Walter wearily, "because my story would have implicated Rhys. I didn't know about his alibi."

"And we didn't talk," cried Val, "because we knew Walter had been in this house at the time of the murder and we thought that — Oh, Walter, Mr. King knows you didn't do it!"

"Not so fast," growled Glücke. "How do I know this man didn't shoot those arrows himself? Couldn't he have been on the Jardin terrace and then dashed over to be in here when that five-thirty-five 'phone call came in?"

"He couldn't have been," said Ellery politely, "and he wasn't. Let me go on. Walter left the house with the arrows and sword, followed by the archer, who attacked him just outside the grounds after Walter climbed the fence, using the Indian club as a weapon. The club, remember, came from the Jardin house, where the archer had been. It was the archer, of course, who dropped the club down the sewer."

"Why'd he slug Walter at all?" demanded Fitz.

"Because he wanted those arrows back. Walter had spoiled his plan — his plan to murder Spaeth and frame Jardin for the crime. He wanted to retrieve the arrows, undo what Walter had done, and leave the scene of the crime as it had been before Walter changed it. But after he struck

350

Walter, he must have found himself unable to go through with the revised scheme. Because we did find the scene as Walter left it. Obviously, then, the arrows were gone by the time he reached Walter near the sewer."

"I'd already dropped the arrows down the sewer," said Walter, "when he hit me."

"So that was it! It puzzled me. But you hadn't had time to drop the sword through, as you intended, nor Jardin's coat. So friend archer took sword and coat, smeared both with the blood streaming out of your own head, went off, coated the sword with poison, and planted both objects in Jardin's closet. If he couldn't frame Jardin with arrows — you'd spoiled that — he was going to use your own little refinements and frame Jardin with the coat and sword. He knew Jardin would find the sword and handle it; and he was the one who wired headquarters with the tip to search Jardin's apartment, so timing his tip that discovery of the sword and coat and search by the police would be almost simultaneous. Very pretty, the whole thing."

The Inspector made a helpless gesture, like a man trying to stop an avalanche.

"His frame-up of Jardin was now complete — in a different form but still effective, even more effective. He couldn't have counted on Frank's identification of Walter as Jardin, it is true; but the rest he was almost positive of."

Ellery took the cigaret from his mouth and said calmly: "You asked before, Inspector, how I could be sure Walter hadn't killed his father. There was one conclusive reason: Walter is right-handed, as he demonstrates unconsciously all the time. But the archer wasn't. The archer was left-handed."

"How do you figure that?" demanded Glücke.

"I don't figure it; it's a fact. In archery, as in any other sport, the favored arm is called upon to do the most work. A right-handed archer will draw back the string of the bow with his right hand. Obviously a left-handed archer will draw it back with his left. Now the shooting glove is always worn on the hand which draws back the bow. On which hand did the murderer wear his shooting glove?"

"The left!" cried Val. "I remember we talked about those prints —"

"Yes, the thumb and little-finger smudges on the table from their relative shape and position came from a left hand, as you accurately observed. Then a left hand wore the shooting glove. Then the murderer was left-handed. That lets Walter out."

Walter shook his head, grinning a little, and Val ran over to him and seized him, her face shining.

"Now let me show you a little trick," murmured Ellery out of a spurt of smoke. "What do we know about the murderer?

"One — he's an expert archer. Fifty yards to hit a man in the heart is no mean feat, even after one bad shot.

"Two — he's left-handed.

"Three — and this is important — *he knew Jardin's coat had a rip in it.*"

"I don't follow, I don't follow," said the Inspector in a fit of irritable excitement.

"He took the coat from Walter and planted it on Jardin, didn't he? To do that, *he had to know it was Jardin's coat.* But how could he have known it was Jardin's coat? Walter was wearing it — a fact ordinarily sufficient to establish an assumption that it was his. Both men owned identical camel's-hairs. There were no distinguishing marks. No, the only means of identifying the coat as Jardin's was *by the rip under the pocket,* which had been made that very afternoon. The archer, then, recognized the coat by the rip. So he must have known in advance of the crime that the coat was ripped in that specific place.

"Four — and this is also a delicate point," said Ellery with a slight smile, "the murderer in order to have been able to use the Indian club on Walter's head, *had to know where to find it.*"

"Say that again?" implored Glücke, who was having a hard time all around.

Ellery sighed. "Visualize our homicidal friend. He has just seen Walter leaving with the sword and arrows. He wants to get those arrows back. What to do? He hasn't anything against Walter personally; he's not out for Walter's blood. A tap on the head will be sufficient. What should he use for a bludgeon?

"We know he used one of the Indian clubs. That means he ran along the terrace, forced the door of the ex-gymnasium, went to the wall-closet where the two clubs hung, opened the closet, and took out the undamaged club.

"*What made him force the door of the gymnasium?* There were lots of other rooms to investigate if he wanted to find a bludgeon. Even if he went to the gymnasium first by mere chance, and forced the door, there was nothing to be seen but a small pile of débris. For Miss Jardin told me Wednesday afternoon that the closet door had been left closed when they moved out of the house.

"No, when he forced that door and went to the closed closet and opened it, *he knew what he was going to find*. He knew there were two Indian clubs in that closet."

Ellery threw away his cigaret.

"I think we have enough now to paint a picture of our 'compleat criminal.' To our knowledge, who fits all four qualifications I've laid down?

"Who is an expert archer, *and* left-handed, *and* knew Jardin's coat was ripped, *and* knew the Indian clubs were in the gymnasium closet?"

For a moment, by some communal telegraphic instinct, the very bees stopped humming; and a final silence fell that was uncomfortably not of this world.

Then Pink burst into laughter, doubling up as he clutched the bows and arrows. "But jeeze," he gasped, "you're 'way off your base. That's *me!*"

Inspector Glücke looked at Ellery with an anxiously questioning triumph, as if to say: "There, smart guy. What do you say to that?"

And Ellery said to that: "Yes, Pink. That's you."

★ ★ ★

"Oh, no," said Valerie, holding on to Walter's arm. "Oh, *no.*"

"Oh, yes," said Ellery. "I knew Pink was an expert archer — wasn't he runner-up to Jardin when Jardin won the California Archery Tournament last spring? You mentioned that yourself Monday night, Inspector. And besides, he's just beautifully demonstrated his marksmanship.

"Left-handed? Ample evidence of that, plus the fact that he just shot an arrow left-handedly.

"He was one of the five persons who were present when Jardin's coat was ripped.

"And he was one of the three who knew about the clubs being left in the closet.

"On the archery point, the only other known archer in the group is Jardin, whose alibi lets him out.

"On the coat-ripping point, the other four witnesses were Jardin, Valerie, Walter, and the gateman Frank. Jardin and Valerie are eliminated because of their alibis. Walter is right-handed. And Frank has only one arm, so he couldn't possibly have been an archer.

"And on the Indian-club point, the other two were the Jardins, eliminated before.

"Pink is the only one who fits all four characteristics. So he must have murdered Solly Spaeth." Ellery sighed. "Take it away, Inspector. I've shot my bolt, too."

During this peroration, they stood motionless, too surprised to think, to take the simplest defensive measure. As for Pink, his crimson neck grew more crimson, and the cords expanded and became visible, and the look of the hunted animal slowly emerged from the sluggish morass of his brain.

But at a certain point something snapped, and Pink demonstrated his amazing nervous and physical versatility. Before they could move a muscle he had bounded off the terrace to a point fifteen feet away and whirled like a tightly wound mechanical toy with an arrow fitted into the bow, the string taut, and the arrowhead pointed directly at Mr. Ellery Queen's petrified breast.

"Don't move," said Pink thickly. "Nobody make one little move."

They were strung out in a straggly line along the terrace, no one behind another. It was absurd, in the sun, with the bow gleaming like a plaything. And yet nobody moved.

"You can get me with a gun," said Pink

in the same thick, dreary voice, "but this guy gets it through the heart first. So don't move. He's got something coming to him." He stopped, and then he said: "He *fooled* me."

And nobody laughed, even at the childish petulance, the plaintive wonder in Pink's voice. His red hair flamed. With his legs widespread and solidly planted in the earth, and the bow grotesquely arched, he was a fascinating object; and faintly in a remote chamber of his brain Mr. Ellery Queen began to recite a small, foolish prayer.

Pink's left arm drew back a little farther and his eye glared at Ellery's breast with an awful fixity.

"Pink," said Valerie. She happened to be standing with Walter near the top step of the terrace. "Pink."

Pink's eye did not waver. "Keep out of this, Val. Keep away."

"Pink," said Val again. Her cheeks were almost blue. Walter made a convulsive movement and she breathed: "Walter. Don't move. He'll kill you. He won't touch me." And slowly she stepped forward and slowly she went down the steps.

"Val," cried Pink, "Val, I swear — go back!"

"No, Pink," said Val in a quiet soothing tone. Slowly, slowly. She hardly touched the ground. She drifted toward him, never taking her eyes from him. It was as if Pink had been a sliver of gold leaf balanced on the tip of a needle; the merest quiver of the ground, the merest breath would send it tumbling. "Don't, Pink. I know there's something horribly wrong in all this. You're not a criminal. You may have killed Spaeth, but I know you must have had a good reason — in your own mind, Pink. . . ."

Fat drops appeared on Pink's red forehead. His body trembled as he stood rooted in the garden, shaken by an invisible wind.

"Pink," said Val, and she went up to him and took the bow out of his hand.

And Pink did a curious thing. He sank down among the flowers and began to weep.

When it was all over and Pink, with a dead look in his eyes, was led away to wait in a police car for Inspector Glücke, Ellery went into Solly Spaeth's study and opened a liquor cabinet and drank standing up from a full brown bottle.

Then, with the bottle in his hand, he

went over to Val and kissed the tip of her ear.

"Just like a woman," he said. Val was crying bitterly in Walter's arms and Rhys was sitting, a little shrunken, and looking old. "You saved my life," said Ellery.

Val sobbed against Walter's chest. Walter glanced at Ellery significantly and he turned away. Walter drew Val off to a corner and sat her down on his lap; she clung to him. "Pink. He was . . . Oh, I can't believe it!"

"It's all right, darling. We'll get him off," crooned Walter in her ear. "No jury will ever convict him in this county."

"Oh, Walter . . ."

Ellery raised the bottle again, and Inspector Glücke said something, and Ruhig and Winni Moon were sent off in custody with their conspiracy to defraud hanging heavy over their heads. And after a while District Attorney Van Every left with a bewildered look; and Fitz, clapping his forehead like a man awakening from a trance, grabbed the telephone, spluttered into it, dashed out, dashed back, found his hat, threw it away, and dashed out again.

Glücke rubbed his jaw. "King, I don't know how to —"

Ellery lowered the bottle. "Who killed

Cock Robin?" he sang. "I, said the sparrow, with my little bow and arrow. . . . It's like a resurrection! Have I sprouted any gray hairs in the last ten minutes?"

"Mr. King." Rhys Jardin rose, working his jaws. For a moment there was no sound except Val's sobbing and Walter's crooning in her ear.

Ellery sighed: "Yes?" He was not feeling terribly fit; there was a bitterness on his tongue not liquorish.

"There's one thing I'll never believe," said Rhys in a troubled voice. "I'll never believe Pink framed me for Spaeth's murder. I couldn't be wrong. He was my friend. I treated him like a member of my own family. It just can't be, Mr. King."

"Look," said Ellery. "A friend may become a greater enemy than an enemy. He was your friend, and you were his. You had advised him to put all his savings in Ohippi. When Ohippi fell, he was furious with Spaeth; and so long as he thought you were Spaeth's victim, too, he remained your friend.

"But Monday morning, in packing your things in the gym across the way, he found a bankbook in your golf-bag which seemed to indicate that you had salted away five million dollars. Were you still his friend?

Not if you doublecrossed him by pretending to be broke while you had five millions to keep you warm against a rainy day. Pink is a primitive soul and he didn't stop to ask questions. In his mind you became one with Spaeth — two crooks who had defrauded him of his life's savings.

"He planned things then and there. He had to take that collection of arrowheads down to the Museum, didn't he? On the way he took two of the arrowheads out of the package, delivering the rest. He fitted them out with shafts, prepared his little broth of molasses and potassium cyanide —"

"But ever since," cried Val's father, "he's been so damned — so damned *solicitous!* He couldn't have been acting."

"He wasn't. When you explained to him late Monday night about the five million, *after* the crime, *after* the planting of the rapier and coat in your closet — when he realized that you'd been with him the entire day on which the five millions were deposited, Pink saw what an awful thing he'd done to you. But it was too late. The crime, the frame-up, were *faits accompli.* There was nothing he could do. He couldn't recall that wire he'd sent headquarters only a few minutes before —

probably by dodging downstairs to the lobby while Val and Walter were in her bedroom and telephoning the wire from the public booth there.

"No, he just had to sit and take it. Every emotion of his since Monday night has been genuine."

Ellery turned to find Val and Walter before him. Val was still sniffling with her handkerchief to her nose, but she looked calmer. "I can't thank you, Mr. King. None of us can. But —"

"Feel better, Walter?"

"We're still a little dazed," said Walter, "but you might be interested to learn that Val and I have decided to do something constructive with my father's money."

"I know," sighed Ellery. "You're going to put it all back into Ohippi and rehabilitate the plants."

"How did you know?" they cried together.

"Because," said Ellery, "you're that kind of damned fool."

"That reminds me," murmured Rhys. "That five million properly belongs to you now, Walter. I'll —"

"You'll do nothing of the sort." Walter smiled faintly. "I hope you'll find me a better partner than my father was."

"Look," said Inspector Glücke, who was still hanging about. "I've got work to do. But I've got to tell you, King —"

Walter said suddenly: "King? Let me show you a trick, Inspector."

"I've had all the tricks I want. King —"

"No, no, you'll enjoy this one." Walter seized a piece of paper from the desk and with a soft pencil began to sketch a face with great rapidity. Glücke looked puzzled. "So what? That's King. I haven't time to look at pictures —"

"You have for this." Walter erased the shaded glasses and replaced them with *pince-nez.* Over the face he smudged a beard. And he put the hair-part in a different place. "Who's that?"

The Inspector gaped from the drawing to Mr. Hilary King. "My God," he screamed, "the pest!"

"I think I knew it," shrugged Walter, "from the moment I saw him. You might fool others, Queen, but you couldn't fool an artist. I sketched your face at the auction."

"Mr. Queen?" said Val, wide-eyed. "So *that's* how you knew what went on here Monday night!"

"I'll be damned," said Jardin, staring.

Ellery reached hastily for the telephone

and gave the operator a number. "Magna Studios? Connect me with Mr. Jacques Butcher's office." As he waited, he said apologetically: "As long as I'm unmasked I may as well go back to work. . . . Hello, Butcher? . . . Who?" He swallowed hard. "Now look here, young woman. This is Ellery Queen, and I — want — Butcher! . . . He *is* there? Put him on!" He said exultantly: "Can you imagine? Butcher at last!" There was a buzzing noise in the receiver and he slowly sucked his lean cheeks in. "Oh, is that so?" he yelled. "So he can't see me — *yet?* Well, you tell your Mr. Butcher —" But there was a click. He stared at the dead telephone and then hurled the whole thing away.

"Uh — Queen," said the Inspector nervously. "I want to apologize — I mean, you've cracked this case and the credit is really —"

Ellery waved his hand. "Don't want any," he said grumpily. "Leave me out of it. . . . Can't see me, eh?"

"That's white of you," beamed Glücke. "Say, I take it all back. How'd you like to meet the Chief of Police and the Mayor? And we could put you up —"

"He's staying with me," said Walter. "That's definite."

"Or maybe you'd like to be appointed Honorary Chief?" glowed the Inspector. "I've got a drag —"

"Wait," said Ellery, frowning. "You're grateful, eh, Inspector?"

"What do you think?"

"You'd have the City run a banquet for me, I suppose?"

"Hell, yes. We could —"

"I wouldn't have to pay any traffic fines, either?"

"Leave it to me."

"You could even see that I met the Governor, couldn't you?"

Inspector Glücke said earnestly: "The Governor, or the President, or *anybody*."

"It's tougher than that," said Ellery in a despairing voice. "Get me in to see Butcher."

We hope you have enjoyed this Large Print book. Other Thorndike, Wheeler or Chivers Press Large Print books are available at your library or directly from the publishers.

For more information about current and upcoming titles, please call or write, without obligation, to:

Publisher
Thorndike Press
295 Kennedy Memorial Drive
Waterville, ME   04901
Tel. (800) 223-1244

Or visit our Web site at:
www.gale.com/thorndike
www.gale.com/wheeler

OR

Chivers Large Print
published by BBC Audiobooks Ltd
St James House, The Square
Lower Bristol Road
Bath BA2 3SB
England
Tel. +44(0) 800 136919
email: bbcaudiobooks@bbc.co.uk
www.bbcaudiobooks.co.uk

All our Large Print titles are designed for easy reading, and all our books are made to last.